A School for Villains

Ardyth DeBruyn

ISBN: 1466378468
ISBN-13: 978-1466378469

For Jonathan Patrick, my first fan for whom this book was written, and for Jonathan Daniel of Guatemala, whose education I hope to aid through this series, may you never stop learning.

CONTENTS

Thus at our friends we laugh, who feel the dart;
To reach our feelings, we ourselves must smart.
Is our young bard so young, to think that he
Can stop the full spring-tide of calumny?
Knows he the world so little, and its trade?
Alas! the devil's sooner raised than laid.

—A School for Scandal, Prologue, R.B. Sheridan

CHAPTER 1

A Dark, But Practical Future

Headmaster Atriz, Master of Evil, Professor of Crime, and dreaded ruler of Dark Lord Academy, sat brooding deep in the bowels of the castle. Normally, he preferred his light and airy office in the tower that allowed him a full view of the villainous dealings of school life below. But the demon pit in his closet needed repairs and he couldn't concentrate with the drafts of fire blasting up or the clanking the repairmen made. So here he was, stuck in the dungeons.

And it all smelled of mildew.

Not that his difficulties would be any less uncomfortable up in his office. Besides, such a dark and dank place was appropriate to the nature of his quandary. Atriz rolled back his thick black sleeves and picked up the list of thirteen names in his pale, almost translucent hands—the final thirteen students who had proven worthy to be admitted to Dark Lord Academy this year. He tucked his long black hair behind one ear. He was the epitome of a dark lord and, as such, knew his apprehensions were true.

One of these thirteen was a mistake. One of these thirteen students ought not to be on this list and would cause considerable trouble. The difficulty was that his sixth sense wasn't telling him which one.

Atriz set the paper down and leaned back in his black leather swivel chair with a sigh. He stared at the boring stone walls of the dungeon, which was empty except for the desk, chair, and Fluff, the white, long-haired cat who sat on the floor a yard away.

"Rowww!" Fluff glared at him with beady red eyes. She wanted a place on his lap.

While Atriz was required by the Society of Master Villainous Leaders of Large Institutions and Associations to keep both the cat and the swivel chair, it didn't mean he had to like either. This was one of the reasons he kept both of them in the bowels of the castle.

"No," he said, "you cannot sit on my lap."

"Merrrowww," insisted Fluff as she jumped up on his lap.

Atriz looked up at the ceiling in disgust, trying not to sneeze as white cat hair spread across his clean black robes. No matter how many times he ran the magic lint roller across them, he never seemed to be able to get all the cat hair off. Still, he was better off letting her stay; she had quite the temper.

The new school year would begin in a matter of days. The board of directors would not be pleased if he delayed it. There wasn't time for another background check on the thirteen students, so Atriz would have to do as many villains before him had done and let things play out in all their evil.

Sometimes patience is the most villainous course, he thought. He would watch the thirteen carefully, as well as his thirteen teachers, and see what developed. Sinking his fingers into Fluff's fur, he stroked. His face lit with a perfect villainous grin. No one could produce so evil a grin as Atriz. One of these thirteen would be oh-so-sorry he ever aspired to be a villain.

It should be quite the evil school year. Only the flick of Fluff's tail across his mouth and its promise of swallowing cat hair prevented him from laughing maniacally at that thought.

***

"Hey! Take a look at the size of this!" Dicky thrust the garter snake towards Danny, its long tail thrashing.

Danny took an involuntary step backwards. He didn't mind snakes, just not so close to his nose. "Yeah, that's a big one. Nice catch."

Dicky cracked a grin, showing his crooked front teeth. "Dare you to put it in Pa's bed."

Danny snorted and turned away to poke in the dirt for more worms for fishing. "Bah, put it in there yourself." He wasn't going to let his younger brother get him in trouble, not so soon after the last time, anyway.

"Coward." Dicky bounced a little. Only nine years old, he was still excited by things like frogs, lizards, and snakes.

"You mean I'm not as stupid as you'd like," Danny retorted. He considered his pranks above that. Nailing Amos's shoes to the floor had been a much more sophisticated crime, and one their older brother had enjoyed a good laugh at after he got over it. "I'm not going to ruin a perfectly good day off getting a whipping. I'm going to enjoy myself."

Dicky made a disgusted noise and tossed the snake away. Danny watched it flailing in the air before it landed in the pond with a splash. Perhaps it was the lucky one, escaping Dicky so quickly.

"Yeah, but *why* do we have a day off?" Dicky asked. "Pa never just gives us one."

"Dunno." Danny decided he had enough worms and headed toward their usual rock to sit. He wasn't going to question a day off from the forge. At thirteen, Danny was now helping Amos with his journeyman work in the mornings and had his own lessons from Pa in the afternoon. While he didn't mind blacksmithing, it was hot, boring work. Fishing, even while putting up with Dicky, was considerably more entertaining.

"But he *never* gives us a day off," Dicky insisted, "only when he goes to market or something. Aren't you curious what's up? Why'd he want to get rid of us?" Dicky followed to take a seat next to him and grabbed one of the worms from Danny's cup.

Danny slapped his hand away. "Hey, get your own."

"Aww, come on." Dicky scooted away, the worm still in his possession.

Danny moved his cup to his other side to prevent more swiping. "Come on, yourself. You should have dug some instead of catching stupid snakes."

"You have no appreciation for wildlife," Dicky said, taking on the schoolmarm's voice.

Danny chuckled, despite himself. He hadn't been to school since his tenth birthday, when he started his apprenticeship in the forge, but he certainly hadn't forgotten Miss Carnworth, the schoolmarm. He copied the thick local farmer accent she lectured them against. "I ken read an' write and make a horseshoe in under ten minutes, 's good enough for me."

Dicky rolled his eyes. "Yeah, well, if I've learned one thing, it's that something's up or Pa wouldn't have gotten rid of us."

For all that he'd discounted his brother's words earlier, when they returned to the house that afternoon, Danny couldn't help but glance at the smoke billowing from the forge chimney and wonder what Pa'd been up to while they were gone. They carried their fish into the kitchen. Dicky got out an extra bucket and Danny the knives when the sound of a door made them jump. Pa walked out of his bedroom. There wasn't any normal reason for him to be there this time of day.

Pa grinned at them and their fish. "Nice catch, boys. I'm looking forward to your dinner." He clapped Danny on the back as he walked passed him.

"See," whispered Dicky. "He's way too happy. Something's up."

Danny didn't have a good argument and glanced out the window to watch Pa heading across the yard toward the forge. Usually Pa had something disparaging to say about them wasting time when they'd been off having fun. "Here, take this. I'm going to check it out." He shoved his fish at Dicky and dashed toward the bedroom.

"No fair, I want to come," Dicky called.

"You're lookout," Danny said, yanking the door open and slipping inside.

Pa's bedroom looked about the same as it normally did; a large bed, even if only he slept in it since Danny's mother had passed away; a mirror, the only one in the house, hanging on the wall; and the dresser next to it. However, something wrapped in cloth on top of the dresser caught his eye. Danny snuck over and peeled back the edge of the fabric.

A piece of twisted metal lay inside, delicate curling lines interlocking in something that looked rather like a collar for a larger animal. The intricate twisted metal links came together around an iron skull in the front. Danny traced the miniature eye sockets and teeth with a finger. This was specialty work. Something about the whole thing creeped him out slightly. Weren't skulls bad luck? Who'd want to put one on an animal collar? Who, for that matter, would want an iron collar when a leather one would be more supple and less of a burden?

Not wanting to overstay his time and get caught, Danny carefully re-wrapped the object. A piece of black paper stuck out from under the fabric bundle. Danny pulled it out. It was a brochure, folded in three parts. On the front, in silver letters, it read: *Dark Lord Academy—We unlock the hidden potential in the most difficult of children.* Danny gaped a moment. Then curiosity won and he flipped it open. The first flap read:

Do you have an unusually bright son or daughter who just doesn't fit the mold? Does your son play pranks? Does your daughter set fires? Is it hard to get your child to follow orders, despite being clever and inventive? Your child might have a future as a Dark Lord.

Wow, Danny thought. *Is this serious?* He'd bet anything if Dicky saw this, he'd be clamoring to be a Dark Lord. Was Pa thinking of sending him? Dicky always had been the brightest at school, even if he drove Miss Carnworth practically to tears over his troublemaking. He opened the final flap to read the rest:

Myth: *Dark Lords rarely have success and are defeated in ignominy by heroes.*

Fact: Most Dark Lords make a highly successful living, have instant name recognition, and no little amount of governing power. Many of the world's most successful governments are run by Dark Lords.

Myth: Dark Lords are self-serving and turn their back on their families for personal gain.
Fact: Heroes are 90% more likely to kill a parent or sibling in the pursuit of "good" than a Dark Lord. The majority of Dark Lords, when polled, say their parents are responsible for who they are today and gave them the foundational skills for their future villainous success.

Myth: Becoming a Dark Lord involves an angst-ridden journey through misery, abuse, and loss.
Fact: Dark Lord Academy's accredited and time-proven methods for bringing out the villainous talents in today's students are safe, effective, and highly enjoyable. Just listen to what some of our students have to say!

Part of Danny knew he needed to get back to the kitchen before Pa and Amos realized he wasn't with Dicky, but he was mesmerized. While Pa claimed to have heard a Dark Lord's speech once on a marketing trip, he'd never satisfactorily described the event or what the Dark Lord said.

"Dark Lord Academy is what gave me the self-confidence to not only to acquire my minions loyalties, but to prepare and run my horde correctly in an economic manner. I never would have conquered six nations without all the valuable training I received." —Dread Lord Hexibold

"Before attending Dark Lord Academy, I was a hopeless

wimp, cringing at the whims of others while plotting make-believe revenge. I trembled like a leaf burning my first village down. Now everyone bows to me and does the cringing. If they cause any trouble, I'm prompt and effective with my revenge."
—Mistogorphos the Deadly

"Dragons, demons, and dashing daredevil villains more than willing to share all their dirty little secrets. Need I say more?"
—Dread Lady Kalipsifix

"Poking around where you don't belong, Daniel?"

Pa's voice made Danny jump. The brochure fell from his hands and fluttered to the floor.

"Er…" Danny's mind raced to come up with a good excuse. He glanced sheepishly up at the doorway and, to his shock, Pa burst into laughter.

"Should have known I couldn't keep anything hidden around you." Pa leaned on the doorframe and beamed at Danny. "Ever since you were a little tot, why, you've always been into everything."

"I…have?" Danny rarely heard his father get nostalgic about them as little kids.

"I knew when the recruiter came by the fair last Saturday it was perfect for you. I sent off the application straight away. Wasn't going to tell you until I heard back, but…"

"You…what?" Danny gaped at Pa, wordless for a moment. It was one thing to admire creepy collars or wonder about sinister speeches in far off countries and quite another to consider *being* a villain.

Pa shrugged. "Well, I'm sure you'll make the cut, son. You always were a bright one."

"B-but villains?"

Pa grinned in a fond way, entirely unlike his usual self. "Why, when I was young, I'd have jumped at this opportunity." Pa leaned forward, a glint in his eye that rather unnerved Danny. Pa was always so practical, reserved, conventional. "You've got to admit they have style. Lightning, reigns of darkness, dragons, magic!"

Danny stared. This was certainly a side of his father he'd never guessed existed. Sure, Pa was a clever businessman and often said ruthless market strategies were necessary for success, but he'd never *hurt* anyone.

Pa's gaze turned distant. "I dreamed of it when I was about your age. Growing up in the maze of the crumbling city of Dorganth, always scrounging for my food out of the trash-heaps."

This at least was familiar territory. Danny had heard Pa's starving-street-boy-to-famed-and-wealthy-blacksmith tale only about a thousand times. But never before had villains come into it.

"The villain students used to come to town for fieldtrips in their long black capes, with their flashy magic and maniacal laughter. They always looked as if they might do anything they pleased. I envied that success, was determined I'd rise above the garbage and make something of myself." Pa pounded a fist on the palm of his other hand dramatically.

"I even applied for a scholarship once, but some snot-nosed genius boy from the capital beat me out for it." Pa glowered a moment. "But I swore I'd have my success, that my family would never have to scrounge the trash-heap for a meal, and look at me now, the richest and best-known blacksmith in all of West Cadford!"

"You're the best, Pa," Danny said, putting on an adoring smile and hoping to turn the conversation away from Dark Lord Academy and onto his future here, with his family. "I want to be just like you."

Pa laughed, but to Danny's surprise, shook his head.

"No, Daniel, I want you to be more. I want all my sons to have what I never did. And thanks to my hard work building this forge, you can really stand out, be someone. Why, your name could be famous across whole countries, maybe into other *dimensions*! Who knows what might be possible? You're a bright boy, for all you're a little reluctant to put yourself out there."

Danny swallowed hard. He didn't want to quash Pa's dreams, but being the next Dark Lord to blight the land with darkness and destruction was definitely *not* on his list of things to do in life. "But aren't villains evil? They… didn't you hear how Girantrius the Terrible burned down a bunch of innocent villages over in Kortia a couple months ago? Dark Lords kill and terrorize innocent people."

Pa waved a hand dismissively. "Bah, that was for show. All those people were carefully relocated before they burned those villages down. I heard it off a goblin I dealt with over by the border."

Danny's stomach tightened. Pa sold stuff to villains? He'd never paid much attention to their customers, but he'd have noticed if they'd been goblins. Then again, Pa did go out with delivery loads and to markets rather regularly. And hadn't Danny just been fingering some evil-looking object? Now he wasn't sure he wanted to know what it was for. Uncertainty clogged his throat.

"Look," Pa continued, "Dark Lords aren't that different from any other sort of government, other than the propaganda. The main thing is, they're filthy rich and highly successful. I never got to have my dream, but you can."

Danny swallowed hard and forced himself to come up with more objections. "Why can't I go to hero school instead?"

Pa sighed. "That's twice as expensive, Daniel, and they only allow first, third, and seventh sons to apply. If we do well enough, I just might be able to send Richard, but that's a big if. Regardless, I want a good opportunity for you, too. Now, no more nonsense. I've thought long and hard about this—I know what's right for you."

Laugher from the kitchen made Danny's stomach tighten. He could hardly believe that Pa was actually planning to send him away to school and to *villain* school at that. He had to explain and fast, before there wasn't a way out of it. He drew himself up a bit straighter and hoped he wouldn't hurt his father's feelings. "Pa, I really don't want to leave home or be a villain. I'd rather just be Amos's assistant. I know he'll inherit the forge, not me, but I wouldn't mind. I like it here."

Pa sighed. His brow furrowed a moment, then his gaze hardened. "I'm your father, I know what's best for you. You'll go and no more arguments. Understand? Now come to dinner." He turned and left the room.

Danny stared miserably at the empty doorway, Pa's words echoing in his head. Anger flickered and he bent to pick up the brochure and crumpled it into a ball. *No, I'm not going to be a villain, I refuse.*

He stalked out of the room and tossed it into the fire on his way over to the table where Amos and Dicky were happily putting out the cooked fish. He paused to watch the flames creep up the ball of paper, engulfing it in flames that shifted from red to blue and then to green a moment, before collapsing into ash. Danny's determination solidified. He'd fight this, stand up for himself, and prove he wasn't a villain.

He glanced up, but Pa didn't seem to have noticed at all.

CHAPTER 2

The Dark Chariot Pays a Visit

Danny woke with a sense of impending doom. The large black envelope, primly propped up against the candlestick on his bedside table, did not suggest today was going to go any better than yesterday. The silver seal, shaped like a devil's head, seemed to grin mockingly at him. Underneath, in lacy silver lettering, read: Dark Lord Academy—*pro peiore potestate*. Danny rubbed his eyes and looked again. Nope, still there. He swallowed hard and reached out to poke it with a finger.

The envelope fell flat.

Danny sat up and groaned. It was much too early to deal with something like this. Should he open it? Could he *not* open it? Danny glowered. He'd let Pa do the honors. That way if it was cursed, it would be justice for Pa to get it. He dragged himself out of bed, carefully picked up the letter, and pinched Dicky's foot as he passed him on the way out.

"Get up, lazybones."

"Oww," Dicky mumbled and buried his head in the blankets.

Danny rolled his eyes and headed into the main room. Amos stood by the fire, stirring the pot of porridge. Pa lounged in his usual chair, discussing horseshoe orders. Resisting the desire to glare at Pa, as it would only get him angry and insistent, Danny shoved the letter at him.

"What's that?" Pa asked.

"Didn't you put it by my bed?"

"No." Pa frowned. "But then, those Dark Lords are uncanny fellows. I suppose they magicked it here." He handed the envelope back to Danny. "Go ahead, son."

That was distinctly not reassuring. They'd responded that fast? Danny needed time to think this through, a plan to prove he wasn't fit for villain school. "What if it's dangerous?"

Pa laughed. "Oh, come on, it's not like they'd hurt one of their well-paying students. Open it."

Danny hid a grimace. Taking a deep breath, he broke the seal. A column of black smoke burst from the envelope. He dropped it and jumped backwards. High-pitched laughter came from inside.

"Muahahahahahahahaha!"

The smoke condensed into a squat and contorted creature. Danny squinted. It was pond-slime green, had pointy ears that stuck out sideways, and a nasty leer on its face. Danny had never seen a goblin before, but this had to be what they looked like.

"Greetings. My sincerest evil wishes. I am pleased to

announce you have been accepted to Dark Lord Academy," it said in a whiny voice. "Transportation will arrive when you have performed your first preparatory dark act. Please do so in a timely manner, because the first day of class is in twenty-four hours. All first year gear can be purchased at the school and this year's new student advisor…" the goblin glanced down at the letter now lying on the ground, "is Mistress Virlyxfrika. Your advisor will arrange your schedule upon arrival. Welcome to Dark Lord Academy, where evil isn't just evil, it's terrifically evil." The goblin grinned a horrible smile that showed about a thousand sharp, white teeth. It vanished with a bang and a cloud of black smoke.

Danny, Amos, and Pa all stared in disbelief at the now-empty black envelope lying on the floor.

"Well," Amos finally said.

"Well," echoed Pa.

Whatever they meant by "transportation," Danny was *not* summoning it. If he didn't, maybe he'd have enough time to change Pa's mind. If nothing else, the horrible letter had driven home the point that dark lords were not only evil, they were proud of it.

Dicky shuffled into the room. "Hey, what's all the noise?" He rubbed his eyes with his sleeve. "Did you drop the pot or something, Amos?"

"Erm," Amos said.

Danny picked up the envelope and tossed it into the fire. He vowed to sweep the hearth and wash the dishes along with his usual chores. Maybe he'd shine Pa's shoes and scrub out the outhouse while he was at it. Trim the bushes in the front yard? Cook lunch for everyone, maybe dinner as well? It sounded exhausting, but surely if he worked hard enough, Pa would have to see he was just too good to be villainous. Besides, it was only one day and then classes would start and he'd have safely missed them.

Dicky scooped himself a bowl of porridge. "What're y'all just sitting around staring for? It's not a holiday, is it?"

Pa stood up. "That's the spirit, Richard! You'll make a terrific hero at this rate. Well, on to the forge." He turned back at the door. "Oh, Daniel, you'd better pack." Then he left.

"What does he mean, pack?" Dicky sat down.

Danny clenched his jaw. Just watching his younger brother's blithe contentment made him want to pummel him. But Pa's decision wasn't Dicky's fault, as much as it might be nice to blame him. "Pa's sending me to villain school. He says it's because Amos is getting the forge and you're gonna go rescue some princess or something."

"I am? Why? Am I going to have to kiss her?" He screwed up his face in disgust.

"All the heroes do it," Amos said. "And you're a third son. Don't worry, no one will expect you to do any of that for at least five or six years."

"As if some girl would want to kiss you," Danny muttered.

Dicky stuck his tongue out at him.

Danny grabbed the broom and swept the hearth right away, before he could forget. He wasn't hungry, anyway.

"You knew all this time and you didn't tell me," Danny complained to Amos.

His older brother shrugged. "You don't like change."

Of all the stupid reasons…Danny gave him an angry look. "But *villains*! Amos, I'm not evil, you know that! Can't you talk him out of it?"

Dicky snickered into his porridge. "I think you smell something pretty evil."

"Oh, shut up!" Danny tried to ignore him and focused on Amos.

Amos gave him a sympathetic look, but shook his head. "You know Pa's made up his mind. How about you just give it a try? You never know. You don't take many risks. Maybe going out there and shaking things up will help you."

Danny's breath caught in his throat. "You think going evil's gonna help me?"

"Nothing's gonna help *you*," Dicky muttered.

Danny took a step forward to slap him, but Amos stood up at just the right moment to "happen" to walk between them. He put a hand on Danny's shoulder and squeezed it. "Don't you think it's worth a shot? If nothing else, you'll learn some insider tips about Dark Lords and then you could be an advisor to a king or hero or something. I mean, what's the worst that could happen?"

Dicky's face lit up. "Hanging, getting burned at the stake, nothing too awful."

Danny jerked out of Amos's grip to take a swipe at Dicky. He caught his brother on the shoulder, sending him backward mid-snicker. Dicky yelped and clutched at the table to try to stop from falling off the bench, but only succeeded in knocking his bowl over before the whole bench tumbled to the floor.

"Oww!" Dicky scrambled to his feet, face red with fury. He launched himself at Danny, fists swinging. Danny blocked with one arm and grabbed Dicky's hair with the other hand, yanking. Dicky kicked him viciously in the shins.

Amos's shout to try and stop them was drowned out by an enormous bang from the front yard. The ground shook, knocking both Danny and Dicky to the ground and a horrible stench filled the air. Amos dashed towards the front door.

Shaken, Danny dragged himself to his feet. "What the—"

"Did the forge explode?" Dicky's eyes went wide.

Black smoke billowed in the front door. Danny scrambled after Amos, trying not to breathe in the fumes. Coughing, he blinked back tears and waved his hand in front of his face. A large, black carriage sat in the middle of the yard. Amos stood a few yards away from it, gaping. Harnessed to it were four of the strangest looking creatures he had ever seen—their heads and necks were shaped like a horse's, but their front legs ended in claws and their backs were snakelike, curled beneath them. Large black wings, similar to bat wings, sprung from their shoulders. While impressively disturbing, they didn't quite look logical. Did they fly the carriage around or slither forward, dragging it? Danny wasn't sure how that worked.

Dicky pushed past him through the doorway for a better view. "Wow," he whispered.

A twisted, green-faced man jumped from the driver's seat—another goblin. He was only about Dicky's height. His beady eyes fixed on Danny and he grinned, showing off the tips of his fangs. "The Dark Chariot is here at your call."

Danny's stomach tightened. "I didn't call anything. There must be some mistake."

The goblin's sneer deepened. "You are Daniel Stronghammer?"

"Y-yes." The cold morning breeze on his sweaty face made Danny shiver and his leg ached where Dicky had kicked him.

"And you have just performed the recent and preparatory dark act of attacking your brother for a thoughtless, but quite harmless comment?"

"But he deserved it!" Danny didn't see how he'd done anything special. Brothers punched each other all the time, right? And Dicky fought back and hurt him, as well. He hadn't done anything evil—they couldn't take him away already. Panic clogged his mind.

"There is no mistake, young Mr. Stronghammer. You have performed your first preparatory dark act, as stated in your acceptance letter. The Dark Chariot will transport you to Dark Lord Academy. Please climb aboard immediately."

Danny glanced at Dicky, who was staring at the goblin slack-jawed. No help there. He looked the other way towards Amos, who stood rubbing his head and looking a bit befuddled. No help there, either. Danny's heart pounded. "Um, I haven't even packed yet."

"There is no need to bring anything, Mr. Stronghammer." The goblin's long ears swiveled back, giving him a displeased air. "The school provides all necessary items. Of course, you'll have to purchase luxuries yourself, but that's the way of it." The goblin tapped his foot. "Well, hurry along, we haven't got all day."

Danny searched for the perfect excuse to prove he wasn't villain material. "But I—"

"Wonderful!" boomed Pa's voice. He had poked his head out of the forge and a smile split his face. "Why, your transportation is already here! They're right timely at this school, I see...I knew I picked the best one for you." He strode across the yard and grabbed Danny into a rough hug before pushing him in the goblin's direction. "Make me proud, son."

Danny wanted to, just not by doing this. He still didn't get how being a villain was something to be proud of.

Amos stepped forward to pat him on the back. "Don't let it get to you," he whispered. "Just give it a chance, I'm sure it'll be alright."

Danny grimaced. *Yeah, right.* But what could he do? Throw a screaming fit like he was half his age? Or would misbehaving only dig him deeper into going?

Dicky's face reddened. "Hey, that's no fair! I wanna go, too!"

"Third sons," Pa said to the goblin. "They're always getting into everything, aren't they?" He ruffled Dicky's hair.

"Hey, cut that out!" Dicky pulled away and flattened his hair. "How come I never get to do anything? It's no fair!" He glared at Danny.

Trading places sounded like the perfect solution to Danny. "Yeah, why don't you—"

The goblin stepped forward, grabbing Danny by the arm. It leered at Dicky, who took a step back. "You'll have your chance in a few years, *hero*. But I suggest you don't take on an Academy Graduate for your villain because you'll not get far."

Danny gulped and tried to yank his arm free. Claws dug into his arm as if the goblin understood his intent to talk his way out of this all too well.

"Well, that was a sweet goodbye," the goblin said, "but let's get on with it." He dragged Danny across the yard with surprising force for someone so small.

Danny glanced back in panic at his family. Pa, still beaming like an idiot, waved goodbye. Amos gave a thumbs up and Dicky thumbed his nose at him. Danny's call for help died on his lips. They didn't care—they were letting the goblin take him away. A lump rose in his throat.

A jerk forced him to look forward and keep his balance. They had reached the Dark Chariot. The goblin flung him at the steps. Danny grabbed the handlebar to steady himself.

"Wait!" Pa called.

Hope surged up as Danny turned to look. Had he changed his mind? Pa took several swift steps towards the carriage, then held up a package in his hand, offering it to the goblin.

"I almost forgot. Special delivery for Lord Atriz."

Danny clenched the handlebar tighter and looked away before he lost his composure. Pa hadn't changed his mind. He wasn't rescuing him, he was just giving that evil-looking collar to the goblin. He really must be working for the villains. Chest tight with despair, Danny pulled himself in. A group of pale, but intensely curious human faces peered at him from the shadows. Children—just like him.

Before Danny could register his surroundings, the goblin yelled, "Gee up," and slapped the reins against the strange creatures pulling the Dark Chariot. The sudden jerk as it moved forward sent Danny flying into the nearest boy, a beefy fellow with dark brown hair and pale skin.

"Get off me, stupid!" He threw Danny across the chariot where he crashed into a girl and boy, both with thin, perfectly trimmed black hair and Asian eyes. They shoved him off of them without saying a word, their dark eyes emotionless.

The boy he had first crashed into flexed his forearms. While large, they looked more fat than muscle. Although thinner, Danny was strong from working in the forge. He guessed they'd be about even in a fight, but he had no intention of getting into another one. If just hitting Dicky got him hauled off to Dark Lord Academy, beating up some stranger was sure to get him locked up there for life.

"Better look where you're falling next time," the boy said with a sneer. "Or I won't be letting you off so easy."

"Right…I'll keep that in mind." Danny rubbed his head and glanced around at the other children.

They stared impassively back at him. Not one smile, encouraging glance, or even hint of sympathy was evident. With a chill, he realized each of these kids was planning to become a Dark Lord—hoping to rule a country as an absolute and evil dictator. He swallowed hard. The odds were definitely not in his favor. He was surrounded by villains in training.

CHAPTER 3

Arrival at the Dark Lord Academy

The Dark Chariot halted with another gut-wrenching jolt. Danny clutched the wall to stop himself from flying into anyone. To his relief, everyone else was too busy doing the same thing to bother him. No one spoke, but the children looked out the window. Danny, squished against the far wall, was between windows and couldn't get a good view. All he glimpsed were trees. He debated making a run for it, but had no idea where they were and getting stranded in some unknown place didn't sound either intelligent or appealing. Better to lie low until he had a better grasp on his options.

The door to the carriage bounced open and the goblin pushed in a girl. Her skin was dark brown and her black hair was done up in little box braids all across her head. She wore a dress the color of moss with flowers embroidered on it.

Danny clutched the bottom of his seat, just in time, as the goblin whipped the Dark Chariot into motion once again. The new girl stumbled. The rude boy shoved her before she could knock into him and she fell into Danny instead. They both tumbled to the floor.

"Don't you look frighteningly evil," sneered the bully.

"At least I'm not as ugly as you," she snapped.

The girl scrambled to her feet and helped Danny up, then began dusting off his clothes. Her braids bobbed up and down as she did so. "You all right? I didn't mess anything up, did I? You hurt at all? Did I tear anything?"

"It's fine," he said, his face burning. He felt everyone's eyes on them.

"So, seeing as we've bumped into each other, I might as well introduce myself." She flashed a quick smile at him and grabbed his hand before he could react, pumping it up and down. "Name's Daisy, they call me Daze for short."

"Danny."

"Well, it's a pleasure to meet you. I was, um," she glanced around at the others, all looking away and pretending not to notice them, "afraid I wouldn't meet anyone nice, you know—afraid of looking stupid. But, as I already looked stupid in front of everyone, I thought, what the hey, you look nice enough."

"Um." Danny wasn't sure if it was a compliment or not, seeing as they were supposed to become villains. But then, Daisy hardly looked frightening and was as cheery as her name. He glanced around, hoping someone would save him from having to come up with polite conversation, but the two Asian kids were studiously looking the other way. He suspected they had anticipated his plea for help and were careful to be unavailable. The boy who had caused the whole problem bossed around a skinny boy with long black hair and glasses. Several others whispered to each other or tried to look invisible. No one would meet his gaze. "So, uh, what made you decide to come to Dark Lord Academy?"

"Oh, that." Daisy rolled her eyes. "Well, my mama's in the Black Action Assistance League. They're a watchdog group that supports racial equality. They did a five-year study and determined that there's a terrible shortage of black villains. In fact, only 1 in 235 villains is a person of color—it's obviously discrimination. The other organizations, however, weren't too keen on taking it on. I suppose they figured it'd be bad press." Daisy shrugged. "But the BAAL decided that discrimination is discrimination, so they sued the Dark Lord Academy and, well, would you guess what they said?" She paused dramatically, waving her hands back and forth.

"I couldn't guess," Danny said, figuring he was meant to say something.

"That they didn't discriminate at all! No black people ever applied! They claimed they'd be happy to accept any qualified candidates who cared to apply. Of all the racist nonsense...they were trying to wriggle out of it. So the BAAL figured they'd just make sure to end it by seeing some fine people of color attend. Only there wasn't anyone but me and Johnny Hannison who were the right age and didn't already have our futures laid out. Well, turns out they rejected Johnny 'cause he had a great aunt who was a witch and, while she didn't have any formal schooling, she was downright evil and you're not allowed to have any evil relations 'cause the children of villains become heroes. Well, Mama says it's baloney, since a great aunt's not the same thing as a mother or father—so she was hopping mad and—"

It amazed Danny how she didn't even need to take a breath between all of that. Out of the corner of his eye, he caught the Asian kids watching them.

"—ready to take the whole school on. Only then came an acceptance letter for me and so, never mind I've never taken much to evil, there was nothing for it but to send me off and even the odds a bit, so to speak." Daisy beamed at him. "Only, say, you two aren't white. I'm Daisy!" She grabbed a hand of the twins both at once and started to pump them up and down. "Who're you two? Don't be shy."

They stared at her wide-eyed and stiff, hardly looking welcoming.

"Oh, well, it's a pleasure to meet you. Oh, hey, and who are you?" Daisy rounded on a tan boy with long, wavy black hair and earrings, and then pounced on a girl with frizzy red hair pulled into a ponytail.

Danny sighed in relief and leaned back against the side of the Dark Chariot. It halted with a jerk that made him bash his head against the wall. His eyes watered and, with a groan, he rubbed the back of his head. As his vision cleared, he saw that the others were piling out of the Dark Chariot in a hurry. Then a hand smashed his head back into the wall again.

"Hey, dorko, need help killing off some more brain cells?"

Some other kids in the background giggled. Danny dodged the boy's next punch and blinked his vision clear.

"I'm not a hero or anything, lay off."

"Nah, you're a loser. I can tell one of those a mile off."

With a guffaw, the bully turned and walked out, his tittering group of admirers following him.

Danny gritted his teeth. If that had been Dicky just now, he'd have pounded the little brat into the ground. But that's what had gotten him here, wasn't it? Revenge was far too tempting, although that idea made Danny stiffen. *No! I'm not evil, I just want to stand up for myself and get even.* Only, if he did that, the bully would retaliate and so on. It was one thing with his brother (or so he *had* thought), but another with a complete stranger.

No, adults had a point about fighting. It didn't seem right, or nice, to go around picking on people just for the sake of being evil. The stupid bully wasn't worth getting stuck here with people convinced that he *wanted* to be like that. He rubbed his head, combed his hair flat with his fingers, and climbed out of the Dark Chariot, trying to look as confident and nonchalant as possible.

Nothing looked familiar. Towering gray cliffs walled off the land beyond, forming dragon's teeth against the skyline. Broken rock covered the valley floor from end to end, except for a clog of dying weeds that choked the rim of a black lagoon. The goblin unharnessed the strange creatures that pulled the Dark Chariot and they slid into the eerie water with a quiet ripple. The spiked towers of the academy loomed in front of the mountains and blotted the sky. The castle's walls bristled with spear-toting soldiers pacing at regular intervals; a moat of lava surrounded them. In the center, a massive tower pushed above the others and belched pillars of smoke. Distinctly not welcoming. Amos was full of it with his "not that bad" line.

The goblin chuckled. "Welcome to the Dark Fortress, luxurious retreat of the rich and infamous, my little munchkins."

Danny wished he wouldn't say the word munchkins as if they were something to eat. It made him nervous. It seemed he didn't have any choice but to play along with this school thing for the moment—he was trapped. Perhaps he could explain to the teachers he just wasn't cut out to be evil and they'd convince Pa he didn't belong.

A grinding screech rent the air as minions lowered a drawbridge. The chains clinked while it jolted link by link toward the blazing moat. With a loud thump that made them all jump, it settled down across the moat, which was blowing large molten bubbles. A dark figure wrapped in a long, hooded cloak appeared in the entrance and paced down the drawbridge towards them. A heavy mist moved with it, keeping its features invisible. The little group of students huddled together, drawn by common fear. Danny realized with a shiver that he stood to one side, entirely by himself.

The dark figure stopped in front of them and lifted its long, black staff in the air, then brought it down with a crack against the earth. Thunder boomed and the ground shook. All the students screamed in terror, knocking into each other as they stumbled, until they all fell flat. Danny, free of the tangle, kept his balance. The mist disappeared, and the figure brought up a thin, pale hand and pushed back the hood.

Danny's jaw dropped. Before him stood the most beautiful, yet chilling woman he had ever seen. Her face was pale, the skin almost as white as porcelain. Her black hair was caught up in a bun, several long dark strands hung down and framed her face. Her bright red lips molded into a sneer as her eyes ran over the group of sprawled and tangled students. Then her gaze strayed over to Danny and her lips curled up in a slight smile.

"There's one like you in every group." Her voice was soft, like velvet against silk, and it sent a shiver down Danny's neck, yet held him still in fascination. "However, it remains to be seen if that means you'll be exceptionally good or exceptionally bad. I shall take my chances."

Danny wasn't sure if this was a compliment or not, but he was fairly certain that now was not the time to bring up his lack of qualifications for villianhood. She turned back to the group as they scrambled to their feet.

"Hurry up, idiots, and follow me inside," she snapped, her abrupt attitude shift startling them. "We haven't got all day." She turned on her heel and walked back towards the dark fortress without glancing back.

The students looked at each other, shrugging. The bully boy squared his shoulders. "I'm not afraid. She's a teacher, that's all." He marched after her. The others followed.

Danny took a deep breath. He wanted less than ever to go inside the school, but this wasn't the sort of place he could just stand around safely. If one of the chariot animals climbed out of the lake, it might consider him an appropriate dinner choice. Besides, the most reliable way to get home would be to convince the teachers he couldn't make the cut. Pa would have to accept him back home then. Danny headed towards the drawbridge.

The lava in the moat fizzed as he approached. A large bubble popped, splashing molten rock up in the air, dangerously close to the drawbridge. None of the other students, almost all across, seemed to notice. *This is nuts.* On the far end of the drawbridge, two goblin guards stood on either side of the doorway, snickering at him. Resentment at appearing cowardly pushed Danny forward. *I'm going to do it—I just won't look.*

The constant popping and splashing made it hard to pretend the lava didn't exist. He fixed his eyes ahead and hurried across. He was so focused on ignoring the lava he didn't notice the foot sticking out from the shadows of the doorway. He tripped and fell flat. His hands stung as they jarred against the stone floor of the hallway. The bully stepped out of the shadows, laughing.

"Hey, idiot, too busy congratulating yourself on becoming teacher's pet? Just remember, there is only one top Dark Lord in this class—me!" He gave Danny a kick.

Danny rolled to avoid the next one.

"Come on, scaredy cat, try and fight me. Let's see what bad moves you've got." The bully chortled. "If you can catch up." He turned and walked off after the others who were heading down the hall.

Danny rubbed his side. Why did the stupid boy think he cared? Not only wasn't he worth it, but Danny wasn't going to let him trick him into looking like he belonged here.

"That was exceedingly pitiful, you know." The grating voice made Danny gulp and look up. One of the guards had apparently deigned to notice him. The goblin flicked a long green ear at him and its gold, flat eyes had a nasty glint. "Best hurry along," it continued, "wouldn't want to get lost, would you? Never know when you might be found again—or what may find you." It flashed its fangs in a sinister smile.

Again, Danny had the impression he looked like a snack to the creature. He shoved himself upward and hurried into the dimly lit stone corridor. It smelled of mildew. Torches in twisted iron brackets lined the walls. Beneath every third torch stood a goblin in full armor with a spear. Danny ignored their disdainful gaze and tried to catch up to the students ahead, who were disappearing around a corner at the far end of the passage. He dashed around it only to find the next corridor empty. Perhaps they'd gone around another corner at the end? Determined to stay calm, he kept going. Passageways going off to the right and left taunted him, suggesting they might have gone down any of *them* instead. Danny turned his head back and forth, trying to check them all without slowing his pace. This place looked like a maze.

The passageway dead-ended in a T, offering a choice of right or left. No one was in sight in either direction. Danny's heartbeat thumped in his ears as he glanced first one way and then the other. Something sounding suspiciously like chains being dragged along the stone floor made him jump and whirl around. The passage behind him was empty, even the goblin guards were gone, although he wasn't sure they'd have offered safe advice even if he dared ask. *Safe? I'm in villain school, the last thing it's going to be is safe.* Danny took in several deep breaths. *Don't panic, it has to be one way or the other, just pick.*

Something clattered distantly down the right passage and then followed the rhythm of thumps that might be footsteps. Taking a deep breath, Danny started down it.

"I wouldn't go that way if I were you."

The voice made Danny jump and let out a small cry. He whirled around first to the right, then to the left, not seeing the person who'd spoke until a boy emerged from yet another corridor off to the side. Danny almost screamed again. By height, the boy might be about his age or a year or two older, but his face was twisted and gruesome in appearance. His eyes were at a slant, his bulbous and misshapen nose torqued the other direction, and his large lips pulled down on the right side, making his whole face look scrunched. Worst of all, a huge scar ran down his forehead to his left ear. Danny tried not to stare and didn't want to imagine what might have happened to him.

"W-what?"

The boy grinned, showing of a set of perfectly normal straight teeth, which glittered white and clean in the torchlight. It somehow made his strange face worse. "I said I'd not go that way if I were you. That heads down to the executions department."

Danny took in a sharp breath. "Oh, uh, thanks. This way then?" He pointed back behind him towards the left passage.

The boy snorted in laughter. "No, no, that leads to Professor Streptococcus's plague collection. Don't want to mess with those really, they're catching, you know." He winked. "Past that is the secret passageway to the dungeons; again, probably not where you're looking to go. You a brand new student? I'm Igor." He held out a hand.

"Um, yeah. I'm Danny." He didn't want to touch the hand, speaking of catching…just in case whatever had happened to him might be contagious, but shook the hand anyway, not wanting to be rude.

"You want teacher offices. They're back the way you came, then the third passage on the left. Here, I'll show you real quick." Igor stepped out farther into the torchlight, revealing a humped back, and pulled behind him a small cart that seemed to be full of stacked mummies, maybe four or five of them. Danny cringed back.

Oblivious, or perhaps just ignoring his discomfort, Igor headed around the corner. Danny didn't have much choice but to follow. He counted the passages, but Igor seemed to go to the fourth, not the third one, before stopping to point. "There, head that way and you'll hit teacher offices." He gave Danny another ghastly grin.

"Thanks. Really appreciate it." Danny walked swiftly down it, not letting himself ponder if following Igor's advice was a good thing or not, but he didn't want to stick around with him and his possibly dead wrapped up bodies a moment longer. He didn't want to wonder how accurate Amos's stories about mummies coming alive were. Nor did he want to wonder if Igor had looked like that *before* he came to villain school or if school had somehow disfigured him. In fact, he didn't want to think about any of what he'd just heard or seen. He picked up his pace and almost bumped into Daisy as he rounded the next bend.

"There you are," she said, smiling at him. "Don't let that jerk get to you. He's just jealous. I wish I had been smart enough not to get all tangled up."

Danny took a moment to realize she meant the bully, not Igor. He grunted in response—that felt almost like a distant memory at this point. He tried to breathe evenly and calm down in the now reassuring presence of the very children who had before unnerved him. *Perhaps it's safety in numbers.* Even the Dark Lady looked a little less intimidating. For the moment, anyway.

This corridor was different; bright globes lit it, hanging from the arched ceiling. Both sides were punctuated by studded metal doors, on each a name written in silver lettering. The Dark Lady stopped by the first door on the left.

"Stand in a line," she commanded.

The students hurried to obey. The bully boy scrambled to the front of the line. Danny stood at the end just behind Daisy, who winked at him before turning forward. The Dark Lady grabbed the bully by the arm and pulled him in front of the first door. She looked him over.

"Typical specimen. You'll suit Mystfolyn just fine."

She tapped him on the head with a wand and he disappeared in a puff of smoke.

The Unpleasantries of Registration

Everyone gasped, staring at the place where the boy had been. Danny couldn't help thinking the bully wasn't much of a loss, but winced since that seemed a bit callous. The Dark Lady was unconcerned as she moved to the next door down, on the right this time.

"Next!"

The girl at the front of the line tried to take a step backward, but someone shoved her forward and the Dark Lady grabbed her, pushing her into position. Danny risked moving to the side to peer around the others and get a better view of what was happening. The girl's eyes were wide and she babbled something incomprehensible as the wand came down. Her words were drowned out as she, too, disappeared in smoke.

This time, the lead boy didn't step forward when the Dark Lady moved onwards. She turned and gave him a scathing look. "Don't get all excited. Each and every student must meet with his or her advisor before being registered for class. I shan't do anything evil to you—yet." She gave them a smile that made Danny shiver. Perhaps catching up with everyone else wasn't such a good idea after all.

The boy, squaring his shoulders, stepped forward at her motion and she vanished him as well. They continued down the hall, although Danny noticed they skipped a door somewhere in the middle. When they reached the last one, only he and Daisy remained. She gave him a thumbs up and a huge grin as she disappeared in a cloud of smoke.

"Disgustingly cute and cheerful, that one," the Dark Lady said, a look of distaste on her face. "Ckriigrihmal has his work cut out for him this year. Serves him right."

Danny shifted from one foot to the other. Now what?

Her gaze turned back to him, cool and distant. "Well now, boy, let's get settled."

She walked back to the door she had skipped. Danny noticed the silver letters: Sorceress Vrlyxfrka. She grabbed his arm and tapped herself on the head with her wand. They were enveloped in smoke, which made Danny cough and blurred his vision. When it cleared, he wiped away his tears.

Instead of the corridor, they stood in a small room, draped in Dark Lord Black. A large window, showing a view of misty dead trees, illuminated the office. The silk draperies were dyed the standard funeral tones, but were quite risqué with their nonstandard silver patterns. Several glittering gems, mounted directly into the wall, also broke the black monotony. A huge, full-length oval mirror hung on the wall as well, with gold skulls on its gilded frame, but Danny saw no reflection in it, only milky white fog. An inky blot of a chair hunched in the corner near an end table adorned with a lamp and half cup of coffee, both nearly invisible against the backdrop of wall and desk. At the other side of the room sat an elegant ebony desk and chair. On the desk, a single, toxically red apple seemed to float amidst the black-on-black accoutrements.

Vrlyxfrka waved her wand, making a plain black chair appear in front of the desk.

"Sit."

She strode over to the desk and sat behind it while Danny plopped into the chair.

"Let's see what the official record says," she said with a grim smile. Another puff of smoke and papers appeared on the desk. Vrlyxfrka produced silver reading glasses from her cloak and perched them on her nose as she scanned the papers. Danny tried to sit as quietly as possible, debating the proper moment to explain.

"Hmf. Blacksmith's son. Original, but not special. A brother with hero potential, typical. Careless and accident prone, refinable. Mostly obedient...we'll stamp that out of you soon enough. I sense a rebel underneath all that." She peered at him over the glasses. "Don't be taking your villainy past the realm of acceptable, young man, understood?"

Danny had no idea what "acceptable villainy" might entail and wasn't sure he wanted to find out. "I don't think I—"

Vrlyxfrka silenced his attempt at explaining he wasn't villain material with a wave of her hand. "Other than that, nothing unusual. Interesting. I'll still take my chances with you. All you really need is a bit of sprucing up." She set the glasses on top of the paper and got up, circling Danny's chair.

Danny didn't dare try to object again. His hopes of explaining wavered. She was a Dark Lady. Who knew what she might do to him? He had to be sure to present his case for going home in the best possible way.

Vrlxyfrka poked his hair with the tip of her wand, making Danny start. "Ugh, the blond hair will have to go. We can't do anything about the blue eyes—yet. You can make them glowing red once you work up to that. And the freckles!" She tsked at him. "Less time in the sun should reduce them until you're good enough to fix that as well. Now for the hair—dye would be best." She clapped her hands. "Drog!"

A goblin lifted up the corner of one of the draperies and stepped into the room. He held a black bottle, which he dumped over Danny's head. Cold liquid stung his scalp, making him gasp in surprise. The goblin worked it into his hair.

Danny grimaced. Pa had always been proud all three of his boys looked just like him. What would he say now? Only that reminded him Pa had made something for the Dark Lords. Had the goblin delivered it? Maybe Pa wouldn't care anymore, maybe he'd agree with the villains; after all, he was sending him here to turn him into one of them. Danny's eyes stung—but that might just be the dye dripping down his face and into his eyes. It smelled like rotten milk and had oozed all over his clothes as well.

"There, perfect!" Vrlyxfrka said as the goblin finished. "When that dries, it should be jet-black!"

Danny reached up to flatten his slimy hair and his hand came away covered in black goop. "Don't I have to wash it out or something?"

"Not necessary. It'll take care of itself. That will have to do towards your appearance for the moment. Black robes, standard school wear, will be brought to your quarters." Vrlyxfrka gestured to the goblin and it nodded and withdrew.

Danny took a deep breath and fought up the nerve to try to explain again. "Um, Sorceress, I—"

"Later." Vrlyxfrka motioned him to silence and sat back down. "First things first, your new name."

"What?" Danny blinked, side tracked. "What's wrong with my name?"

Vrlyxfrka frowned at him. "Seriously? Danny the Dark Lord? Don't make me laugh. Even Daniel brings up images of god-fearing prophets, not sorcerers and villains. A villain needs a proper name." She wrote out a name on piece of paper and handed it across the desk to him.

Danny looked down at it. Zxygrth. He frowned. "How do I say this?"

"Any way you like." Vrlyxfrka beamed at him. "All villains have difficult and unpronounceable names. Standard issue. On to your courses."

Danny didn't dare test her patience further so close to the last time, but a lump formed in his throat. He hadn't known they'd take away his name. *Pa always called me Daniel*...But it was getting harder and harder to keep fighting this school thing when no one seemed inclined to care or listen.

"These," continued Vrlyxfrka, ignoring his discomfort, "are your regular classes." She handed him another sheet. It read:

Elementary Dark Magic: Exploring the principles and theories of dark magic. Learn to summon monsters and demons, as well as enchant beautiful women and throw heroes against walls. Also an overview of the specializations of Dark Magic: Necromancy, Demonology, Enchantment, Mind Control, Meteorology Control, Channeling, and Illusions.

The Elements of Personal Style: Design your own Dark Lord look. Learn about the conventions of appearance and attitude. Perfect your maniacal laughter, design your personal accent, and learn to properly monologue. As the year progresses, we'll cover witty battle banter, how to properly berate your minions, and issues of Dark Lord etiquette.

First Year History: Study the great villains of the past, their mistakes and flaws and how to avoid them. In particular, we'll look at the ten top reasons villains fail historically and explore world domination and why it's such a popular idea.

Elementary Tactics: Ruling the world is complicated business. We'll be exploring minions, the pros and cons of the different races, and the benefits and drawbacks of created minions. Plus, different methods for establishing control and organizing your Dark Army.

"I make all my first year students take a study hall," Vrlyxfrka said, "which leaves you one elective. Some of the more ambitious students take a language, which can be challenging in your first year, so I don't require one from you. If you start a language next year, you'll have plenty of time to fulfill the language requirement. Besides, you couldn't possibly know what sort of Dark Army you'd want at this stage, so it's hard to say which language would be best. Of course, Demonic is a good standby in that case, it always comes in handy."

Danny had no desire to speak to demons or any other sort of evil creature. Just the thought of meeting some made him feel sweaty and weak. "I don't really think—"

"Any musical talent? You could take Organ, it's impressive. Or Art. Here, take a look." She handed him another sheet. "Physical education is done through sports, of course. I expect you to sign up for a fall sport and join at least one club, but you'll have a month to settle in first."

Now was the time Danny ought to speak up again and convince her that he just wasn't up to being a Dark Lord, but morbid curiosity won out. Danny looked at the list with trepidation.

First Year Electives:

Architectural Planning: Learn to design the perfect Dark Hideaway. Decide if castle, fortress, cave, or other structure is the perfect setting from which to rule the world.

Art: Learn to express your evil side through images.

Deadly Engineering: Designing exceptionally elaborate and slow mechanisms for hero disposal.

Health: If you haven't got your health, then you haven't got anything.

Languages: Demonic, Goblinese, Orcish, Trollese, Wraithish, and Creative Linguistics—Designing your own evil language (prior language experience required).

Magical Weapons: An overview of the array of choices for slaughtering innocents.

Math: You never know when you might need to count.

Monsters and Terrors: An overview of the scariest things out there and how to control them.

Music: Add to your evil aura by learning to play impressive mood-altering pieces on the organ.

Zombie Economics: How not to break your bank account on your first invasion.

He certainly didn't feel up to a language; it was bad enough he'd have to take one next year if he couldn't find a way to escape. Danny frowned at the list, trying to find something easy. He considered Art, but he'd never liked being creative and he wasn't sure he knew how to "express his evil side."

"Um, Magical Weapons, I guess." At least he had some experience making the occasional spear or sword as a blacksmith.

"Good choice, practical, and not too difficult for your first year, although very popular." Vrlyxfrka nodded. "Perhaps you are worth the effort—let me see if I can get you in quickly enough."

She muttered and the paper in Danny's hands exploded in a puff of smoke, making him jump. Vrlyxfrka cocked her head, as if listening to something, then nodded. "Very good, I slipped you in just in time, the very last spot. I think we are finished for the moment. However, remember to consider the sports and clubs carefully—"

Smoke erupted in the middle of the room, cutting short their conversation. When it cleared, Danny gazed into the gray eyes of the most wizard-like person he had ever seen. The man was bald, but had a long, black beard. He had a long nose, noble features, but somehow they made him look as cold and uncaring as if he were chiseled from stone.

Danny gulped and glanced back at Vrlyxfrka. His advisor pressed her lips into a thin red line. "Screkvox, I'm with a student at the moment. Don't you have your own to be orienting?"

"This is of the utmost importance and I have finished with my student." Screkvox made a careless brushing movement with his gloved hand. "You must gather all the first years back together immediately. One of them is an imposter."

Danny's heartbeat thumped in his ears. Did he mean *him? I'm not an imposter, I just want to go home.*

Vrlyxfrka did not look impressed by the declaration. "I shall do nothing of the sort. I have already divided them up and if you object to your student, speak to the headmaster."

"This is not some petty concern!" Thunder rumbled as Screkvox stepped forward. "The school meter shows both goodness and honor up at near alert levels—we have been infiltrated."

"New students always skew the meters a little." Vrlyxfrka shook her head. "There's no reason to incite panic. When the headmaster returns, you may take it up with him."

Screkvox's expression turned downright murderous, making Danny wish he could sink into the floor. Maybe he should explain this was all an accident, that he tried to get out of it, but no one would listen. Only Screkvox hardly looked like someone he wanted to confess to. He looked angry enough he might kill him on the spot rather than let him go home. Danny was going to have to be careful around these teachers and pick who to reveal his lack of villainy to with more discretion.

"I'm telling you, a hero has—"

Vrlyxfrka held up a hand, stopping Screkvox mid-rant. "We can discuss further investigation, but in the meantime, it is crucial the new students are situated before classes start tomorrow morning. At the very least, there is no need to subjugate Zixygrith to this debate. Drog, escort him to his room."

Screkvox's icy glare fixed on Danny as the room dissolved again into annoying smoke, forcing Danny to concentrate on breathing.

CHAPTER 5

Getting Situated in an Uncomfortable Environment

The goblin showed Danny to his room. It was a small box of a space, just enough room for a single bed and nightstand. An empty bookshelf stood at the end of the bed. A black cloth hung opposite it like an ominous strip of darkness. The goblin pushed it back, revealing a closet full of black robes.

"Your school wear, lordling," sneered the goblin, somehow making the title into an insult. "Supper bell rings at six. Dress appropriately. School rules require you wear your nametag." He slapped the tag on the nightstand and left.

Danny stood a moment, his hair still dripping. The room seemed hardly bigger than a jail cell—perhaps he could write a letter convincing Pa the school was a rip-off. Only if he got a letter back telling him to stop whining and stick it out, that'd be more than he could bear. Screkvox's tirade on imposters not-withstanding, it just might push him over into accepting his evil fate.

He stripped off his dirty clothes, muddy from his fall in the corridor and stained with hair dye, and put on a black shirt, pants, and cape. He supposed this was what the goblin had meant by appropriate. The room looked very empty, but since he hadn't been allowed time to pack, he hadn't brought anything. Suspecting his own clothes would soon disappear because of their lack of conformity, he sorted through his pockets and found a couple of nails he had made and a bit of paper on which Amos had sketched some plans for making a plow and an axe.

A lump rose in his throat. Around this time, Amos would be finishing up at the forge and usually Danny would be sweat-covered, but satisfied from a long day of work. It would be about the time that Amos would teach him more blacksmithing, with Pa looking on, making suggestions. Was Amos teaching Dicky now instead? Or was it later than he thought and they were already sitting down to supper?

The clanging supper bell interrupted his thoughts. Danny put the paper on the nightstand, with the nails on top to weigh it down. They didn't particularly matter anymore, but he'd keep the small reminders. Then he piled all the dirty clothes on the floor near the door. He grabbed the nametag, pinned it to his shirt, and hurried out.

Noise assaulted his ears. The hall was full of students, all in black, although the clothes were diverse in style. They hurried down the hall, talking animatedly. Some of them looked quite wicked, with red eyes, horns, or fangs. Danny eyed them cautiously; these confident villains could kill him in a moment if they wished. But he didn't dare be late, either, so he edged down the corridor in the same general direction, careful not to touch anyone else.

"Danny!"

Daisy came dashing over to grab him by the arm. For a second he didn't recognize her. Her braids were gone. Instead her hair made a soft black halo around her face, hanging down to her shoulders. She was dressed in long black robes and the total effect went a long way towards turning her from cute to scary, but her big white smile and the sparkle in her eyes made her seem more a mischievous witch or fairy than a true villain.

"Or, should I say..." she squinted at his nametag, "Zixegreth?"

Danny shrugged. He noticed her nametag had said Hglifthea, but she had crossed it out and wrote Dazidethia instead.

"I shall call you Zixy!" she proclaimed, beaming at him. "Don't mind the tag, the name's Daze, just like I said before. I talked to The Prof, you know, my advisor. We decided on a happy medium, after much debate."

Danny guessed that "The Prof" had met his match in Daisy. She looked innocent enough, and way too cute, but he guessed she was something terrible when she didn't get her way. She might turn out to be the most evil of them all. He almost burst out laughing at that thought and ended up coughing instead.

"Ooh, careful," Daisy said, slapping him on the back. "Did you swallow something?"

"No, no, I'm fine," he said hastily, lest she try and help him further.

The hall opened into the dining room. Tables draped in

black filled the space and large black banners hung over them labeled "Year One," "Year Two," and so on.

"Hey look! There's those Asian kids. Did you know they're twins? They're real nice." Daisy grabbed his arm and dragged him across the hall to join the line for dinner.

The bully stood at the end of the line, talking to a skinny boy with glasses and his hair spiked straight up. Next to them lounged a tanned boy with earrings.

"Why hurry? Let's look around a bit more…" Danny wished they could wait and stand behind someone else, but Daisy was oblivious to his protests.

"Hey, what're your new names?" she shouted, waving her hand at the twins who were standing farther ahead in line.

The bully turned and caught sight of Danny. He smirked. "Nice hairdo, loser. What, blonde hair not allowed? Surprised they didn't send you packing after one look at you."

He shoved Danny, but since he expected it, Danny was able to move with it and not send Daisy sprawling.

"Hey! That's not nice!" Daisy protested. "And it's prejudiced, too."

"I'm a Dark Lord, fuzz-head, I'm not supposed to be nice."

"Tell me you didn't just call me fuzz-head, lump-brain."

"Fuzz-head, I'm surprised they didn't toss you right out by your pigtails the moment they caught sight of you." He sneered at her, stepping closer so he loomed above her. Danny noticed his nametag said Tlkyzefrl. He was beginning to think that, awful as it was, he had one of the best names so far. *I guess I'll just call him Tulk.* He realized what he was doing and almost groaned out loud. *I'm sounding just like Daisy! If I hang out with her anymore, she's going to drive me insane.* And if she wasn't careful, she was going to get them in more trouble irritating everyone around them like this.

He tried to pull her away, mumbling something about how it wasn't worth it, but Daisy marched right up to Tulk. She puffed up and thrust her index finger in his face. "Now see here, just 'cuz you've got big muscles, you think you can boss everyone around. Well, I ain't gonna hear none of your idiotic and Neanderthal comments. If you don't stop —"

Tulk took a swing at her, which would have smashed into her face about level with her left eye if Danny hadn't shoved him at that moment. Forget not fighting, he wasn't going to let the bully hit a girl—it just wasn't right. Tulk rounded on Danny, who blocked the next blow. Before he could retaliate, the two of them were jerked apart by older students. The one holding him had spiky purple hair and a nose ring. He wore black jeans with silver chains hanging from them. A girl with long black hair, silver-streaked highlights, and a slinky black dress had an iron grip on Tulk. Danny couldn't help but think Tulk had gotten the better deal. A boy with bleached-blond shaggy hair that went every which way and dressed in flowing black robes stepped between them.

"No showing off in the dining hall," he said, fixing them with his strange stare. His eyes were silver with no pupils. Tulk's eyes looked like they were going to bug out of his head. "Evil attitudes are allowed, but no physical fighting except when in a zone designated for that sort of thing. I'll see you both in detention if I hear of you doing it again." He turned his silver eyes on Tulk. "And I'll know if either of you try it again. I'm watching you, Tilkyzefril, and you..." he turned to Danny, "Zixygrath. I won't forget either of you and I don't think the pair of you want the attention of Demigorth the Destroyer!" His eyes flashed red and he laughed. "Muahahahahahahha!"

Both the kids holding Danny and Tulk joined in, their maniacal laughter echoing across the hall. All the other kids from the Year One cowered. Demigorth turned away and cut in the line ahead of them all. Danny was released when Demigorth's friends went to join him. He rubbed his arm and grimaced. *Looks like fighting isn't allowed here after all, or, well, only in "designated areas."* As he turned to find Daisy, Tulk leaned forward and hissed, "Watch yourself, Zixy, 'cause I'm gonna get even with you real soon."

Tulk grabbed a tray and turned to get served. Danny sighed and waited until he moved away before holding out his tray, mostly wondering how long he would have to put up with Tulk before he managed to find a safe teacher to convince he didn't belong. He was distracted by a suction noise, followed by a loud plop. His eyes widened as he noticed the large formless lump of gray on his tray. He wrinkled his nose in disgust.

Someone grunted unpleasantly and he looked up into the narrowed eyes of the evilest fat woman he'd ever seen. Her round face curved into a frightening frown, her triple chins jiggled in annoyance, and she curled her right arm into an enormous fist with bulging biceps. She might be fat, but he was sure one punch from her would send him flying across the cafeteria.

"You wanna make something out of my food, boy?"

"No, no. Looks properly evil," Danny blurted. "Um, well, you know, an evil school should have evil food, right?" He hoped he was giving her a compliment. He knew it would be safer to shut up, but he rambled on stupidly. "I was, em, afraid the food wouldn't be up to code, but you've proved me wrong. It's of the same... quality as the rest of the school."

She seemed mollified, but she shook an enormous forefinger in his face. "For now, I'll take that as a compliment, but I'll be keeping an eye on you, *Zexaygreth*."

Danny gulped, hoping she wouldn't watch too closely, so he could throw away this slush at his first opportunity.

Daisy, beaming, pulled a miserable Danny down to the Year One table. "Wasn't that awesome, the way Demigorth's eyes did that flashing thing? Oh, I can't wait to learn it. Don't mind Tulky, he's just jealous. Oh, hey, did you guys see how he did that?"

The last question was directed at the twins, who sat together on the other side of the table. They looked the same as they had before with their tidy, close cropped black hair, only they both wore Chinese style black shirts and pants. Neither of them spoke. Their name tags read Shaidazgx and Aundrwtl.

"So, what electives did you guys pick?" Daisy asked. "I picked art, of course. I hope you did, too."

"Eh..." Danny didn't know how to tell her he hadn't. Although he was relieved he wouldn't be sharing the class with her, he didn't want to hurt her feelings. "I actually picked Magical Weapons."

"So did we," said Shai, the girl. She gave Danny a small smile. "Have you picked a sport yet? We were leaning towards dueling."

Danny managed a tentative smile back.

"Don't know I'd be any good at that," Daisy piped in. "I was thinking of minion tossing myself. Once I get my magic down, of course."

Shai nodded. "I hear that a temper is essential to minion tossing. I think it's a good choice."

Daisy chuckled. "Mama always did say I had a temper a mile long, like a blizzard in the summer." Both Shai and Daisy fell into uncontrollable giggling at that.

Danny glanced at Aun, who lifted an eyebrow and shrugged.

"So, you know much about weapons?" Danny asked, to try to steer the conversation elsewhere from girl nonsense.

"A bit." Aun shrugged again. "My father taught me some stuff."

"I wish I knew more. I've learned the basics of sword and axe making, but we never did anything fancy."

"You made swords?" Aun looked impressed.

Danny flushed. "Well, Pa and my brother Amos did, they were teaching me...until Pa decided I'd be better off here, since Amos is getting the forge..." He trailed off, realizing it wasn't such a good conversation after all. Aun had a far away look on his face, as well.

Danny turned to poke his gray lump with his fork, searching for signs of life, and decided he wasn't hungry.

A crack of thunder resounded through the cafeteria, making him drop his fork. It clattered onto the table. Shai gasped and many of the other first years went pale. However, the older students only grew quiet and turned to face the stage at one end of the dining hall. Lightning flashed and thunder cracked again. When Danny blinked the spots out of his eyes, he saw on the stage a tall, pale man with long, dark hair dressed in (of course) black robes.

"A dark elf," whispered Aun, sounding awed.

"Now why is it that 'dark' elves are always white people with black hair?" muttered Daisy on Danny's other side. "I'm just saying..."

The dark elf raised a hand and the hall lapsed into complete silence. "Greetings! For the benefit of our first years, let me introduce myself. I am Atriz, Headmaster of Dark Lord Academy."

So *this* was who Pa had sent the mysterious collar to. Danny wasn't sure if it made Atriz a better choice as someone to convince he wasn't villain material to or a worse choice. Either way, he had to make sure of his words before trying.

"Tomorrow marks the beginning of a new year of evil and I hope you all will show unprecedented progress in that regard," continued Atriz. "I have returned from my meeting with the school's board of directors and they have high expectations that this year's graduating class will bring a new level of terror to the various worlds." Atriz nodded at the sixth years, who let out a cheer, then waved his hand again and they were silenced.

"I am often asked by both parents and students how it is that such a place as this most venerable institution can exist." Atriz smiled, which sent a shiver down Danny's back. "I would like to remind you all of our school's great philosophy. Perhaps we must work together a little, but if we keep our own personal desires in check, we can do much for the Greater Evil. Think of it! Instead of each of us trying to add a little evil where we can, every year Dark Lord Academy unleashes thirteen highly qualified villains to wreak havoc across the dimensions. This was the great vision of our dear founder, Lord Xonios the Plotter, who vanished mysteriously while on an expedition to map hell and was never heard from again."

Atriz shrugged. "But no matter. What is important is that each and every one of you keep the larger goal in sight —the Greater Evil."

Wait a minute, Danny thought. *If one of the students is an imposter, they aren't working for the Greater Evil at all...but something good, right?* Danny's heart pounded with excitement. *What if Pa is wrong and I am a hero?* Maybe it didn't matter as much as people thought, being a third son. Only he didn't feel very heroic, other than not wanting to be evil. Maybe that was enough to qualify as a hero anyway and he could find another way to make Pa proud of him. If he was a hero, perhaps Pa wouldn't be so upset at him for failing to fulfill his dream.

"So." Atriz held up a warning finger. "Only make each other miserable within the bounds of school rules and plot ahead for the day when you may take out your full wrath on the miserable masses and their heroic leaders. That and detention in the dungeons is highly unpleasant. I expect evil things from all of you." He threw back his head and laughed. "Muahahahahaha!"

The whole cafeteria broke out in maniacal laughter. Most of the first years just stared. Daisy giggled. Then Atriz snapped his fingers. Lightning crashed down in front of him, thunder rolled, and the ceiling broke out in a downpour of rain.

Some of the girls shrieked and students jumped up, shielding themselves with food trays or their arms as they dashed for the exits. By the time Danny registered it was actually raining indoors, cold water already ran down the back of his neck. He sighed and slowly pushed his chair back, not bothering to try and shield himself at this point. Then he noticed that Daisy, unlike all the other first years, hadn't moved.

Her wet hair plastered to her face, she turned to him with a huge grin. "Isn't this so cool?"

CHAPTER 6

A Terrible Day of Horrible Classes

Danny slid into a desk as the bell rang. He breathed a sigh of relief and then took a moment to examine the classroom. The walls were dark gray stone, like a dungeon. Chains hung from several twisted hooks and a couple of old bones littered the corner. At the front, a black cat stretched out luxuriously next to a human skull on a tidy stone desk. Its amber eyes regarded Danny with disdain. He looked away to watch the other students shift nervously in their desks and talk in low voices. Only Tulk, sitting near the front, seemed cool and confident.

"Nice *ambiance*." Tulk smirked at the others. "Wouldn't you agree?"

"Yeah, you're right about that." The boy next to him nodded so fast his glasses bounced. "Very, um, ambient."

Danny leaned forward to see his nametag: Spleglrtyk. He guessed Spleg didn't know what Tulk was talking about any better than the rest of them, but was trying to act superior.

Tulk sneered at Spleg as if he guessed the same thing.

Thunder interrupted them. The cat stood up on the front desk, arched its back and hissed. Purple lightning cracked across the front of the classroom, making everyone, including Tulk, scramble to the floor and hide under their desks. Danny felt his newly colored hair fizzing up in the static electricity and tried to flatten it, but only succeeded in shocking himself as his hand brushed the metal leg of his desk.

"Ouch!" He jerked back, hit his head on the bottom of his desk, and sent it tumbling over. "Owwww!" He clutched his head with his other hand and stumbled to his feet away from the desk. It briefly occurred to him that sitting beneath a desk with four metal legs during an indoor thunderstorm was worse that standing up on his own.

The lightning massed at the front of the room into a large ball of energy. It crackled with white and yellow and purple light, then started shrinking. A dark figure emerged behind it, until the lightning was reduced to a sphere of electricity at the end of a long staff. The light flickered onto the caped figure's face.

He had closely trimmed black hair that came together an elegant widow's peak in the middle of his forehead. His large, dark eyes were rimmed with finely arched black eyebrows and his thin mustache curled up at each end. His small beard was also curled primly. He wore a long and flowing black cape, although his shirt and pants were dark red. One of his feet poking out from under the cape was actually a cloven hoof. Danny couldn't decide who was more intimidating, Vrlyxfrka or this new teacher.

The man held up his left hand to the globe on the end of his staff and caught hold of one of the strands of electricity. He drew his hand away from it, as if pulling the staff away from his body. A bolt of purple energy crackled between the staff and his hand. Out of the corner of his eye, Danny noticed the cat flatten its ears and sit back down on the desk, tail lashing.

The Dark Lord coldly regarded the class, still cowering under their desks, until his eyes lit on Danny. Then the left side of his mouth twitched upwards in a half smile. "Students, up and into your desks," he ordered. Everyone scrambled to obey. Danny bent and picked up his fallen desk to straighten it. "And you!" The teacher pointed his staff to Danny. "Come up here."

Danny seemed to be making a habit of standing out. Perhaps this time he could explain he really didn't belong and this new teacher would listen. Tulk sniggered as Danny passed him and he glared back. The Dark Lord, however, didn't give him an opportunity and launched immediately into a lecture.

"I am Mystfolyn, terror of nations, more deadly than a demon, but as polite as a king, worker of the dark arts, and master of fates!" Mystfolyn snapped back the staff and the lightning curled back around it into a subdued ball of purple light. "Most particularly, master of your grades." Danny saw wide eyes and a few open mouths staring at Mystfolyn. Tulk, however, looked smug. Danny longed to wipe that expression off his face with a well-aimed punch, but refrained.

"Welcome to the Elements of Personal Style, where you will learn to transform yourself from pathetic evil wannabes like this—" He pointed at Danny, whose face burned despite himself. "To evil and mysterious Dark Lords, like me!" He swirled his cape around him, threw back his head, and laughed. "Muahahahahahahaha!"

The class shivered and Danny wanted to crawl into a hole and disappear. Maybe he was planning at ditching Dark Lord Academy at the first opportunity, but that didn't mean he wanted to be made into a public spectacle.

"Now," continued Mystfolyn, "the cape swirl and maniacal laughter are the foundation from which every villain must build up his or her reputation and personal style. Watch carefully."

He swirled his cape, slower this time, and Danny, not wanting to provoke him further, watched carefully. Mystfolyn twisted his shoulders and flicked his wrist, making the cape flap around him, the thin silk material swirling and dancing as it moved. Then he tilted his head back and laughed again. It was a deep and undulating laugh that shook Danny to his bones. "Muahahahahahaha!"

As impressive as it was, the cat only flicked an ear, which steadied Danny a little. Mystfolyn had just implied it was for show, right?

"Now then—" Mystfolyn squinted at Danny's nametag. "Zuxy-gruff, let's see you try that."

Now didn't seem the right time to try talking—maybe after class he would be more sympathetic. Feeling the weight of everyone's gaze on him, Danny took a deep breath. He twisted his shoulders and his cape moved a couple inches, not the huge swirl that Mystfolyn had done. He twirled harder, so hard that he turned around in a circle and almost fell down, but managed to hang onto his cloak. The class tittered, Mystfolyn frowned, and the cat put its ears flat in disapproval.

Danny felt his face get even hotter, but attempted the

laugh. "Muh-hehe-ha?" It sounded more like he was clearing this throat instead of laughing.

"Muw-ahaha!" Tulk started laughing at him, doing a passable impression of Mystfolyn's laugh.

"Wonderful, wonderful." Mystfolyn applauded. "Come up here, Tulkyzefril, and give us a demonstration." He pushed Danny back towards his desk. Tulk strode forward, looking rather haughty, to the front of the room. Danny slunk back to his desk.

"It wasn't that bad," Daisy whispered.

Danny could see the pained looks on Shai and Aun's faces.

"Yes, it was," he muttered and wished he'd stayed in bed this morning and skipped class. So what if it got him in trouble; he didn't want to be here anyway. To make matters worse, Tulk managed an admirable cape swirl on first try. *I don't want to be any good at this, why should I care?* Danny glared at Tulk. *If I was a hero, could I get away with attacking him?* His heart beat pounded in his ears in sudden excitement. The idea had a strong appeal to it—he could attack Tulk and, when stopped, declare he was the hero who had infiltrated the school.

Then reality hit him like a punch in the stomach. Declaring himself a hero in front of all these villains, teachers, and students alike would be suicide. Didn't villains kill heroes? Better stick to claiming it was a mistake and he only now realized he simply didn't belong due to his horrible incompetence. While embarrassing, it was far safer.

Mystfolyn interrupted his musing by breaking the class up into small groups to practice the laugh and cape twirl. Danny made several feeble attempts in hopes of showing how incompetent he was, but wasn't sure if Mystfolyn noticed him. Daisy took up most of his attention, laughing uproariously, but not at all maniacally, so loud that no one could hear themselves over her. The cat hid under the desk and Mystfolyn looked relieved when the bell rang. "I want everyone's maniacal laugh perfected by Friday," he called as the class hurried toward the exit.

Danny took a deep breath and walked over to Mystfolyn's desk. "Um, professor? I…don't think I'm any good at this."

Mystfolyn gave him a scornful glance. "Of course not, you miserable little excuse for a villain, thus your homework." He gestured at the door.

Danny winced, but bravely made a second attempt. "No, I mean I really am not any good at all, so bad in fact I shouldn't be here. I'm just not—"

"Shoo, I'm busy." Mystfolyn grabbed him by the shoulders, turned him around, and gave him a shove towards the door. "Before I get annoyed and zap you."

Danny stumbled forward. When he glanced over his shoulder, Mystfolyn was preening in a mirror behind the desk, ignoring him. The cat, now spread full-length on the desktop, gave him a baleful look and lashed the tip of its tail. Then the next class of older students burst into the room, talking noisily. One of them grabbed Danny by the collar and tossed him through the doorway. He tumbled to the paving stones.

"Hey, there you are!" Daisy bounced over beaming at him. She grabbed him by the arm and hauled him up.

"Thanks," Danny muttered, rubbing his head.

"What happened?"

"I tried to ask Mystfolyn a question, but he didn't want to let me." Danny sighed. "I don't think he likes me."

"Bah, don't let style class get you down." Daisy slapped him on the back, flashing white teeth at him. "It just takes practice. Myst-face said I kept laughing like a heartbroken hyena. I think he's just that way to everyone."

"Everyone but Tulk," Danny said crossly. Even if he didn't want to be a villain, Tulk getting all the praise rankled.

"Well, he's Tulk's advisor, isn't he? So it's only natural. We better get moving so we're not late!" Daisy glanced at her schedule. "Looks like it's Dark Magic! Awesome, I can't wait." She grabbed Danny's arm again and pulled him forward, not giving him time to respond.

Danny hoped that the Dark Magic teacher would be easier to talk to, although by the way things had been going so far, it didn't seem likely.

The Dark Magic classroom was shrouded in darkness, the only light a small, glowing orb in the center of an oblong table. Danny had to blink several times in order to see inside the room.

"Ooooh," squealed Daisy. "Scary. I *like* it."

Danny suppressed a shiver. Niceness and all aside, sometimes Daisy seemed to really manage all this evil stuff. If he was a hero, would that make them enemies? It wasn't like they were friends, but the idea made him uncomfortable all the same. He decided not to think about it.

Daisy skipped into the room and sat down. Shai and Aun came up behind Danny, making him jump.

"Are we supposed to just walk in there?" whispered Shai. She seemed as apprehensive as he did.

"Come on in!" Daisy shouted and Danny winced.

"What's the hold up?" someone's impatient voice sounded behind them.

"I guess we should," muttered Aun, stepping into the room, and Danny followed him.

Danny groped around in the dark and chose what felt like a seat. The rest of the students filed in, sitting around the table, their faces glowing in the pale light. Slowly

Danny's eyes adjusted. They glanced back and forth at each other, wondering what it all meant.

"But where's the teacher?" whispered a boy across the table. Danny squinted at his nametag, which possibly read something like: Brxlygf.

"Right here," said a quiet, low voice that sent shivers down Danny's back. He turned to his left to see, seated in their midst, a hooded figure, the light only illuminating the bottom half of a young female face. "Today, for our first class in Dark Magic, I am going to teach you the most important and basic principle: getting in touch with your inner villain."

Somehow, Danny didn't think he'd be any better at Dark Magic than Style Class. Hero or not, only a real villain could manage Dark Magic and he was sure to stand out again as an imposter. Still, she was quieter than Mystfolyn and not nearly so cold sounding as Vrlyxfrka. Perhaps he'd finally found someone he could confide in, someone who would help him get home.

"I am Nyshlza, master of Necromancy, and you are privileged to have me as your Dark Magic teacher this year." Nyshlza held out a hand towards the globe in the center of the table and it grew brighter. Nyshlza was dressed in flowing black robes that covered her completely and a huge dark hood. Her face was still only dimly visible. While her introducing herself as a necromancer made Danny feel cold and sweaty, she spoke in a soft, kind voice. "Dark Magic, that is, *truly* Dark Magic, comes from deep within us."

Nyshlza's gaze rested on them each in turn. "You must bring it up from your depths and feed it, let it grow until it fills your senses. Only then may you do great and terrible things."

This was exactly why Danny couldn't let himself be a

villain. He had zero desire to do terrible things. While he wasn't sure he wanted all the excitement of being a hero, he was certain he didn't want to be evil. Most people wanted to make a quiet living and disturbing them didn't seem right. This was why blacksmithing appealed to him. It was lucrative and productive and well-admired. Plus, he had three years' head start on learning it. Why did Pa have to have delusions of grandeur for him?

"Hold out your hands," Nyshlza told the girl next to her. She then reached below the table and pulled out a dead chicken, depositing it in the girl's outstretched hands. The girl dropped it with a little scream. Danny locked his jaw to keep himself from gagging. Nyshlza didn't even blink. "Pass it on down," she ordered, handing the boy on the other side of her a dead rat. "Everyone gets an animal. Go on—do it!"

The girl, who had been looking horrified, grabbed the leg of the dead chicken and shifted it over to the girl next to her. Nyshlza put a dead possum in front of her. The girl swallowed hard, but didn't protest. Danny was immensely relieved that he sat directly opposite from Nyshlza. He only had to accept the rat when it was put in front of him, not pass it on. Daisy, next to him, got the chicken.

"Poor little thing," she murmured. Then she grinned at Danny. "Perhaps I'll have it for lunch when we're done with it."

Danny started at that comment. Daisy went from kind to evil with such rapidness he had no idea what to think of her.

Daisy giggled. "It'd taste better than the cafeteria slop."

Danny had to agree with that—anything would.

"And chickens do scare me when they're alive," Daisy continued. "My brothers always used to laugh when that infernal rooster would chase me around the yard when I was young. They set it on me on purpose. The lot of them should have been sent here."

"Dark Lord Academy has been reinforced with a special set of enchantments that allow us to access our dark magic more easily and thus make learning it easier," Nyshlza said, ending their conversation. Daisy watched her with rapt attention. "This room has been designed to call the magic up in you and magnify it and, while here, you need only learn the proper way of reaching for it and it will flow naturally. This allows you to learn some control before facing more difficult situations."

Danny couldn't help but be a little fascinated. If he was a hero, would he have *good* magic instead? The idea did excite him a little, as unlikely as it felt. He'd never done anything magical—ever.

Nyshlza smiled and, for an uncanny moment, Danny thought she could tell what he was thinking, but perhaps it was just sitting in her direct line of sight that gave him the impression. "My own specialty, Necromancy, uses the energy of death, making it an excellent starting point for exploring our darker selves. Today, we will begin learning the basics of animating objects."

Nyshlza gestured to the dead animals across the table. "Anything may be given movement, a life of sorts. You will not yet bring these creatures truly back from the dead, that is beyond you, but animation is the first step towards necromancy."

Danny met Shai's troubled gaze on his other side. Everyone looked understandably nervous, except Tulk, who still had a self-satisfied smirk on his face. *As usual, I expect he'll excel at this.* Danny wasn't sure why that bothered him, it wasn't like he wanted to do well at necromancy and dark magic.

"Everyone, shut your eyes and concentrate on my voice." Nyshlza's tone was musical, almost singsong, and rather mesmerizing. "Feel the warmth inside your chest, the life force of your body."

Danny shut his eyes and concentrated. At first he felt nothing, only his heartbeat hammering in his chest. Yet sitting like this, he relaxed, letting go of the tension of the last two days.

"Under that warmth, feel for darkness, hate, jealousy, spite, the desire to kill, to control, to manipulate." Nyshlza's words seemed to surround him, as reassuring as they were disturbing. "Look for these things deep within you and you will find the darkness."

Danny didn't really want to have those evil things inside him, did he? The sense of calm spread and his nose and hands and feet started tingling, as if they didn't quite belong to him or as if he might move out of his body.

"Let that darkness grow inside you until it brings you power, and then command the animal in front of you to float, to move, to animate."

Deep within Danny, something dark stirred—fear, panic, not knowing what to do in this strange and unpredictable place. It shifted, bringing in jealousy and anger at Tulk, the desire for revenge, to make *him* embarrassed and flustered in front of everyone. The emotions built, moving to fury at Dicky's cocky smile and wanting to go here when he so desperately wanted to stay at home, wanting to pummel him, then resentment at Pa, a howl of inner betrayal that longed to burst out with evil intent. Danny realized with a rush of fear that he didn't want to find his inner darkness and make this dead rat move. He most definitely didn't! He didn't want to know the extent of what he might find inside himself and the terror of possibly hurting his family interrupted the feelings.

The darkness slipped away from him. Only some of it lingered, making his hands tingle even more.

"Now, slowly open your eyes. Look at my right hand." Almost against his will, Danny did so. She twisted it in a strange, but somehow fascinating movement. "Make this motion and order, quietly, the creature in front of you to move. Command it to do what you wish of it."

Danny twisted his hand. "Move," he muttered. The tingling in his hands forced itself outward in a small whoosh of air that hit the rat. It went up in the air, fell, hit the table with a dull thud, and rolled across it. It ricocheted off the table, bouncing several times, and hit Tulk—who was concentrating on his dead crow—with a disgusting splat.

"Hey!" Tulk screamed, slapping at his head, and jumped backwards, knocking over his chair and falling to the floor. That broke everyone's concentration. Several dead animals flopped to the table and people started snickering.

"Silence," Nyshlza commanded. She waved her hand and Tulk's chair righted itself. Tulk went flying up into the air, landing back into it, and the dead rat jumped off the floor and plopped right in front of Danny, who gulped.

"He did that on purpose!" accused Tulk, pointing at Danny.

Did I? Danny's hands shook. He didn't mean to do that, did he? Only he couldn't be sure, part of him had wanted to get back at Tulk, despite trying to cut off the emotions. *I didn't tell it to though, I didn't! It did that on its own.* He glanced at Nyshlza, trying to control the fear. For a second her eyes seemed completely white, but he blinked and saw they were normal.

"Very good, Zixygrith," she said, a hint of a smile in her voice. "However, concentrate more fully next time on what exactly you want the object to do, so it doesn't go wild. I want everyone to show as much, if not more, concentration as Zixygrith and your object will move with as much strength."

Tulk's glare intensified and Danny looked away. Somehow the fact she knew it was an accident wasn't reassuring. Daisy beamed at him. "I only got the chicken to twitch a little. You're an amazin' villain, Zixy."

"Um," Danny mumbled, glancing down. He immediately regretted it. The dead rat stared up at him; its body was torn a bit and intestines hung out. He glanced at Nyshlza instead, hoping she wasn't facing him. She wasn't and he let his breath out in relief.

"Now, class, let's try that again." She started the routine over again, only this time, while he closed his eyes, Danny didn't try following her suggestions. Instead, he slitted his eyes, examining a little slice of the table and following the grain back and forth to distract himself from her instructions and voice. When she commanded them to try again, he held up his hands and made the motion. His rat didn't even twitch.

Tulk's crow levitated half a foot off the table, as did about half of the other students' animals, including Daisy's chicken. The chicken flopped to the table after a couple of minutes and Daisy turned to him, beaming. "I did it! I did it!" She hugged him, then turned and hugged Aun on her other side.

"Good job, everyone," Nyshlza said, although her eyes lingered on Danny and he sensed she knew he hadn't really tried this time. "Practice your focus until next class." She shut her eyes, her face peaceful for a moment, and when she opened them, they were solid white. She spoke in a strange language and the room seemed to close in on them. Although it didn't get darker, it felt darker, like the walls were collapsing inward. Most of the students gasped, a few cried out. Nyshlza said something in a strange language and suddenly all the dead animals on the table came to life.

It wasn't simply animation. Danny could somehow tell, as they all twittered to life, that Nyshlza had brought them back from the dead. Several people screamed and stumbled backward. Tulk didn't move, but his eyes bulged and his face turned as white as a sheet. Paralyzed, Danny stared in morbid fascination. Nyshlza made a sweeping motion across the table. When she spoke, her voice was a low hiss, "Back to your cages."

The students scrambled backward as the animals raced across the table and into the darkness behind her. Danny's rat, its intestines still hanging out, scampered off.

"Class dismissed," she hissed.

The students took off running for the door. Danny sat frozen as Nyshlza walked over to him and put a hand on his shoulder. Her white eyes peeked at him from under the hood. Though in an unsettling way, she was beautiful. "You have the gift, Zixygrith, and you know it," she said in her usual, musical voice. "Make your peace with it and it will be yours."

"I—I don't know what you're talking about," Danny stuttered.

"Have it your way, young necromancer," she said in a quiet voice and turned away. Danny rushed from the room, feeling sick to his stomach.

CHAPTER 7

VILLAINOUS COMPLEXITIES

Danny hurried down the hall, trying to ignore the panic building inside of him. Nyshlza's words echoed back and forth in his head. *She can't be right, she can't! I misunderstood her.* Flashes of excuses or other crazy possibilities swept through Danny's mind, but nothing changed the fact that Nyshlza thought he had a talent for necromancy. His earlier hopes of unknowingly being a hero evaporated.

He paused to steady himself against a wall. Other students moved past him, talking and laughing. No one seemed to notice him. Danny took several deep breaths.

It was obvious teachers and students would be of no help; he was on his own. No matter how angry Pa was, it would be better to escape first and work up an excuse between here and home. Everyone seemed busy, perhaps he could just walk out and head toward the nearest city and find transportation from there. He had the lunch break before his afternoon classes—right now might be his only chance. They wouldn't know he was missing.

"That's it, I'm getting out of here," Danny muttered. No way was he going to make a career out of bringing people back from the dead. He wasn't staying to find out what else they might make him do, either.

The trouble was, with Vrlyxfrka's vanishing smoke moves, he didn't have any idea where the castle gate was. *If I keep wandering around, I'll find it eventually.* Trying to look confident, he headed down the hallway in the opposite direction from his classes. Older students filled the halls here, chatting in small groups.

"Hey, kid!" a boy with a flat, snake-like nose called, stepping in front of Danny. He wore a black shirt with a white skull on it and baggy black pants with lots of chains hanging from them. "What're you doing here?"

Danny swallowed his nervousness. "I was looking for the teachers' offices and I got lost."

The student sneered. "I'll say. Get out of here." He gave Danny a shove back the way he came.

I suppose it would be too nice for a villain to offer directions. But the boy was nearly twice his size so he hurried away. Only, somewhere along the way, he must have made another wrong turn because he ended up in a different hall full of classrooms he hadn't seen before.

Wandering deeper into the fortress, he heard the lunch bell ring, but ignored it. It wasn't like the food was edible, anyway. Finally, the passage he was following dead-ended into a door leading outside to the school courtyard. Ahead were some buildings, perhaps stables, and to the left a black lake, but there on the right were the walls of the castle, jagged against the sky. Below them was another wing. On a hunch, Danny decided to cross the courtyard and try the part of that building instead.

This wing smelled of mildew, its unadorned and twisting passageways familiar from yesterday. Danny passed the teacher offices and headed into the maze section he'd gotten lost in before. Now what had been Igor's directions? If he could only follow them backward...

"And where do you think you're going?"

Danny startled, noticing the arched hallway before him was guarded by two goblins in full armor, each leaning on a spear. *Stupid, stupid, of course it'd be guarded.* Their golden eyes fixed intently on him—their fangs flashed ominously in the torchlight. Danny's mind whirled for the right thing to say. Showing any fear would be stupid. As far as they knew, he was just a student.

"Er, I'm...I've got an important errand in Executions," Danny stammered. Probably not the smartest story, but he couldn't be sure of the teacher's name who owned the plague collection, so best to stick with what he remembered.

The goblin on the left snickered while the one on the right sneered. The right one, however, waved a claw through the doorway, indicating Danny could pass. Trying to look like he knew what he was doing, Danny strode forward, relieved they'd believed him, or at least had no intention of stopping him. He didn't dare look back to see if they were watching, it seemed un-dark-lordly to be so concerned with the minions.

Passageways turned off to the right and left, all looking identical, dark stone walls with torches, the sound of water dripping in the distance the only thing he could hear. Then a scream echoing distantly made him jump. Danny clenched his fists. No, he wasn't going to run, he didn't have any idea what was where. For all he knew, he'd run right toward danger. He tiptoed along, listening harder, but silence had fallen on the maze again, other than the eerie drip, drip, drip. The passageway teed. Right or left? He had to pick one or the other.

Danny lost track of time, although gradually the maze fell into a pattern, confirming his fear that he was going in circles. One by one, he tried the passages, only to end up at the same intersection. Fast losing patience, Danny kicked the suffocating dark walls. Soon someone would notice he was gone. Lunch had to be over by now, didn't it? Or maybe it just *felt* like he'd spent forever wandering in circles. Danny collapsed against the wall and glanced up at the oppressive stone ceiling—and stared.

A rune was carved in the beginning of every passageway in the middle of the ceiling. The maze was marked, only he'd never thought to look straight up. *Brilliant. Even though I can't read them, I can at least remember them.* Danny pulled himself upright and began tracing his steps through the passages again. When he came out at the same intersection, he glanced up and saw the rune was different. It only appeared to be the same intersection. Keeping that in mind, Danny focused on trying different tunnels, checking each one's ceiling, until he turned a corner to see natural light shining in the distance.

Too excited to be cautious, Danny dashed forward. He'd found the front gate and not only was the drawbridge down, but no goblins were posted here, either. The moat blazed on either side of the bridge and across it he could see dead grass and the jagged mountains. He took in a deep breath of the fresh air and glanced both ways. No sign of anyone. Not even the unnerving moat could stop him now. Sticking to the middle of the drawbridge, he started across.

Slow at first, he soon picked up speed and confidence. The hot air moving up from the moat ruffled his hair and it felt good to be outside…only he didn't seem to be getting any closer to the other side of the drawbridge. Danny walked faster, then started to run. He looked down, watching his feet move across the wood, definitely moving forward, yet when he glanced up, the other side looked farther away than ever.

Magic. Danny skidded to a stop. He should have known it was too easy, without guards or anything like that. He turned around, looked back, and found he was still only a few yards from the gate. He tried running forward again. No progress. Danny ran his hand through his hair, now damp with sweat. Defeat was the last thing he wanted to admit, but what else could he do? *There must be a spell or something special I have to do to get across.* Maybe if he started over from the castle passageway he could find runes or something like before. With a sigh, he turned around and headed back toward the castle—only to find he couldn't make it back *inside* either. The more he walked, the farther and farther away he got from door.

Now what? Danny halted, looking first toward the castle, then away. The drawbridge had somehow elongated, leaving him orphaned in the middle. He was trapped. How long would it take before someone noticed him? Or would the villains even care? Perhaps he'd be marooned out here permanently until he wasted away from lack of food, water, and shelter. He took a few steps backward—wait, perhaps that was it. Making sure he kept evenly in the middle of the drawbridge, he faced the open doorway to the castle and started walking backwards. The doorway started to look a little father away and hope rose in him. He didn't dare try looking backward in case that ruined the effort.

Wham! He slammed into something hard, tangled with

it, and fell. Danny tensed, gripping at the wood, suddenly afraid he'd get knocked off the drawbridge.

"Oww, watch where you're going!" He'd run into another person.

Danny pulled himself free and turned to meet the gaze of two bright blue eyes. It was a boy, perhaps a year or two older. The boy rubbed his head, mussing up his red-blond hair. He wore a bright red tunic and purple pants and was that a hint of *glitter* on his cheeks? Danny stared.

The boy pushed himself up and put a hand on the hilt of the sword he wore. "You could have knocked me off this thing. Be more careful." He held out a hand. "I'm Alec."

Danny took it cautiously and the boy hauled him to his feet. "Um…Danny. I mean, Zixy."

Alec quirked an eyebrow and considered him. Danny self-consciously flattened his hair and shook out his black robe. Alec's friendly expression hardened. "Wait! You're a villain!"

"Aren't you?" Danny realized the second he said it that Alec was too brightly colored and honest-looking to possibly be a fellow student.

"*I* am a hero!" Alec drew his sword.

Danny took a step backward. "W-what?"

"A *hero*, oh, Agent of Darkness. Your evil plans will be foiled, your conniving schemes thwarted, you dastardly hopes defeated!"

"Wait, I just got here yesterday and I'm trying to leave," Danny said. "I'm not the villain you're looking for."

"A likely story!" Alec waved his sword, making Danny wince. This was going to hurt unless he did something fast. "I'm not fooled by your filthy lies. You might think you've trapped me here, but Alec the Brave will not be deterred." He jabbed his sword skyward to emphasize the point.

"Goodness and Right will prevail. On guard, Emissary of Evil!"

"I'm stuck here, too, and I'm unarmed," Danny protested. He glanced first right, then left; nothing but lava. This was not looking good. "It's not fair to attack me. Isn't killing unarmed people against the rules?" He had no idea what the "rules" of being a hero were, but it was worth a try.

"Hah! I've got a spare." To Danny's dismay, Alec reached behind his back to pull out a sword. It was half as short as Alec's regular one, but looked just as sharp. He held it out, making Danny take another step backward.

"Why don't I just surrender and you take me prisoner without a fight?" Danny suggested. That'd at least get him out of the school, right?

"No can do, I have to infiltrate Dark Lord Academy and defeat a villain before I get the extra credit badge. We'll have to fight, although if you beg for mercy like the coward you are, I might consider sparing your miserable life." Alec bent and slid the sword toward Danny across the wooden planks.

Maybe I should have gone to magical weapons class after all. He could use a magical weapon about now. Danny had practiced fighting, but only in play with his brothers. Fighting with a sharp sword for real was not his idea of a good time. "I can't, sorry, I'm a paci—"

Alec didn't give him an opportunity to make up any further explanations—he attacked with a war whoop.

Danny didn't have time to grab the sword from the ground; instead, he ducked and crashed into Alec. He grabbed Alec's wrist and tried to pry the sword away from him. The hero yelled and yanked backwards and shoved Danny with his left arm. Danny slammed his shoulder into

Alec's chest and fought to keep his grip and prevent Alec from using the sword. Getting run through might get him out of Dark Lord Academy, but only in a body bag.

Alec slapped Danny hard on the face, then pulled on his hair. Gritting his teeth, Danny pulled away a moment to then ram Alec in the stomach with his head. Alec dropped his sword.

"You will pay, Evil One!" he roared, trying to trap Danny in a headlock. Struggling to breathe, Danny tripped Alec, only to stumble on one of the swords himself. Lava flashed before Danny's eyes and he realized too late that their fight had gotten them too close to the edge. He clutched at Alec and Alec at him, but they were too unbalanced. With a scream, they both tumbled over the edge of the drawbridge.

Danny shut his eyes, waiting for the searing heat, and hit something solid instead. His head throbbed with pain and when he opened his eyes, all he could see were flashing spots. The surface under him was hard and cool and as the spots cleared from his eyes, he saw dark stone. With a gasp, Danny sat up, rubbing his head.

He was sitting on the stone floor of the castle in the doorway in front of the drawbridge. Danny gaped, then noticed on the far side a dazed Alec also pulling himself up. They had both been returned to their respective starting points. *The lava must have had a protective enchantment.* Danny let out a breath in relief, only to then realize he'd gotten no farther on his escape.

Alec got to his feet and waved his fists at Danny, shouting, "You dastardly Dark Lord! You, cruel, conniving Corrupted One! Beware! Alec the Brave will be victorious!"

Despite this speech, Danny noticed he didn't try to cross the drawbridge again. Even if Alec hadn't been determined to kill him, Danny didn't want to risk the enchanted drawbridge again. There was no guarantee a second fall into the lava might not be deadly or perhaps he'd just end up trapped on the bridge for days until he starved. It seemed walking out of Dark Lord Academy was not an option. He'd have to make them send him home.

Swallowing his disappointment, he turned back into the castle.

"Come out and fight! Coward!"

Danny ignored Alec. He had a maze to re-figure out.

By the time he made it out again, the bell was already ringing for dinner. The entrance hall near the cafeteria was filled with students, all still busy and oblivious to him. Did anyone even notice he'd been missing? While he originally had hoped they wouldn't, it felt a bit lonely that even missing class went unnoticed.

"Zixy!" Daisy's cry was a welcome relief. "I wondered where you got off to." She dashed forward to grab his arm.

Danny winced as it was the one he'd landed on when he thought he was falling in the lava. "Just took a wrong turn and got a little lost." He was going to have to come up with a new plan. Perhaps if he could find the real hero and ask for help—that's what heroes did, right? Help people? *Well, people who aren't villains…*Alec hadn't seemed inclined to listen, but perhaps if he approached the problem right, the infiltrator would be more inclined to assist him. He scanned the cafeteria, trying to speculate on which of his classmates might be the one.

Daisy headed towards the diminishing dinner line. "It's a shame you're not in Art. What was your elective again? Oh, hey, look, there's—"

Danny lost track of her rambling as a sudden idea wriggled to life, altogether too much like his rat when raised from the dead. Maybe Daisy *was* the student who didn't belong. She didn't behave like the other kids. She was as sunny and friendly as her name and she'd been nice to him since the very first day he met her.

The cafeteria lady, the one who looked like a sumo wrestler, slapped a spoonful of reddish-brown glop on his plate. The food splattered across his robe and he looked up into her menacing glare.

"Uh." Were villains supposed to say thank you? "Nice aim."

She flexed her hand with the spoon and he was sure if she hit him, his brains would go flying out.

Thankfully, Daisy pulled him away toward their table, but Danny could feel the woman's stare following him.

"Hey, Zex-guts!" Tulk called, shattering Danny's thoughts. "You need a bib or something?" He pointed at Danny's splattered clothes. "Muahahahahaha!"

Spleg, sitting next to him, pulled off an evil chuckle.

"Oh, shut up, bat-brain," Daisy yelled back. "You didn't look so cool with rat guts all over your head this morning."

Tulk's smirk twisted into a scowl.

Danny snickered before he realized she was being mean again. It baffled him how quickly Daisy went from one to the other. Of course, the absence of villainy did not necessarily mean heroism. Despite her general disposition, she hadn't *done* anything heroic. Then again, none of them were very villainous yet. Perhaps the student only had hidden hero potential.

"I thought you were in Magical Weapons," Aun said, distracting him. "I didn't see you."

Danny looked up to see both the twins watching him from across the table.

"Um…I wasn't feeling well." Danny picked the first excuse that came to mind. "I feel horrible about missing it. What was it like?"

"She's a tiny old lady," Aun said, grinning. "She must be eighty or something and she's short, but man, you should have seen her demonstration. I wish I could move that fast. She explained the correct stances and some attack positions —it was awesome."

"Wow, maybe you can show me what you learned and help me with the homework so I can get caught up."

Aun started to nod, then stopped and frowned. "Wait, you skipped and now you want me to help you?"

"I didn't skip," Danny protested, even though he had.

Aun gave him a lofty glare rather similar to the one Mystfolyn had used that morning. Then he flicked his black cape over his shoulder with a passable swirl. "Hah! You just want to copy my answers. Well, I'm onto your game."

Aun stood and held up his fists, ready to fight, although they shook a little with the effort. "Just you try it and you'll see my incredible defensive powers." Aun took a deep breath and paused, a look of concentration crossing his face before he managed the proper maniacal laugh. "Muahahahahaha!"

Shai and Daisy giggled.

Brex, however, looked impressed. "Awesome. Say, could you, like, teach me Kung Fu or something?"

Aun scowled. "I'm the Fearsome Fighting Fright, who conquers all alone! I'll...leave you all behind in the wake of my villainous success." He turned and stomped off, leaving Danny at a loss as to what that was all about.

"Hey, we could do Dark Magic homework together," Daisy suggested.

"Er, I'm gonna study for Weapons in my room. I'm kinda tired." Danny sighed, feeling like an idiot for having suggested any form of cooperation in the first place. He spent that evening wracking his brains for a new plan, but nothing came to him. It seemed he'd just have to play along a little until he thought of something.

Danny wondered if someone would take him to task over skipping class, but found he had a different set of classes the next day. The first was History, taught by Screkvox. Looking as thoroughly disagreeable as when Danny first met him, he immediately made them take a comprehensive pre-test that Danny suspected was to try and ferret out the imposter of the class. Danny failed it. The way Screkvox looked at him after that made him almost as nervous as the way Screkvox punctuated his lecture points with lightning.

Study hall was the opposite extreme—dreadfully boring. Everyone sat silently working on their assignments because the gray-haired matron who oversaw it screeched, "Sit down and shut up!" every time anyone said a word.

After lunch was Danny's final new class—Strategy. Trying not to dwell on when his skipping yesterday would catch up with him, Danny let Daisy drag him along to find the Strategy classroom. Danny hoped that whoever taught it would agree with him better than the lunch rebelling in his stomach. He'd been foolish to try it after the look he'd gotten from the cafeteria lady at his comment of, "horribly scrumptious," when served something that resembled guts.

"Hey, I think we go up there!" Daisy pointed to stairs that went up in a curve, into one of the towers of the fortress. They started climbing. By the top, Danny was out of breath, but Daisy seemed as eager and bouncy as ever.

The walls of the classroom were covered with maps, some which had pins stuck into them at various positions representing troops. Tables were grouped together and various scrolls lay around haphazardly. The windows looked down on a field of dry grass next to the school with various obstacles and other equipment lying around. Shai and Aun came up behind them to stare as well.

A curtain on one side of the room pulled aside and a young man stepped out, blinking at them through half-circle-lensed glasses. He grinned and pushed his shaggy blond hair out of his eyes. He wore a red silk suit with a purple bow tie and cape, which reminded Danny a bit of Alec the Brave.

"Oh, hello, there. I thought I heard someone."

"We're looking for Strategy class." Danny felt his face get red. Where had they ended up? He hoped he wasn't about to have another duel.

The man beamed at them. "You're in the right place." He gestured his hand over the messy tables. "Go ahead and find a seat. I'll be right with you." He went back behind the curtain and they could hear him moving something around.

"He's a Dark Lord?" Shai whispered, looking as confused as Danny felt.

Daisy shrugged. "Perhaps they get tired of wearing black all the time. I know *I* would." Then, louder, she said, "Come on. Let's sit down."

Danny and Aun followed her and Shai over to a table and watched the rest of the class arrive. Danny breathed a small sigh of relief when Brex (the boy with earrings) joined their table, so that Tulk had to sit at a different one when he arrived. When they were all assembled, the colorful young man returned.

"All here? Good, then let's begin."

"Wait!" called Tulk. "You can't be the teacher."

A bemused smile crossed the man's face. "And why not?"

"Because you don't look like one."

"And you are confident in your answer?"

Tulk frowned and shrugged.

"Well then," the young man paced in front of the room. "What makes you think a teacher must look a particular way?"

"Because they're Dark Lords," answered Spleg, the boy with glasses. "And you don't look like a Dark Lord."

"Ah, but there the two of you have kindly shared your ignorance with the rest of us," the man said, smiling at them. Tulk and Spleg looked confused. "Nowhere in school policy does it say teachers or students must dress a particular way."

"But Mystfolyn said—"

The man held up a hand, cutting Tulk off mid-sentence. "That, young man, would be the difference between personal opinion and school policy. I suggest you study the difference between the two before confusing them. Just because something looks evil, doesn't mean it is, and vice-versa. Unfortunately, most people are very stupid, and so think that appearance reflects nature. That is why someone intelligent like me can rule thirty kingdoms as absolute lord and despot, remain undefeated, and retire in style, while your ordinary Joe in a black cape is beheaded by the first third son of a farmer he encounters."

"You ruled thirty kingdoms?" blurted out Daisy. "But you look so young!"

"He probably has an age spell, stupid," said Brex.

"No, he doesn't, stupid yourself."

Brex winced as Daisy stomped on his foot beneath the table. Danny's hopes rose, listening. Here, finally, was someone friendly and open. Perhaps he could confide in a teacher after all.

The teacher laughed, an honest laugh, not a maniacal one. "I happened to be an evil child genius. By the age of fifteen, I was emperor of thirty nations and after ten years of ruling them, it got boring. But enough about me." He flashed a smile at them. "Let's get on to strategy! Strategy is what makes or breaks you as a Dark Lord or Lady. If you follow the confines and stupidity of tradition, you will end up like the other 99% of Dark Lords—dead!"

He slammed his hand on the table to punctuate his words and everyone gasped. His expression was now grim. "I, Mordryn, stand undefeated, because I think before I act, plan before I attack, and use my brain!" He jabbed at his head. "Where is my black cape and glowing red eyes, you want to know?" His icy blue eyes flashed. "Vanity of vanities! That is what is wrong with Dark Lords past and present. Vain idiots! And I'll tolerate none of those in this classroom."

Everyone fell silent. Mordryn walked around the room, staring down each student, until they looked down at their desks. Danny risked a glance at Tulk and saw he looked white as a sheet after his stare-down. He heard footsteps and looked up to see it was his turn.

Mordryn's eyes were as blue as his own or perhaps Amos and Dicky's, although he had no freckles. His expression was still friendly. Nothing in his face hinted at evil and yet Danny got a sense of blackness and hardness, like the center of dark magic that Nyshlza insisted they all had. This was not someone he could confide in. This man could watch him die and do absolutely nothing. Danny glared back at him.

Look down, something in him whispered. *You're going to stand out and make yourself look stupid if you keep this up.*

No, I don't care. He was tired of being intimidated and humiliated in every single class. So what if they expelled him? It would be a welcome relief. In fact, that was a brilliant idea—if they expelled him, they'd have to send him home. He already had a good start since skipping Magical Weapons was sure to catch up with him soon.

"Ahh," said Mordryn, "you are not what you seem, are you, Zixy?" He turned his gaze away first and beamed down at Daisy, who grinned up at him. "Just like Dazydethia here."

The class tittered. *I'm not like Daisy at all!* Danny wanted to object, but he also didn't want to hurt her feelings.

"You would all do well to watch Daisy carefully. But enough said!" Mordryn clapped his hands, summoning a goblin. "On to today's lecture. We've much to learn before you battle each other for midterms—if you hope to survive." And his grin looked very evil this time.

CHAPTER 8

Dirty Dish Detention

Pondering a death-and-torture-proof method of getting expelled, Danny didn't notice Tulk on the stairs until he bumped into him.

"Watch where you're going, Zitty." Tulk elbowed him.

Danny wasn't in the mood. "Watch it yourself, dork." He managed to avoid knocking into Sleg by grabbing the railing. He put on a burst of speed to get ahead of Tulk and the rest of the class.

"That's a lame comeback!" Tulk called after him.

"Not half so lame as you telling Professor Mystfolyn what he should wear," Daisy said. Her steps pounded on the stairs behind him as she sped up to catch him.

Danny didn't look back, but could hear the rest of the class laughing. A bit of satisfaction at Tulk getting ridiculed instead of him flashed through him, followed by guilt. He ignored it. After all, Tulk was a villain, that meant being enemies was a good thing, didn't it? It ought to be okay to punch him sometime for all his bullying, only he didn't fancy having Demigorth the Destroyer stepping in again.

He joined Aun and Shai at the back of the dinner line in the cafeteria.

Getting expelled was more important, anyway. If he refused to do his homework and failed all his tests, perhaps he could flunk out. He already looked stupid in most of his classes. If he could just stand the ridicule, he could look stupid in all of them, enough so the teachers would give up on him. Pa would be furious, but it would serve him right.

The cafeteria lady shocked him out of his reverie by handing him a plate with something that looked alarmingly like a large dead cockroach on its back, stuffed with smashed brains. Danny grimaced as its smell wafted upward.

"Now don't try and get away with your half-assed compliments this time!"

Danny looked up, surprised, into her scowling face.

"No, no, I was just thinking about something else..." he stammered. He glanced at the roach, swallowed hard, and grinned back at her. "This looks terrifically evil, ma'am, sorry I wasn't paying attention before."

She grunted and motioned him onwards. Danny hurried past, trying not to think about her eyes boring into the back of his head. He had to be more careful if he didn't want to end up the main ingredient for breakfast tomorrow. He looked down at the so-called dinner. The smell of it made him gag.

He took a step forward and tripped over someone's leg

sticking out in his path. Danny tried to catch himself, but the tray went flying out of his hands and his palms struck the ground with a painful jolt. The foot he had tripped over kicked him in the ribs and Danny rolled away. Tulk grinned smugly down at him.

"Muahahahahaha!" Tulk laughed, getting Mystfolyn's intonation down almost perfectly.

Getting to his feet, Danny glanced ahead for his tray and his gaze met the angry faces of the second year students covered in his dinner. A girl wiped slime from her hair and reached for a handful of her own mush, while a boy picked up the roach by one of its legs.

"Uh, oh!" He ducked as they retaliated. The food hit Tulk right in the face, wiping off his sneer mid-laugh.

"Hey!" Tulk grabbed a handful of the meal of the person at the table next to them and launched it back at the second years. It missed them, hit the table behind, and splattered food across the third year table, landing bits of bright color on black robes. Shouts filled the cafeteria. Danny ducked under the table as everything predictably erupted into a food fight.

The cafeteria dissolved into a mass of yelling bodies and flying pieces of goop. One of the giant stuffed roaches bounced off someone's foot and slid across the floor toward him. Danny blocked it with the bottom of his shoe. He decided the safest course was to stay under the table.

"Hi, there."

Danny turned to see Shai crouching next to him. She grinned. "I don't fancy getting covered in slop."

"Yeah," Danny said, unable to think of anything cool to say. He wondered whether her sitting under there meant that she might not be a villain or if she was simply a fastidious person. It reminded him of the imposter hero. Maybe, unlike Alec, his classmate would actually help him.

He smiled tentatively at Shai, wondering how to tell for sure which classmate was the right one.

A crack of thunder distracted him and the lights went out, then on again. Danny and Shai peered out from under the table to see the teachers had arrived. The cafeteria lady's face was bright red—she flexed her muscles. Several other teachers in black robes and capes were snapping out orders to the shame-faced students. The cafeteria lady marched straight over to Danny and Shai. Danny tried to duck back under the table, but he was too slow. She grabbed him by the collar before he could get away and hauled him up.

"I've got him!" she roared, shaking Danny until his teeth rattled. "Here's the little demon."

"Good," said one of the other teachers Danny didn't recognize.

"I didn't throw any food," Danny protested. "Tulk tripped me!"

"Hah! I saw the way you looked at my fine meal!" The cafeteria lady continued to scowl at Danny. The other teachers looked away and coughed. "I'm taking you to your advisor right now!"

Danny wanted to object again, only it occurred to him, here was his perfect chance. While he hated to let Tulk get away with it, wasn't he just plotting to get in trouble? The woman shoved Danny forward and marched him forcibly out of the cafeteria and down several corridors, until he recognized where he was—in front of Vrlyxfrka's office door. The cafeteria lady rapped on it. "Virly!"

The world dissolved again and Danny found he was standing in Vrlyxfrka's office, the cafeteria woman still holding his collar. Vrlyxfrka leaned back in her chair behind her desk and gave him a measured glance. "I thought I'd be seeing you again quite soon." The left-hand corner of her mouth twitched upward, the only clue she was amused behind her impassive face and cold eyes. "Yes, Carly? What have you to say about my student?"

"He started a food fight with *my* dinner."

"Did he now?" Vrlyxfrka raised an eyebrow. "I told you I expected a lot of you, Zixygrath, but I suggest you leave Carly's fine cooking out of your exploits."

Was that sarcasm or not? Danny couldn't tell.

"I want a month's daily detention of kitchen work," Carly snapped and Danny's stomach sunk. He wasn't sure if he had the guts to go through with his new plan for expulsion.

"Every day for a month?" Vrlyxfrka's face wore a polite look of disbelief. "It seems a tad harsh, don't you think? Weekends seems plenty to me."

"Fine," grumbled Carly. "But if I catch any sass from him..."

"Yes, yes, by all means if he doesn't behave, you may extend it." Vrlyxfrka's eyes sparkled with amusement. "I'm flattered, Carly, that you picked out the same one as me, but I do want him keeping up in his classwork and I'm sure he'll be serving detention with someone else soon enough. We wouldn't want to clutter up his schedule."

Carly gave a sour laugh. *Mystfolyn wouldn't rate that one very high*, Danny thought, *but it fits the rest of her image*. He also wondered if that meant Vrlyxfrka already knew about Magic Weapons.

"You do know how to pick them," Carly said. "Although you took a bit of a risk with this one."

Then she disappeared in a cloud of black smoke that smelled of burnt bacon and made Danny hack.

Vrlyxfrka sighed. "First skipping class, now starting food fights. I was hoping you'd settle in a little longer before giving yourself over to misbehavior."

"But it wasn't my fault," Danny objected before he

could help it. His plan was working, but the way she was eyeing him made him highly uncomfortable. He'd forgotten how intimidating she was.

"Half of villainy is being in the wrong place at the wrong time." Vrlyxfrka shook a finger at him. "You'd do well to remember that. And this as well: there are rules here to evil behavior and you would fare better to obey them, because the consequences for breaking them can be quite villainous. Understand?"

Danny swallowed hard and nodded. He wondered what extra punishment he would get for skipping class, but wasn't going to let her threats deter him from his new plan.

"You will serve cafeteria detention directly after dinner every weekend for the next month. Osweggi is at liberty to assign whatever other detentions and assignments suit her. You are dismissed." Vrlyxfrka waved her hand at him and Danny was engulfed in smoke. Coughing, he waved it away and found himself in the hallway outside of the cafeteria. Students poured out the doors into the hall.

"Zixy! There you are!" Aun waved. "Great food fight."

"Yeah, right." Danny headed over to Aun and Shai, grateful for their support. His stomach rumbled, but he wasn't about to ask Carly for something new to eat. One of them might be the hero, but how could he pick between them? He liked them both.

Daisy caught sight of them and rushed over. "Hey, you're not in trouble, are you?"

"Got detention on weekends for a month," Danny muttered.

"Oh, that's not so bad." She grinned. "That cafeteria lady's kinda interesting, don't you think? Maybe you'll learn to cook something fun."

Danny pictured her having him boiling cockroaches and scooping out their guts and wrinkled his nose. Aun and

Shai made gagging motions and dissolved into giggles. Danny couldn't help but grin. "Fun to poison Tulk with."

Daisy laughed and Danny smirked before realizing he was feeling evil again. Or was he? He never used to think anything of making fun of Dicky. No wonder picking the hero was so difficult, they all seemed to be a mix of good and evil.

As if drawn by their merriment, Tulk sauntered over. "I'm surprised to see you still in one piece, Zitty."

"Yeah, you were too scared to take the fall, weren't you?" Danny replied. "She doesn't scare me because I'm not a wimp like you!"

Tulk snorted. "You eyes bulged like a frog's with terror when that woman grabbed you. It was priceless watching that, why—"

"Here comes a teacher!" Shai's call cut him off and Tulk moved away from Danny. Nyshlza, hood up, headed down the hall toward them. Swallowing hard, Danny grabbed his books and headed the opposite direction. Detention in the kitchen was at least better than detention with her. He'd have to be careful who he got in trouble with—he didn't want to end up collecting dead bodies or something.

The next day he finally made it to Magical Weapons. The teacher, Osweggi, was a tiny old lady, like Aun had described, her white hair done up in a bun, but age didn't stop her from giving him quite the lecture. Worse, Tulk apparently had the class as well and watched the whole thing, smirking. On top of that, he liked to make snide comments in class when the teachers weren't watching. After considering heroes more thoroughly, Danny was inclined more than ever to retaliate. Attacking a villain couldn't be evil—Tulk deserved to be answered in kind.

Only he had precious little time in which to plot something. Osweggi had him spend his breaks for the next few days polishing armor until his hands ached. The incredible patterns worked into them were fascinating, but irritatingly difficult to get properly clean. He was also assigned to write a report on the proper use of battle-axes compared with long-swords. Aun, to Danny's surprise, offered to help him find the right books in the library, although it turned out it was mostly so he could write a report of his own in hopes of extra credit. Danny found the research as fascinating as it was grueling, but it wasn't like Magical Weapons were evil on their own, or so he told himself. He was sure to make his report far inferior to Aun's in hopes of a poor grade.

The weekend arrived with much trepidation on Danny's part. His earlier determination wavered as he wondered what Carly might force him to do for detention. He shifted back and forth from foot to foot while waiting in the food line.

Aun turned around in line and gave Danny an evil grin. "I'm sure it won't kill you or anything." Danny wasn't sure if he meant that to be a friendly comment or a nasty one.

"Next!" bellowed Carly and Aun stepped up to get his plate of glop. As Aun stepped out of the way, Danny held his breath and moved forward, suddenly realizing that perhaps food was not a good idea at this moment. Carly narrowed her eyes at him. "Ah, the little trouble maker— you'll make a lot less by the time I'm through with you. I expect you in the kitchen the moment you're through with dinner."

She dropped a spoonful of sludge from a good height and it splatted on Danny's face as it landed. Then she leaned forward, her face inches from his. "If you're not careful, you'll be the next main ingredient."

"Um…thanks," muttered Danny and edged away, searching for the first year table. He sat next to Shai and

Brex and pushed his slop back and forth with his fork, wondering what Carly was going to do with him.

"Hey Zitty!" Tulk sat down across from him, thumping his tray down with a clatter. "So, what's this I hear about you quaking with fear over kitchen duty?"

Danny narrowed his eyes at Tulk. "You started the food fight, not me."

"Yeah, that's why I'm ultra-cool, bad-ass Tulkyzefril the Evil and you're Zits-face the fall guy." Tulk sneered at him, then threw back his head and laughed. Inspiration hit Danny and he flipped his plate of glob at him. "Mauahahaha-uck, ack, ack, ack."

Danny set his tray back down, watching with satisfaction as his unappetizing dinner slid down Tulk's face. While Tulk spat it out and wiped his eyes clear, Danny switched plates with him.

"You little—"

"Want to start a food fight and join me in detention?" Danny asked with a smile. He dug his fork into Tulk's dinner and gulped it down. It made his stomach lurch, but Tulk's horrified expression made it worth it. He opened and shut his mouth a couple of times, but seemed lost for a response.

Danny stood up, grabbed the tray, and winked at him. "If you want to get me back, you know where to find me."

Shai snorted into her dinner while Brex stared at Danny open-mouthed and awe-struck. Danny sauntered off, but had to correct his gait to normal when he almost crashed into an older student in the aisle. His warm feeling of success at momentarily winning against Tulk leaked away when he noticed Carly standing by the kitchen door, watching him and tapping her foot. He took a deep breath and came over to her.

Carly grabbed him by the ear and shoved him through

the kitchen doors. It was all Danny could do to keep from moaning. An enormous stack of dirty dishes covered one wall of the kitchen.

"Better get going, boy," boomed Carly, shoving him toward the dishes. "They won't wash themselves."

"What about magic? Or minions?" Danny muttered.

"Hah! Why use minions when I have disobedient little students like you?" Carly chortled her sour laugh again. "But if you think you can use Dark Magic to get them clean, go right ahead."

Danny knew better than to respond to *that*. He rolled up his black sleeves and started scrubbing. Carly sat in a chair, put up her feet, and started reading a huge book entitled: "The Better Dungeons and Graveyards Cookbook."

"Soup tomorrow…lemme see," she said cheerfully. "What'd ya think, Zixy-boy, Eye of Newt Chowder or Rat-tail Broth? Oooh, look, Bat-wing Lasagna with deep-fried chicken feet on the side—I bet the students would love that! Mwehehe! So, what'd ya say, Zixy-boy?"

"Umm…" Danny mumbled from within an enormous pot he had to practically crawl into to get to the bottom. It stunk like rancid oil, making it hard to breathe. Why the food tasted as it did was becoming all too clear.

"Can't hear ya, speak on up?" Carly sounded jolly.

Danny took a deep breath, gagged, and searched for an appropriate answer. "What about dessert?"

"Ah ha! I like the way you think!" Carly slammed the book on the table so loudly Danny jumped, spraying suds in the air and banging his head on the side of the pot. "I've got just the book—Dargroth's Deadly Delights! I haven't read that in years!"

Danny rubbed his head and stared after her a moment as Carly went to fetch it. Then he set back to scrubbing the pot as hard as possible, hoping against hope he could somehow finish before getting a list of grossed out desserts. But it was more likely Armageddon would arrive, considering the stack of dishes still tottered up near the ceiling.

Things Get Worse, Not Better

Monday morning dawned gray and drizzly, the sort of late fall morning that made Danny want to stay in bed with a cup of hot tea. Unfortunately, that didn't sound villainous enough to be allowed. Danny hadn't seen a hint of tea since arriving at Dark Lord Academy. On top of that, the thought of facing Carly and the spider pancakes she had promised this morning was more than he could take. He rolled over and went back to sleep for another half an hour until the bell rang for going to class. Then he yanked on a black robe and dashed off.

He realized halfway there he was lost. Rubbing sleep from his eyes, he tried to wake up enough to recognize his surroundings.

"Zixy!" Daisy beamed at him and waved from way down the hall. "Cool evil 'do. Hey, where were you at breakfast? I told that nice cafeteria lady you weren't feeling too well; she asked after you. Oh, and I grabbed you a biscuit."

At her first comment, Danny reached up to discover his hair on the right half of his head stuck straight out to the side while the hair on his left poked out in the opposite direction. He patted it down and grimaced at Daisy. "How were the spider pancakes?"

Daisy hurried them through the halls. "Crunchy, and I didn't take any of those, they looked rather burnt. The dog-breath biscuits and gravy were much better. Oh, here's our class."

Danny eyed the pictures in heavy gold frames of various unpleasant-looking people spotlighted on the walls. They always made him feel as if his answers in History were overseen by a panel of judges intent on seeing him fail. Maybe that would help him flunk out, but he still could have done without them. To Danny's dismay, Daisy sat in the front row and motioned to the chair next to her.

"Come on!" she ordered. Not wanting to be rude, Danny sat. Daisy rummaged around in her bag while the other students filed in. "Here they are." She pulled out two biscuits wrapped in a napkin and put them on Danny's desk.

"Th—" Danny didn't get the words out before a black-gloved hand closed around the biscuits.

"That's very kind of you, little girl," said a cold voice. "May I mention that all food in my classroom belongs to me?"

There was no speck of kindness in Screkvox's dark gray eyes as he took the biscuits from the table and popped them into his mouth. Danny's stomach rumbled, but his tired brain reminded him he needed to get in trouble some more and this was a perfect opportunity. It was now or never.

"That was my breakfast!" He glared at Screkvox, trying to copy the "menacing look" they'd been practicing in Style.

"So sorry for you." Screkvox sneered, brushed the crumbs from his beard, and walked away. His black boots clicked on the stone floor, his long black cape flapped behind him. It wasn't working.

Danny needed to do something drastic. He reached out and tugged on Screkvox's cape. The dark lord whirled around, flicking his hand and an invisible something smashed into Danny, shoving him, chair and all, backwards. He gasped for breath.

"You will show up for detention at seven this evening for that." Danny didn't meet his iron gaze, but nodded and tried to collect himself. Screkvox then turned to the class.

"Today we begin considering the complex history of the Dark Lords of Durindank." Something in the sneer of his voice felt familiar to Danny, but he couldn't place it. His heart was still pounding over whatever the teacher had just done. He needed to be careful—he wasn't necessarily safe just because he was a student.

Screkvox linked his gloved fingers together, apparently distracted from Danny. His eyes flashed with evil delight as his voice rose in intensity. "The long and unforgiving search for world domination, the clashes, the fights, the *death!* Oh, how many the villains who searched and how few who succeeded." His voice dropped lower and darker. "And fewer still who survived the heroes. Oh, no, students, becoming a Dark Lord, an ultimate villain, is no simple or carefree task. It is a struggle—a dark struggle!"

He spread his hands outward and lightning clashed down from the ceiling, making Danny scrape his chair backwards in surprise. No matter how many times they did that, it never seemed to fail to make his heart race.

By the afternoon, Danny was seriously dragging. How did they expect him to function if they kept him up all night doing dishes? Sunday evening shouldn't count as part of the weekend—not that he wanted to spend Friday night doing detention instead. He shuffled down the hall, hoping Magical Weapons would somehow keep him awake.

A goblin stepped in front of him. Danny hadn't been paying close enough attention and stumbled into it. He blushed. "Uh, sorry." He pulled back, intending to hurry off.

"A moment, lordling." The goblin gave him a disgusted look as it stopped him with a hand on his arm. "You have mail."

Danny gaped at him, dumbfounded. The goblin shoved a letter into his hands and hurried off. For one glorious moment, Danny thought someone from home must have written him. Perhaps Pa had changed his mind. Only the handwriting on the envelope was unfamiliar. It said: *To the Young Dark Lord Danny-Zixy*. Danny ripped it open and unfolded the letter.

Dear Dreadful Dark Lord Danny-Zixy,

Your underhanded and uncalled for attack on me on the drawbridge will not stand. My skills grow; my heart is true and full of courage. One day in the near future, the hour of your reckoning will come. My distaste for your evil ways increases with every word I write and I give you fair warning that we are now enemies and nothing will deter me from seeing your ruin.

Yours truly,
Alec the Brave

P.S. I will discover your real name—you cannot hide it from me.

Danny stood, staring at it, as other students rushed by him toward class. He didn't even know what to think about it, other than he really had no intention of ever fighting Alec again if he could help it. Getting stabbed by some hero was the last thing he needed. Not to mention getting a letter made him wonder why he hadn't heard from his family yet. Didn't they miss him? The bell sounded, making him jump. Danny crumpled up the letter and dashed off to Magical Weapons.

Fortunately, Magical Weapons today was a practical lesson held outside in the courtyard. The day was still cloudy, but it no longer rained. The courtyard was empty, gray stone, but Danny appreciated the fresh air. Besides, he needed to know how to fight properly more than ever, just in case Alec ever did manage to show up again. Goblin aides lined up in rows and handed out swords enchanted to be blunt and thus safe for sparring. Danny managed to get in between Aun and Shai on the opposite side of the courtyard from Tulk.

Osweggi seemed smaller than ever out in the courtyard. "Show me your opening stance, students, just as we talked about in class," she said in a quavery voice. A slight breeze ruffled her white hair, drawn up in a bun. Determined to learn properly to defend himself, Danny tried to hold his sword steady. Before, he had thought to get more detentions in this class, but now he needed to learn this. Besides, sword fighting by itself didn't have to be evil, it was just practical.

Osweggi adjusted her pale gray kimono and patted the enormous scabbard attached to her belt. Her wooden sandals clicked on the stone as she walked up to them.

"What a lousy bunch of idiots I've got this time. I hope you fight better than you look."

Danny glanced at Aun, who was staring at Osweggi, open-mouthed.

"Well, any of you want to try and take me?" she challenged.

The older students all stepped back, leaving the first years in front. That wasn't a good sign. Before Danny could step back, she spoke again.

"Only you newbies, eh? Try your best." She drew her extra-long sword and passed a hand over it, muttering an enchantment.

"EIIIIII-YA!" the little old lady yelled at the top of her lungs and charged at them. Danny yanked the sword up in front of him, but he was too slow. She knocked it aside, hit him on the shoulder hard enough to make him stumble, and sent Aun flying with a kick at the same time. She tripped Shai and hit Tulk across the wrists as he tried to block her. Her next blow knocked Tulk backwards into the air and the crunch he made landing sounded nasty. It took all of five seconds.

"New recruits," Osweggi sighed. "Never much of a challenge." She sheathed her sword. "Now then, let's get down to business. The first and foremost rule in the practical side of weapons is to examine your weapon *before* using it. Without proper weapon care, your sword will be useless." She turned to the first-year students. "You have each been given a practice sword that will be yours through the rest of the term for our practical classes. Make sure you take good care of it."

"Do they have magic powers?" Aun asked, fingering his sword hilt.

"Boy," snapped Osweggi, "learn to use a normal one

before you start interfering with magic. The way you fight at the moment, you're more likely to blow your head off with a magical one than do anyone else any damage."

Aun wisely shut his mouth. Danny supposed it was good after all that he didn't have a magical sword when he faced Alec, although he would have liked to have had a weapon of some sort. Osweggi shouted out instructions, pairing them up and making them go through sword moves. In short order, Danny was sore all over. His shoulder ached horribly from where Osweggi had thwacked him and the older students were merciless about pounding him whenever he dropped his guard. Still, he felt a lot more confident about what to do when someone came at him swinging a sword.

In the final round, he found himself facing Tulk. Both of them quickly turned away in an attempt to find another partner, but Osweggi would have none of it. She blocked Danny and shoved him towards Tulk.

"Come on, now, let's see what you got!" she cackled.

"Yeah, right," muttered Danny.

Tulk gave him a lofty glare. "Frightened?" He swirled his cape a little, looking appropriately dark-lordly.

"Not of you," Danny replied, glaring back, although he sounded more obstinate than evil.

They closed in on each other. Tulk swung at Danny's head. Danny raised his sword to meet Tulk's, but winced at the force of the blow. It jarred all the way up his arm to his sore shoulder. He gritted his teeth and blocked Tulk's next blow at his side. He was going to look stupid in front of everyone if Tulk won, not to mention how many more bruises he might get. *If Alec is allowed to hate me, just because he thinks I'm a villain, then there shouldn't be anything wrong with me hating Tulk.* Danny's resolve hardened and he attacked, driving the bully off-balance. He pushed aside Tulk's sword and aimed at his head, planning to hit Tulk with the flat of the sword, just to be safe. He might not like the bully, but he didn't want to kill him.

Inches from Tulk's face, a fireball exploded out the back of Danny's sword. It burst into a shower of sparks, peppering Danny's face and clothes. He yelped, dropped the sword, and rolled in the dirt to put out the flames. Everyone started laughing, except Tulk, who stared wide-eyed and pale-faced down at Danny.

"Now that," chuckled Osweggi, "is the danger of a magical weapon." She straightened up, giving Danny a piercing stare. "I don't know how you managed to end up with a magical one, young man, but it's an excellent example for everyone. You never know when it might prefer the person you're attacking. You must know your weapon intimately to make sure it doesn't turn on you. Swords especially have been forged for specific reasons and if the wrong person tries to use it—" She waved a bony and gnarled finger in warning. "You'll find yourself on the wrong end of it!"

The rest of the class gasped.

"So remember what, class?"

"Know your weapon!" the older students chanted back. "Check your weapon before using it."

"That's all for today," Osweggi snapped. "Dismissed."

As the others went to put away their practice swords, Danny got to his feet with a groan. His legs were about as steady as Jell-o. "But how did I end up with a magic sword?" He felt his head and realized with horror the explosion had singed off half of his hair, leaving the rest sticking straight up in an unfortunately uneven punk hairdo.

"Let me see that." Osweggi held out her hand and Danny gave her the sword. She narrowed her natural eye at it. "Wait a minute..." She waved her hand over the sword and there was a bang and a huge puff of black smoke that made Danny gag.

"This is not a practice sword!" Osweggi's brow wrinkled. "This belongs to a staff member. You can't use this—you'll need a different one. I wonder..." Her eyes snapped over to the goblins stacking the swords. "Someone has been playing pranks!" She marched towards the goblins. Only after she was gone, did Danny realize he'd missed an opportunity at another detention.

CHAPTER 10

Lightning Conductor

Danny clutched at the stone side of the small balcony, trying to ignore the prickly feeling in his feet, the way the wind tugged at him, and the sense that any movement he made could tumble him over the edge. The slopes of the main roofs and the many towered tops of Dark Lord Academy rose around him. Farther above, a blue sky had small clouds scuttling across it. The pinnacle of the nearest roof stood about equal to his head, sloping down on either side. Danny stood with his back to it, trying to soak up the reassuring feeling of wall. He hadn't known his detention would be on the roof. *This does it—I'm never trying a Screkvox detention again.*

"Move." The goblin who'd brought him up here gave him a little shove. Taking in a sharp breath, Danny scooted over. It seemed the wall he'd been clutching held a small closet. The goblin opened it with a key from his belt and started rummaging around inside.

Danny tried to not look down, but from his vantage point, it was impossible. From here the school grounds spread out much too far below. The practice courtyard, stables, a race tack, a stretch of something that might be dead grass, the black lake, and the distant walls and guard towers surrounding all of it. Looking the other direction, there were the many roofs and towers of the main school. The biggest one in the middle loomed up even higher than where he was now and Danny was relieved it wasn't that roof he'd been sent to.

Trying to focus and use the perspective to good purpose, he searched for a way he might leave Dark Lord Academy without passing through the gate, but he couldn't see past either the wall or the school enough to see the lava moat. If it wasn't for that, he could consider just scaling the castle walls. Although from here, looking around in every direction, he could see the dark, jagged mountain range surrounded the entire school as well. He had no idea, once out of the school grounds, how to get out of this valley and in which direction, or possibly dimension, home lay.

No, it was better to see this through and flunk out with detentions and bad grades. Then they'd send him home, or so he hoped.

The goblin took out a bucket, a paint scraper, a spray bottle, and some rags. He thrust the items at Danny.

"You'll need all this. You're to clean the moss off the lightning rods and then polish them up so they're in proper working order."

Danny gulped at the thought of climbing over the

rooftops to the various lightning rods he now noticed were spattered across the top of the school. "But I can't carry all this stuff, I'll need my hands!"

The goblin rolled its eyes and thrust a leather utility belt at him. "If you don't like it, lordling, you shouldn't have gotten in trouble in the first place."

Not daring to protest any further, Danny put it on and attached the various tools. He only half-listened as the goblin barked out instructions, his mind still on the impossible task of navigating the sloped rooftops. With a final sneer, the goblin gave him a shove toward the roof. Not wanting to end up getting pushed off, Danny swallowed his terror and clambered up on the slanted roof. *Just don't look down and try this first lightning rod.* He stood up and tried to pretend he couldn't see the far-off ground. He still felt like he was walking on pins and needles.

The first lightning rod wasn't far from the balcony. It was gold and about his height with a red glass globe halfway up it, at least he thought it might be red under the thick moss and grime that covered it. Right above it was a weather vane, an arrow on one end like usual, and some sculpture, perhaps a dragon, on the other, although its detail was obscured. Danny held on to the upright pole with his left hand, propped the bucket against the base of it, and grabbed the paint scraper from his belt with his right. Wanting to start with something simple, he slid it up the straight part of the mossy rod.

A horrible scream rent the air, making Danny gasp and jerk backwards. He clutched the lightning rod harder to keep his balance.

"Ow, ow, ow. You're killing me," the voice moaned. "Don't *do* that. It hurts!"

Danny wrinkled his forehead and stared at the rod in disbelief. *The lightning rods talk?* He ran a finger down the smooth metal now uncovered, but it seemed unscratched or hurt in any way. "I didn't—you're fine."

"Not the dumb rod, stupid. You imbecilic, scrawny excuse for a student! Me! The one you're tearing from my humble home to toss in that dreadful bucket of yours. What comes next? Fire? Torture? Tossed out in the barren wasteland to dry up slowly under the unrelenting sun?"

Danny gaped. "You're talking moss?"

"No, I'm a conifer. Of course I'm moss, you bat-brained idiot. You have no right to come up here and rip me from my home, to tear me about like this. Oh, the pain, the cruelty." The moss started sobbing.

Danny wasn't sure what to do. "But...but the goblin said I had to clean the moss and polish the lightning rods."

"Heartless, so heartless. Woe, woe, woe. The cruelty!"

Danny grimaced. Did the goblin know the moss was alive and talked? If he did, did he care? "Can't you grow somewhere else? I really have to do my job here."

"Can I grow somewhere else!" The moss sounded indignant. "Here you come to *my* home, ripping me up when I've spent all this time and energy establishing myself, and ask *me* to move. Grow somewhere else, you say. It's not like *you* are using this lightning rod. It's not like it hurts it any to be a little less shiny for my presence. This is a villain school, anyway. Old, moldy, and decrepit is a better sort of décor."

"Um...how about I be real gentle?" Danny gingerly tried to carefully pry the edge of the moss up with the corner of his paint scraper. The moss screamed again and he jerked his hand back.

"The pain! The pain! Oh, cruel world!"

"I hardly touched you," Danny grumbled. He glared at the moss, unsure what to do next. How was he going to get the lightning rod clean?

"Still only on the first one, *lordling?*" The taunting, dry voice of the goblin made Danny jump again and clutch the lighting rod as he turned to look for him. Only the place he grabbed was mossy and the moss screamed again under his grip. Terrified of falling, Danny didn't let up. Below on the balcony, the goblin was back. Aun stood behind him, looking a bit pale and putting together a work kit like Danny's.

The goblin flashed fangs at Danny. "You dawdle that long and you're never getting off the roof. Both of you are to stay up here until every last lightning rod is cleaned, no matter how long it takes."

"But it hurts the moss to scrape it off," Danny objected.

The goblin burst out laughing. "Some villain you are, if you're afraid to hurt the poor little moss." It gave Danny a nasty smile. "No skin off my ears, though, if you want to spend all night up here, but I hear there might be a storm tonight. Be so sad if you got fried by lightning."

Danny swallowed hard and turned back to the lightning rod. The moss moaned under his hand. Moss didn't even have feelings to hurt, did it? Danny certainly didn't want to spend the night up here, especially not in a thunderstorm, but something felt wrong about hurting something that could make so much painful noise. Danny adjusted his hand to a moss-free area of the lightning rod.

"About time." The moss sniffed. "You've flattened me, pressed my spore capsules flat into me."

Danny sighed. He tried gently prying the moss up again, only to have his ears assaulted by more screaming. "I'm being gentle. I don't have a choice," he snapped. He tried prying the moss up with his fingers instead, but it clutched the lightning rod with a tenacity that made it impossible, even with his fingernails, to get it up.

"Boy, that's noisy." Aun clambered up next to him on

the roof. While pale, he seemed to be balancing fine. "Whiny stuff, isn't it?"

Happy for the momentary distraction, Danny asked, "Why're you up here?"

Aun glowered. "I should have gotten 100% on our last History test. I had all the answers correct, but for no discernable reason, Screkvox gave me only 80%. I went to complain to him and he said that perfect scores were too good and so he marked me down for being too smart and getting everything right!" Aun clenched his hands and his face flushed a bit.

That wasn't the sort of problem Danny had ever had, his score had been abysmal, but obviously Aun was outraged and upset. "That's…really unfair."

"Damn right it is. I tried to tell him about what Professor Mordryn says about evil intelligence and Dark Lords, but then he did his lightning thing and insisted I was cheeking off and gave me detention."

"Well, I think he's an irritating bully." Danny shrugged. "Maybe he's just afraid you're going to end up smarter than him, which you probably are already." He was glad for the company, not that it would help any if he lost his footing and fell off the school roof to an ignominious demise.

Aun brightened a bit. "Maybe. I just studied real hard for that test. And don't let that stuff bother you, yeah? It's probably just magicked to make you feel guilty and slow you down. It's something they'd do, yeah?"

"Am not!" the moss retorted. "I'm being cruelly scraped and slashed into bits, ripped from my home—"

"Oh, shut up," Danny said, his confidence boosted by Aun's take on the situation. Danny didn't see he had any choice but to get the job done. If he didn't, he'd be spending the night on this stupid roof and who knows what other awful thing Screkvox would give him in punishment to do for not completing this task. He dug his paint scraper into the moss and scraped to another piercing scream.

Aun grimaced and covered his ears. "Um, I'm gonna find another lightning rod to work on...hope it's not as noisy. Oh, wait, I've got some ear plugs in this belt. See if you have any."

Danny discovered he did, in a small pouch on the belt. "Thanks." Ears plugged and the moss's screaming down to a dull annoyance, he watched Aun walk carefully along the ridge top to the next lightning rod. It was a group of about six spikes branching out like metal fingers. *That was really nice of him and he's so brave about the height.* Danny felt warm, despite the cold wind that buffeted him. He sort of liked Aun, he was fun to hang out with, and the idea he might actually be a hero felt comforting.

With new evil abandon to the moss's feelings, Danny scraped and scraped. The red glass globe finally looked red and, with a great deal of care, the dragon in flight on the end of the weather vane emerged as delicately sculpted, its claws and wings spread out as if grasping at unseen prey, beautiful in their detail. It made Danny wonder if there were dragons here and if he'd get to see them up close. While he was sure they weren't pleasant, the idea also excited him a little.

The polish smelled something terrible, but at least it didn't scream as Danny applied it. He had a flash of victory as he regarded the shiny, moss-free lightning rod, before realizing with a heavy sinking in his stomach it was only the first of who knew how many.

Even with Aun's help, the lightning rods seemed endless. Danny's hands ached and his stomach rumbled with hunger. He even missed Carly's abysmal food. Kitchen detention was far better than this. Dusk came, shading the western horizon the color of blood. Dark clouds, ominous and foreboding, gathered on the eastern horizon, growing thicker and thicker. The storm seemed not to have been just an idle goblin threat.

Danny worked on a row of blue lightning rods, their globes slightly different shades of the color, looking strange and luminous in the dusk. He glanced around for Aun and felt a bit queasy when he noticed him. Ignoring the extra height, Aun was perched on a steep tower roof, polishing a rod that had three different globes on it, one of them done like a planet with smaller globes orbiting it on a metal framework. It spun as Aun cleaned it. Danny looked away, shivering, his own fingers and toes tingling. Darkness fell as he worked on.

A few stars poked out between gaps, but the rising storm darkened the already gloomy evening sky. Lightning flashed in the distance, urging Danny to work faster. He wasn't sure the last few lightning rods were all that polished, but how were they going to know, anyway? Not like they could check them all tonight.

Aun also noticed the storm. "Hurry!" he yelled over the wind, which was picking up with evil intent. "You get that one on the far end and I'll get the other tower past this one."

Danny turned. The lightning rod on the far end of the roof was the most peculiar one he had seen yet. Instead of a single tall spike at the end, or even several tall spikes, it had thinner wires fanning out in all directions, forming a globe shape at the top of it. It reminded Danny of a chimney brush.

"Oh, don't forget to get the mushrooms off the roof on the way there," Aun called.

"What? We have to do those, too?" Danny scowled at the white fungi—they seemed too bent and strange in shape to be properly called "mushrooms." Danny swiped at them half-heartedly with his paint scraper. The fungus he touched burst into flame and red and orange sparks spurted up into the air like a geyser.

"Ahh!" Danny stumbled back, losing his balance, his palms hitting the sloped roof, his knees scraping as he slid down toward the gutter. He tried to grab at the shingles to stop himself. Terror coursed through him, but he slid to a stop just shy of the gutter.

A trap door banged open from the middle of the roof, just inches from his nose, making him bite his tongue to keep from screaming and flinching backward into nothing. A disgruntled goblin popped up, nose to nose, glaring at him. "Watch out for the Anti-aircraft Warning Attack Fungi, you little pathetic villain, or next time I'll see to it you're knocked clear off this roof and your innards splattered all over the courtyard."

"Wha—"

The goblin smacked the trap door down with a bang. Heart pounding, Danny tried to catch his breath. He was all too aware of the drop just inches past his feet.

"Muahahahaha!"

The laugh made Danny look up. Aun hung on to his lightning rod with both hands, his head tossed back in a maniacal laugh. Framed by the gathering storm, Aun had never looked so evil.

"You knew! You told me to do that on purpose!" Danny dragged himself to his feet, hands and knees stinging. He clambered up away from the edge. "You could have killed me!"

Aun just smirked at him. Danny felt extremely stupid for even thinking for a moment Aun might have been a hero. *I should know better than to trust anyone here, hero meter or not. Even Screkvox could have just been lying about that in the first place.* The wind was now so strong that he had to practically crawl along the ridge-top to avoid being blown off the roof. Despite that, he was careful to avoid the roof fungi. Wet misty drops stung his left cheek and the lightning rod glittered in the fading light ahead like a beacon calling him onwards. *Hurry, hurry.* He needed to get this done and off the roof before the storm hit.

Fortunately, the many thin points at the end of the rod weren't covered in moss, although Danny had to be careful not to bend them as he wiped them off. He practically hugged the rod itself to keep his balance. A flash of light behind him made him whip his head around, terrified lightning had already arrived and was striking down. His heartbeat thumped in his ears and his throat tightened, but it wasn't lightning. Screkvox had appeared on the roof. Danny somehow doubted he was here to release him from his detention. Another brilliant light flashed next to him and Mystfolyn also appeared.

"I'll take this end, then?" Mystfolyn pointed in Aun's direction.

"Fine with me." Screkvox's curt tone was not comforting. Were they going to check all the rods? Danny wasn't sure they'd managed all of them.

Screkvox strode along the ridge of the roof, not with a foot on either side like Aun, but one after the other on the very tip. He didn't even sway in the increasing winds, but marched right out to the very edge of the roof parallel to Danny. He pulled out a wand, bent, and made a tapping motion in the air in front of him. Something started to rise out of the edge of the roof, thin and pointed. Danny's stomach sunk, as it occurred to him that Screkvox and Mystfolyn might be creating *more* lightning rods for them, but the top of the rod then opened up, large and flat into something that looked vaguely familiar.

Screkvox took out a paper from his coat and placed it on the flat end and Danny realized it was a music stand. Then the professor raised his arms and brought the wand down like the first beat of a symphony. The clouds above closed in with an evil finality. Mesmerized, Danny forgot his job and stared as Screkvox drew them closer and closer, until with a sharp wave of his wand, he pointed at the nearby tower. Lightning jagged down from the sky with an ear-splitting crack to hit the lightning rod on top of it.

Danny cried out in surprise and horror, dropping his paint scraper. It fell off the roof, vanishing into the darkening school grounds below. Danny clutched the rod before him with both hands, then realized exactly how bad an idea that was. He yanked himself backward, throwing himself flat on the roof, hands pressed to the shingles.

It wasn't a moment too soon. Screkvox's next swing directed the lightning to Danny's rod. It cracked out long, bent fingers, striking the strange brush-like end. Blue light cracked and sparked as energy jumped back and forth across it. The air sizzled with heat and electricity and Danny smashed his face against the roof and held his breath. A piercing scream made him jerk his head back up. He had left the bucket leaning against the lightning rod and the electricity had zapped the moss in the bucket. Smoke clogged his nose and static hummed and snapped. He didn't need to feel his hair to know it was all standing on end. Body tingling, Danny pushed himself backward, still lying flat on the roof. He wasn't about to stand up and make himself a target for the next bolt of lightning.

Somehow, he doubted Screkvox cared much if he got fried.

CHAPTER 11

A Disappointing and Irritating Situation

Despite avoiding future Screkvox detentions, Danny found his plan for expulsion was truly harrowing, if not to mention far too time consuming. Mystfolyn had him de-cat-hair and press fifty black capes, making his arms ache, and a detention he got in study hall for setting his desk on fire almost got him sucked into a magical toilet. Then Carly had him feed mice to a set of large flesh-eating plants in her garden. Only his forethought to bring his practice sword along saved his fingers from getting bitten off.

The next weekend she had him scrub some rather disturbing stains off the kitchen floor. Danny did not ask what caused them. He gritted his teeth and tried to ignore

Carly's monologues on the subject of evil cookery. That was supposed to be his last detention with her, but by managing to mix just the wrong jars in the kitchen together, he successfully exploded several stacks of dishes and got time added. Still, his patience at his plan was starting to wear thin.

Virly called him to her office, but unfortunately it wasn't about the detentions. Instead she gave him another hate-letter from Alec and congratulated him on making a personal enemy so quickly. Danny cursed Alec out in private after that for making him look more villainous than ever, but couldn't think of a way to undo the damage.

The school work also picked up pace. While giving him plenty of opportunity to fail, it kept him rushing from detention to homework to class non-stop. Mystfolyn insisted on daily demonstrations of personal aura. Danny felt dizzy from all the cape twirling and his mouth hurt from grimacing practice.

Nyshlza seemed to be breathing down Danny's neck every time he turned around in Dark Magic, despite the fact he gave in and levitated a dead rabbit.

Screkvox gave them so much homework that Danny couldn't carry it all to study hall, let alone finish it.

And to top it off, his hope that Strategy Class would remain at least tolerable was crushed when Mordryn announced it was time to start practicing for the fast-approaching midterms.

"While you are progressing in your strategies, it is imperative that you experience the practical applications of command," Mordryn said, "and so, starting next week, we will be meeting on the ground for you to practice for that eventuality against your fellow students."

"You mean we're going to fight each other?" Tulk's face lit up with excitement.

Danny grimaced, not fond of the idea. On the other hand, part of him wanted to beat Tulk to a pulp in front of everyone. That would mean trying to win instead of fail, though, and might prolong his already sadly delayed expulsion. Still, what if he could find a way to manage both to humiliate Tulk *and* get expelled in doing it? While it sounded a bit nasty, maybe if he hurt Tulk somehow in the process, they'd think he was too dangerously clumsy. He paid Mordryn closer attention.

"That is how I will test your knowledge of strategy: we will hold a series of battles and, depending on your standing of battles won and lost, everyone will be given a final score."

Mordryn grinned. "And, most importantly, each of you will have your very own second-in-command, the one who will direct your evil minions in battle according to your orders. Each of these creatures has also been separately accepted to the Dark Lord Academy's Second-in-Command-Minion Training Program and the two of you will work together for the extent of your schooling here. This program is highly acclaimed and I just happen to be the founder of it. Today is the exciting day when you will meet and learn to work with your very own SICM."

The class wriggled in their seats. Danny wondered what sort of creatures the SICMs were. Perhaps goblins?

"Are they ready, Trog?" Mordryn motioned to a goblin standing at the side of his desk.

A sinister smile crossed its face and it bowed low. "Yes, Master Mordryn." It licked its lips and Danny hoped the SICMs weren't goblins.

"There are, of course, several strategies for handling your SICM and you must find the one that fits you best. You will randomly pick a number here at the front of the room." Mordryn shook a small basket full of slips of paper and set it on his desk. "Your SICM, waiting in the room beyond," he gestured at the curtain on the right side of the room, "will also have that number. Ready?"

There was a chorus of mumbled yeses from the class. Students scuffled their feet or fiddled with pencils.

Mordryn motioned to Aun. Flipping back his long, black bangs, Aun sauntered to the front of the room. He pulled a number out of the basket.

"Twelve."

"Ah, an excellent choice!" Mordryn gestured to the goblin.

Trog grinned and walked out the door. It returned, leading forward a young orc with a large nose ring, who viewed the proceedings with scorn. Aun looked a bit unsettled, but said nothing.

"There you go." Mordryn beamed at Aun. "Next!" He pointed at Daisy.

Grinning, she skipped up to the front of the room and received a creature that had the upper body of a boy, but the lower body of a bull. Daisy beamed at it. Danny grimaced. What would he do with some enormous creature?

"And you!"

Tulk got up at the teacher's urging and was given the ugliest creature Danny had ever seen. A dark gray color, it looked a cross between a bulldog and a dragon. It had orange beady eyes that gazed up at Tulk reproachfully.

"It's hideous!" Tulk protested.

"All second-in-command minions are hideous," Mordryn said with a shrug. He motioned to Danny to come pick a number.

Tulk gave the teacher a sour look and kicked his minion in the ribs. "Hurry up then, ugly." It grunted and followed him to his seat.

Danny walked up and drew a paper from the hat. He looked down to see the number six. He took a deep breath. What sort of hideous and fearsome creature would he have to order around? The goblin dragged in something small—a lump the color of vomit—that quivered and sobbed on the ground.

The goblin kicked it. "Get up."

The lump cried harder.

Danny wrinkled his nose. "What is it?"

"Not like I know," sneered the goblin. "Have fun with it."

"Er…" Danny's cheeks burned. "You gotta get up and come back to my desk."

The creature lifted its head. It had a flat nose and human-like ears, reminding Danny of a monkey. Short, mottled fur of pink, green, and yellow covered its body, longer along the back of the head, so it stood up in tufts, like wispy hair behind a mostly bald head. Its huge, liquid eyes stared up at him between long, thin fingers it held up over its face. It shivered and whimpered, pressing its hands closer to its face.

Danny nudged it with his toe gently, half expecting it to ooze puke all over him. "You gotta come."

It whimpered again.

"Hurry it up," snapped Mordryn, frowning at them and tapping his foot on the floor. "You're keeping everyone else waiting! Get back to your desk before I throw the both of you across the room."

Danny steeled himself and grabbed the creature by the arm. It shrieked and locked onto him with a surprisingly tight grip with both its hands and feet. Its body seemed monkey-like, only it lacked a tail. Danny wasn't sure if that made it an ape rather than a monkey, but whichever, it was also annoying. He carried it back to his table. When he got there, it wouldn't let go. He had to pry its fingers off one by one while it whimpered.

"What *is* it?" asked Shai, wrinkling her brow.

"I dunno." Danny shrugged.

"I hope I don't get one," she muttered.

Danny glanced forward to see Brex receive a young goblin. Danny looked back at the strange creature that was now "his." It shivered.

"Don't beat me, Great Master," it whined in a high, piercing voice.

"Shh," Danny hissed. "I'm not going to beat you. Just keep quiet."

"Yes, Great Master." Its shrill voice made the other students look at it with increased interest and Mordryn glared. Danny settled for looking at Daisy and trying to ignore it.

Daisy beamed at the half-human, half-bull creature. His human half looked about their age. He stared wide-eyed, his reddish hair sticking straight up, and looked kind of scared. His bull legs were curled up and, kneeling on the ground, he was about level with their table.

"So, what's your name?" Daisy asked. "Oh, I'm so excited to be working with you."

"W-we...t-they said we'd get new names from our new masters," the boy stuttered, looking positively terrified. Why, Danny wasn't sure. Daisy was the least terrifying person he knew. "But Mom always called me Orro."

"Orro, huh? I like it!" Daisy held out her hand. "I'm Dazydethia, up and coming Dark Lady! Pleased to meet you." She pumped his hand up and down while Orro looked rather stunned. Daisy turned to Danny. "Oooh, I like him. We'll make a good team." She gave Danny's new second-in-command minion a long look. It whimpered and hid its face again under her gaze. "Well, you sure got a strange one. What's it called?"

"I dunno." Danny felt like an idiot. He glanced at the creature, which was still shivering on the table in front of him. Compared to Orro, it seemed tiny. He gently poked it to get its attention and it nearly jumped off the table. "What're you called?"

"Whatever you like, Great Master." Its eyes huge, it nodded its head up and down, its lower jaw quivering.

"I'm not going to hurt you." Danny's patience was growing thin. It was as bad as the shrieking moss, only less talkative. "Don't you have a name?"

"No, Great Master," it howled, and then started bawling.

"It looks like something puked all over the table," Aun observed rather unhelpfully. "I've decided to call my orc Sneegblood—doesn't that sound cool?"

Danny glanced at Sneegblood. The orc sneered back at him. Danny supposed it only had one expression. Across the room, he saw Tulk kicking his unresponsive gargoyle while it lay on the floor. Spleg, next to Tulk, tried to untangle his arm from something with a lot of tentacles. Up at the front of the room, Shai was receiving what looked like a gray wolf. He turned back to his puke-colored monkey and decided he had gotten the raw end of the deal in this second-in-command minion situation. Puke, as he mentally dubbed the creature, was too pitiful for his hideousness to have any effect at all.

"So," Daisy said, chatting obliviously on with Orro, "how'd you lot end up here?"

Orro shrugged. "Non-humans don't have many options for the future. My family thought if I became a second-in-command evil minion, I'd have a good, secure future. Some of my older brothers got killed off by heroes and they didn't want the same thing happening to me." He looked wistful. "I don't know much about being evil, but that's really your job. I'm just supposed to follow orders. We had a class about it…" He tapered off, glancing fearfully at Daisy, as if he had said too much. Danny felt a rush of sympathy for him; they weren't that different.

"Don't worry, I'll evil you right up." Daisy grinned at him and Orro quivered.

That'll be interesting, Danny thought, then looked at Puke again. When it noticed, the monkey resumed howling.

"Stop it—you're embarrassing me," Danny muttered, wanting to poke it into silence. He doubted that would have any positive effect, but only make it howl louder.

Mordryn stood up and frowned in Danny's direction.

"Stop whining or…Professor Mordryn is going to stick both of us in a dungeon with no food or water," he hissed. To his relief, the creature stopped howling.

"Now that I have everyone's attention," Mordryn said, beaming at them again. "I'd like to bring home the most important concept of strategy! Simplicity!" He turned and wrote on the blackboard: Simplicity is the best strategy.

Tulk waved his hand in the air. "But Professor, that's not very evil. Isn't complex more evil?"

Mordryn frowned at him. "And who, young idiot, has ruled thirty nations? You or me?" He waved the chalk at Tulk. "If you don't like my advice, feel free to ignore it and listen to those other idiots out there who think complexity equals evil—just keep your mouth shut in my room."

Tulk's mouth clamped shut and he gave his gargoyle an extra vicious kick. It sat in stony silence. Tulk winced and rubbed his foot.

"The second most important point of Strategy," Modryn continued, tapping his chalk on the blackboard. "Remember that in nothing is the power of the Dark Lord more clearly shown than in the estrangement that divides all those who still oppose him."

Puke kept making little whining noises and wringing its hands, which was horribly distracting. Danny hoped they'd get around to expelling him before he actually had to use any of this stuff.

When the bell rang at the end of class, Mordryn held up his hands. "Alright, all SICMs will stay with you for the duration of a three-day adjusting period, then they will continue with their own courses while serving as your personal servants in their off time. Everyone is dismissed!"

Tulk headed out the door first and most of the others hurried behind him, their expressions ranging from relief to wariness to eagerness. Danny paused to shove his books into his black shoulder bag and contemplated how he was going to get Puke to go downstairs with him. Did not-quite-monkeys even walk or was he going to have to haul him like a second book bag everywhere?

"Hey, professor!" Daisy waved to Mordryn, calling him over. "How's Orro gonna get down the stairs?"

Modryn smiled. "He can take the lift, which is how he got up here."

"Can I go with him?"

Mordryn shrugged. "If you wish."

Daisy got up, then turned around. "Hey, professor, you really meant it when you said we don't have to be like everyone else around here, right? 'Cause everyone else says I'm not evil enough and..." She scuffed her feet against the ground.

Mordryn's eyes crinkled behind his glasses in amusement. He flicked one of Daisy's dreadlocks over her shoulder. "Just be yourself. That'll be all the evil you need."

Daisy beamed. She put an arm around Orro and led him off. Danny was not so easily convinced. Despite his looks,

Mordryn was a Dark Lord. "You were really nice to them. What for?"

Mordryn turned his blue ice gaze back on Danny. "Sometimes, a little kindness can be more evil in the long run." Then he turned away and walked behind the curtain, leaving Danny alone with Puke.

CHAPTER 12

A Puke Disaster

"I'm hungry," Danny told Puke. "Come if you want, but I'm going to lunch."

To his surprise, the monkey creature jumped up and clambered on his shoulder. "I a-coming, Great Master!" it said in a squeaky voice.

Danny sighed as it clutched his neck with its sticky hands and resigned himself to carrying it. It wasn't all that heavy. He headed down the stairs. The last thing he wanted at the moment was to handle another exchange with Carly, but his stomach cramped with hunger pains and he knew he wouldn't be able to concentrate in class if he didn't eat something. So, with a feeling of foreboding, he went to the crowded cafeteria.

Maybe she won't notice me for once, he thought as he stood in line. He kept his head down and thrust out his tray, but had no such luck.

"What's that—that thing—doing in my cafeteria?" boomed Carly.

Puke dug his fingers into the back of Danny's neck, making him wince as he met Carly's glare.

"My Second-in-Command Minion," Danny mumbled.

"Do you see any other minions here?" Carly snapped.

Danny looked around and noticed in surprise that none of his classmates had their minions by them.

"We don't serve *their* kind!"

Danny took a deep breath and tried to sound reassuring and casual. "Hey, minion, you've gotta go eat with the other minions." Puke didn't move.

Danny next tried to peel it off his neck. It started wailing. "Save me, Great Master! Don't make me leave you!" Everyone's eyes fixed on them. Danny blushed.

"Can't it stay?" he asked lamely.

The student behind Danny snorted. "Who's in control, you or the minion, kid?" Those around them started laughing.

"I won't waste any of my food on it," Carly said, glaring at Danny. She slapped a casseroled something onto his plate. "Get it out of my sight."

Danny sighed and walked toward his table. "Are you sure you can't eat with the other minions?" he asked Puke. It started crying again. "Fine, fine," he said, shaking his shoulder to try and shut it up. "I won't make you. You can have some of mine, just this once." He found an open seat next to Daisy and was thankful for once because she didn't comment on Puke, only smiled at him.

"I think Professor Mordryn is the best, don't you?"

"Mmm…" Danny took a bite of whatever Carly had given him and stuffed his mouth to avoid answering.

"Orro's so cute," Daisy continued. "It'll be so much fun working with him to battle everyone else. I think Strategy is going to be my second favorite class, you know, right after Art. Hey, I wonder if Orro would pose with that demon for the haunted paintings we're doing in there. What do you think?"

Danny had just swallowed his food and so was forced to answer. "Uh, I guess so. You could ask the teacher."

"Lordling?" The dry voice of a goblin at his elbow made Danny jump, splattering Puke with the food that'd been on his fork. The monkey licked his fur clean.

"Your mail," the goblin said, shoving a letter at him.

"You got a letter from home?" Aun asked from across the table. He leaned forward to peer at it. The hint of jealousy in his voice made Danny wonder if no one got any mail. Swiping any letters from their families sounded like something Dark Lords might do.

"No, it's…" He blushed, unsure how to explain Alec.

"A love letter?" Spleg asked, reaching over to try and snatch it out of Danny's hand.

"It's a hero." Danny yanked the letter out of reach.

"Riiight," Tulk said. "Why would a hero write you?" He narrowed his eyes at Danny. "And why would they let him?"

"It's a long story." Danny glanced from one face to another and could see that none of them would believe him. He ripped the letter open. The only way to end speculation was to share. "Um, here, you read it." He handed it to Daisy.

"Oooh, it *is* a hero!" Daisy cried. "Listen to this: Dear Zixygrath the Evil, now I have found your real name. You cannot hide from me. Your destruction will be at my hand unless you mend your evil ways. Even now, I am growing in my knowledge and skills. You cannot hide in your dastardly lair forever. You and your minions will not prevail. Your True Enemy Forever, Alec the Brave."

Danny glanced at Puke, who eyed his lunch plate wistfully, and didn't think Puke looked like he'd prevail in anything. He cut the monkey off a bite of his lunch and pushed it in its direction. He felt everyone's eyes on him.

"Wow! A real enemy...how did you meet him?" Aun asked.

"I...ran into him trying to break into the school and stopped him."

Everyone oohed and aahed, except Tulk, who glowered jealously, and Danny swelled with pride, deciding not to mention it was all entirely unintentional.

"Are you going to write him back?" Brex asked.

"You should!" Daisy handed Danny back the letter.

"Tell him he'll never win because you're a master villain," Aun said excitedly. "That you'll—"

"Watch out, your minion!" Daisy poked Danny's arm in sudden alarm.

Danny turned to see Puke gulping down the rest of his food. "Hey, that's—" He never got through the sentence. Puke went pale in the face and then threw up all over Danny's robes. Shai, next to him, ducked in time, but barf splattered down the table, catching Spleg and Tulk as well. If looks could kill, he'd be rolling in his grave already, puke and all.

Daisy wrinkled her nose and fanned her hand in front of it. "That doesn't look so good."

"It reeks!" Aun offered from across the table. "Ewww, get it out of here."

"Yeah, you'd better change before Study Hall," Daisy said, trying to look cheerful about it all, but not succeeding.

"Sorry, Great Master," whimpered Puke, cringing.

"I guess naming him Puke was appropriate," Danny said, getting up. The laughter as he walked out of the cafeteria, Puke trailing him, made his face burn. *Trust Puke to ruin the moment—no wonder no one else took their minions to lunch.*

Back in his room, Danny peeled off his clothes, but only had time to shove them into the corner before the bell rang for the next class. "Stay here—we'll do laundry after Study Hall," he told Puke and hoped the creature would obey.

He rushed into Study Hall as the bell rang again and sank into an open chair.

"Hey, Puke-face!"

Danny glanced up to see a murderous Tulk leaning over a desk, leering at him.

"Sit down and shut up!" yelled the teacher.

Tulk jumped and they both looked up at the front of the room. The teacher's long gray hair stood out in thick strands from the back of her head, curled this way and that in the air like tentacles. They swirled rather unnaturally as she paced forward and brought a ruler in her left hand down on Tulk's desk with a nasty crack. He yelped in pain as it clipped his fingers. The rest of the class giggled.

"Get to work or else!" She revealed a set of disconcertingly pointed teeth.

The classroom was deathly still as the teacher paced back up to her desk, then there was a rustle as everyone hurried to get out their books. Danny fumbled with his bag.

Style was first thing the next morning. He flattened his homework on the desk and read, "One: List the five essential elements of personal style. Two: List the most popular looks of male and female Dark Lords. Three: Explain in a full paragraph why personal style is important when confronting heroes." He rubbed his forehead and sighed. *If nothing else, I guess Alec had style, although I wouldn't be caught dead in glitter. I wonder if I'll get detention or extra assignments for doing this badly.* He'd learned already after the first five or six assignments if he simply didn't turn anything in, the teachers would require him to stay in study hall until he did. As much as he wanted to get expelled, that got dull fast.

As soon as class was over, Danny shoved his books in his shoulder bag and rushed out, avoiding Tulk and his comments. He hurried down the hall to get to his room. To his relief, Puke was still sulking in a corner on top of the rest of Danny's dirty laundry.

"Come on," Danny ordered. "We've got to get this in the wash or it'll stain." He scooped all his laundry into a dirty black cape from yesterday and slung it over his shoulder. "Do you happen to know where the laundry room is?"

"Puke doesn't know, Great Master," Puke said mournfully.

Danny sighed. "Well, we'll just have to go looking for it."

The hall was mostly empty, as it was the afternoon break. He searched up and down trying to find where the laundry room was, but with no success. Danny heard a quiet sob and turned to see Shai sitting in the corner, half-hidden behind a drapery. He shook his head, unsure if he'd heard right. She couldn't be crying. She hid her face as he approached, but he saw his first guess was right. He thumped the cape full of laundry down next to her and sat on it. For a long moment, he didn't say anything, not wanting to upset her further.

"It's stupid," she said thickly. "I'm fine, really."

Danny shook his head. "Tell me about it." *If it's Tulk, I'll get him, somehow. It's bad enough that he picks on me all the time, but he ought to leave the girls alone!*

She paused, tears still glistening in the corners of her eyes. Danny waited. Then Shai nodded, as if realizing he wasn't going to tease her. "I took music because I like to play the cello. But the teacher said the cello wasn't evil enough and I ought to give it up and learn something truly evil, like the organ." She sniffed. "I've never played a keyboard instrument, it's totally different. And I don't really want to. I miss the cello."

"Hmm." Danny thought for a moment, relieved it was nothing serious. "Why don't you play the viol?"

"The what?" Shai gave him a puzzled look, blinking away tears.

"The viol. It's an older version of a violin, only a bit lower...I think." Danny couldn't remember too much about it. Amos's hobby was musical instruments and he used to talk for hours about them while they worked together in the forge. Danny had only half-listened, not being all that fascinated by them. At least now it might come in handy. "But with such a vile name, they're bound to let you play a viol. At least you can make a good argument for it."

Shai's face curved into a small smile. "I guess it's worth a try."

Seeing her perk up made Danny feel warm inside. "Of course it is! You just gotta know how these people think. And hey, taking advantage of the system is perfectly evil, so they can't even complain about that!"

Shai snorted in a quiet laugh and put a hand on Danny's shoulder. "You know, you're the nicest villain around— even nicer than Daisy."

Danny's cheeks burned.

"I wish I could do something to help you in return," she said. "You always seem to have everything together and worked out."

He did? Danny squirmed uncomfortably, although he wasn't going to disillusion her by letting slip exactly how wrong she was. "Well...there is something..."

Shai smiled hopefully.

"By any chance, have you seen the laundry room?" Heat crept all the way down the back of Danny's neck, as well. Just what he didn't want to remind anyone of—Puke's little disaster at lunch.

"Oh, yeah, actually I have." Shai blushed as well. "Hey, follow me." She got up and quickly strode down the hall.

Relieved at the chance to get over his embarrassment, Danny followed a pace behind, Puke at his heels. He wondered if maybe Shai really was the hero in disguise. She seemed a great deal kinder to him than Aun. Surely a true villain wouldn't have said such nice things to him.

Shai led them down several corridors to a room full of piled linens and a fountain in one corner for beating out laundry. Several goblins were busy washing things and ignored them. Danny sighed, not looking forward to facing his dirty clothing. He dumped the clothes on the floor next to the fountain.

"Well, well, if it isn't Puke-face."

Danny turned around to see Tulk standing in the doorway.

"There are no words to describe the hatred I am feeling for you at this moment." Tulk's eyes glistened with anger as he repeated one of the evil monologue lines Mystfolyn was having them practice in style class. "You ruined my cape at lunch with that barfing machine of yours and then made me look stupid in front of everyone in Study Hall and I'm not going to let that stand." His voice dripped with sneering hate, just like Mystfolyn had impressed upon them.

He thinks he's quite the villain, doesn't he? Danny clenched his fists. "It wasn't me who did anything," he said, glaring back. "And you're not exactly my best friend."

Shai rolled her eyes, expressing what she thought of his comeback.

Thanks for backing me up here! Danny gave her a sarcastic look in return.

"Muahahahahaha!" Tulk leaned his head back, producing the ear splitting laughter Danny couldn't even begin to approximate. He pointed a finger at Danny's laundry pile. "May your laundry strangle you to death, you simpering idiot!"

The black robe rose from the laundry, dumping the rest of it on the floor, and turned towards Danny. If it had had eyes, he'd have sworn they were looking right at him. He took a step back. The robe rippled threateningly and three crumpled socks also rose in the air.

"Um, I think you ought to get out of here," said Shai, backing away from Danny. "This doesn't look good..."

"Yeah," Danny muttered. The last thing he wanted was for everyone to see him chased across the school by his dirty laundry, but he suspected that Tulk's curse was genuine and it really was killer laundry.

The robe and socks—dripping with puke—came flying towards him as the rest of the laundry launched itself into the air. Danny turned and ran. He'd worry about his image after he managed to escape.

CHAPTER 13

Life is No Fair

Danny sped down the school corridors, each glance back verifying that, yes, indeed, his dirty laundry was still after him, and gaining. Shai had disappeared, but that hardly mattered since the killer laundry was after him, not her. Other students dodged out of the way of the puke-dripping socks and robes. The hall rang with maniacal laugher.

He dashed down another hallway, one with classrooms, but the laundry made the turn as well. And as luck would have it, older students were pouring out of one of the classrooms, clogging up the hall. They stopped to add their laughter to that behind him.

Danny took a deep breath and shoved between students,

frantically trying to outrun his laundry. They shoved back and Danny careened back and forth through the hall, jarred one way and then another, until he tripped over someone's foot and landed face-first on the stone floor.

"I would think you of all people would know better than to run," said a quiet voice and Danny looked up in horror to find he'd landed right at Nyshlza's feet. Danny gulped—so much for avoiding another little chat with her. Nyshlza flicked her hand at the arriving killer laundry and it dropped to the floor. Danny sat up, rubbing his head.

"You there, goblin." Nyshlza motioned again and a goblin emerged from the shadows of the hallway, leering at Danny with amusement. "Take care of that properly." Nyshlza pointed at the laundry. From here, her face was shrouded by her hood, giving him no hint of her expression.

The goblin bowed and gathered it up with a sneer.

"Now then," Nyshlza said, offering Danny a hand. "You ought to have been able to take care of that on your own."

Danny didn't want to touch her, but he was more afraid of offending her, so he took her hand. It was cool and dry. She pulled him up. The other students snickered at them, but when Nyshlza glanced in their direction, they quickly hurried off.

Danny scuffed his shoes together. "You didn't teach us that curse or how to counter it."

"But, then, you didn't try, either," Nyshlza answered dryly. "If you had, you would have realized it was all the same principle. Tulkyzefril simply wished for the clothing not only to move, but attack."

Danny glanced up in surprise, wondering how she knew it had been Tulk. Her white eyes looked back at him, making him want to look away, but somehow, he couldn't.

What he could make out of her face looked so young and gentle, but he couldn't trust it at all.

The corners of Nyshlza's mouth curved upward. "And you prefer to play the victim rather than the villain. A pity and a waste—but I suppose that is up to you." She turned away and, with a flick of her robes, disappeared into her classroom.

Danny took a deep breath. It unnerved him that she saw through his whole plan so easily, or most of it, the failing on purpose part. With a sigh, he went to find out what had happened to Puke and his laundry. He poked his head in the laundry room and caught a glimpse of the goblins teaching a terrified Puke how to wash laundry and decided he wanted no part of that. Instead, he headed to the cafeteria to get dinner before Puke tried to find him. Despite all that had happened, he was hungry.

To his relief, all Carly did was remind him about detention. Danny hurried to his seat, the first one in his year to sit down, and started eating quickly.

"What's the hurry?" Aun asked as he joined him.

"I want to get an early start on my homework," Danny mumbled, the first excuse that came to mind.

"Oh, you look all right," Shai said, joining them. "So you managed to undo Tulk's spell?"

"Mmm," Danny said and took another bite.

"Spell?" asked Aun.

Shai told him about Tulk, giggling over the laundry, and Danny's face burned red. He noticed she left out the part about her crying over her cello playing, but he just couldn't find it in him to make fun of her, even if it was cruel of her to do the same to him. *You idiot, she's a villain in training, not your friend.* It didn't matter—it still hurt. After the fiasco with Aun on the roof, he should have known better than to hope Shai was a hero, but it seemed he couldn't help but hope anyway.

He finished his plate in a hurry. Ignoring the arriving Tulk's gleeful cries of, "Oh, still alive, Zitty?" he hurried off to his room. He lay there glaring at the black cracks on the ceiling, feeling more alone than ever. Detentions and extra assignments were exhausting enough without also constantly dealing with crushed hopes. He silently vowed to stop looking for the stupid hero.

Danny wondered bitterly if Screkvox had been mistaken. Maybe everyone here was a villain. The meters were simply all wrong because he, Danny, was terrible at this villain business and had no desire to be one. At least he had to be well on his way to flunking out at this rate. But despite his resolve, Danny was sick of detentions, embarrassments, and feeling stupid in front of the others. He tried to tell himself it didn't matter what they thought, that they were villains and he shouldn't care about them, but he liked hanging out with them. Usually that was a good thing— only because they were villain students, did that make it bad?

Danny rubbed his head. He was no closer to solving what exactly was good and what was evil than on his first day here. Everyone else seemed to think it was an easy question and assumed he should already know the answer, but the more he considered it, the more complicated it got. Alec, it seemed, could get away with all sorts of insults being a hero: writing a villain, attacking him, even possibly *killing* him. Danny didn't feel evil. In fact, he was trying hard not to be. How was that any fair?

I'll just have to hope he doesn't actually follow through on his threats. At least Alec hadn't been smart enough to get past the drawbridge. *Wait a minute!* Danny sat up as a new idea smacked him as hard as Osweggi with a practice sword. *What if I did write him back? What if I incited him to attack Dark Lord Academy? Maybe not just him, but his friends as well!* Danny filled with hope. If he got a bunch of heroes to attack the school, all because of him, surely that would be out of the realm of "acceptable" villainy. Or if nothing else, he could escape the castle in the midst of the confusion. This had to be a faster plan than flunking. Danny jumped up and grabbed some paper.

Dear Alec the Brave...

Danny considered a moment. He needed to be inflammatory, but not so transparent his letter couldn't get through the school censors.

*You will never defeat me because I am far more powerful than you could ever imagine. Not only that, but I have lots of evil...*He couldn't call them friends, could he? *compatriots who will aid me in your destruction. We will not let you live, if you even make it past our front gate, which you are apparently too stupid to even manage. You are pathetic and not worthy to be called a hero.*

Evilly yours,

Zxygrth, Master of Darkness

P.S. Get my name right, you pathetic jerk. Or can't you spell?

That ought to do it. Surely a few rounds of this and Alec was bound to return for a second try. With a practiced cackle of glee—Danny surprised himself by actually sounding half-good—he stuffed the letter in an envelope and went to find a goblin to go mail it for him.

The week sped by without a reply from Alec, but Danny was sure he would get one soon. On Saturday, when he reported to detention, he was surprised to find Puke waiting for him. Ever since Puke had gone back to his own classes after their three day "adjustment," Danny had been quite relieved only to have to endure him lurking around his room during their breaks. He wasn't sure if this new SICM arrangement meant Puke would now be sharing all his detentions.

"Puke will help Great Master!" The monkey-like creature bowed deeply. Danny could have groaned out loud.

"Excellent, excellent!" Carly bustled into the room. "You and your minion can clean out the grease traps and scrub the grill down."

Danny did groan aloud this time.

Carly's eyes sparkled with an evil glint. "Get to it, Zixy-boy!"

It wasn't until after eleven that, greasy and reeking of oil, Danny and Puke dragged themselves to bed. Or rather, Danny dragged Puke. He pulled off his ruined clothing, dropped the filthy and half-awake Puke on top of them, and crawled into bed. In the morning, Puke still slept on, so Danny quietly got dressed and hurried off to breakfast before the creature could wake and beg to be taken along. He was in such a hurry that he almost crashed into an older student. Dodging to one side just in time, he mumbled, "Sorry."

The boy grabbed his arm, bringing him to a stop. Danny glanced up and met unnerving silver eyes and recognized the shaggy bleached hair and red-brown skin—Demigorth the Destroyer.

"Hey, there, Zaxygrath, you remember me?"

"Um, yeah…" Danny muttered.

"Yeah, well, you and that Tilkyzefril boy are just what I need. You haven't signed up for a sport yet, have you?"

"Uhh." Danny found himself tongue-tied. He'd almost forgotten Virly's talk of school sports by now. He hadn't planned to be around this long.

"Well, the troll wrestling club meets tonight and I want

both you and Talky-what's-it there!" Demigorth shoved Danny forward, clapping him on the back. "We need newbies with your spirit. Talk some more people into it."

"Talk us into what?" Daisy asked, catching Danny as he stumbled into her.

"Troll wrestling, 4:30, Saturday afternoon. Don't forget!" Demigorth beamed at them, his eyes flashing and blinding them for a moment, then he was gone.

"Wow! That sounds exciting!" Daisy beamed. "We should go."

"Sounds too exciting, if you ask me," Danny said under his breath, deciding he'd conveniently forget. Wrestling trolls with Tulk did not sound like his idea of a good time. He followed Daisy into the cafeteria.

"Hey Zixy-boy!" Carly boomed at him as he held out his tray for breakfast. "Where's that Puke of yours?"

The kids behind Danny started snickering.

"Er, he was tired, so I let him sleep," Danny said hastily.

Carly's expression softened. "Poor little thing. Yesterday before you showed up for detention, he said he'd never had anything like my cooking before and begged me to let him come with you, did you know that?" She shook her head. "I don't know what they feed those minions…I suspect goblin food. No wonder the poor dear can't take it. Hey, bring him in with you tomorrow."

Her voice suggested Danny didn't have a choice about it. He bobbed his head and hurried away.

Yet, detention wasn't as bad when sharing it with Puke. Perhaps it was true that misery loves company, or maybe it was that Carly seemed friendlier with the monkey present. Danny was impressed by the compliments the overly-subservient Puke came up with, even if he did feel a little put out having to learn flattery from a cringing, puking minion. And Puke had almost gotten him in trouble with

Mordryn—he might be useful for racking up more detentions.

With both detentions already piling up and waiting for a reply from Alec, Danny's most pressing problem was to find a way to get even with Tulk for the laundry trick. Tulk and Sleg did impressions of the incident whenever they could and, to Danny's annoyance, Aun and Shai seemed to find it highly amusing. People even pointed him out in the hall as the "laundry boy." Danny had enough. He didn't see how not being a villain meant he had to be a doormat.

Unfortunately, his schedule left little time for plotting revenge. Style class was the worst, where Tulk continually garnered compliments. Danny's attention wandered from Mystfolyn teaching them how to twist mustaches and turn their eyes glowing red, but Mystfolyn's periodic demeaning comments and Tulk's snickering meant he had to at least pretend to be trying to make it work. Class dragged on forever until the bell rang and Danny was the only student who didn't leave with his eyes glowing red. Not because he couldn't, but because it looked stupid.

"This is awesome!" raved Daisy. "I bet I look wickedly evil."

"Me too!" Aun said. "Hey, I wonder if we'll scare Professor Nyshlza."

Danny's relief at Style class ending evaporated the instant he realized it was now time for Dark Magic class. His breakfast felt like lead in his stomach. Today the mere thought at muddling through another day of making dead animals twitch was enough to make him consider ditching class—except detention was sure to involve dead animals if he tried that. He dragged his feet, but Daisy would have none of it. She grabbed him by one arm and Shai grabbed his other.

"Hurry up, Zixy, we're going to be late!"

"Yeah, and why not change your eyes to match with us?" Shai asked.

"Don't you remember what Professor Mordryn said about just being yourself?" Danny retorted, irritated.

Shai shrugged. "He's just weird. Come on, everyone else has them! You'll stand out."

Fortunately the discussion ended because they reached the Dark Magic classroom. To Danny's surprise, the table with the globe of light in the center was gone. Instead, the globe hung from the ceiling, dully illuminating the room. Chairs, without desks or tables, were arranged in a semi-circle on one half of the room. Thick fabric hung against the far wall they faced and that half of the room also had a thick carpet on the floor.

"What—" said Aun as they all stared.

"Come in." They saw Nyshlza standing in the shadows, smiling. Danny noticed her eyes were solid white again and he looked away. He could feel her gaze following him, though, as he picked a seat.

"Today," Nyshlza said in her silky voice once they had all gathered, "we are going to do something a bit more active. You will be learning how you can throw someone against a wall."

Whispered excitement filled the room, but grew quiet as Nyshlza continued. "This basic move is important for confronting heroes or dealing with annoying minions. I assume all of you have been practicing finding your core energy."

There was a chorus of murmured yeses. Danny cleared his throat to avoid saying anything, but he doubted Nyshlza was fooled, as she looked right at him.

"That same center is where you draw the power to animate something, although you are not trying to animate the human you wish to move. Controlling someone takes considerably more power and skill than any of you have at the moment. You merely want to push them with that energy, hard enough to send them flying into the wall." Nyshlza gestured at the fabric-hung wall. "It has been properly padded so that no one will be damaged. Now, may I have a volunteer?"

Everyone looked at the floor, except Daisy, who waved her hand back and forth. "Ooh, ooh, me! I want to!"

Nyshlza beckoned to her. "Now, you hold your hand like this and find your core. Fix in your mind your intent to throw the person and thrust that outward with the energy along with the word." The quiet, velvety sound of her voice lulled Danny and he felt the darkness inside of him move, connecting with his senses. He pushed it back and focused on Nyshlza's hand.

She flicked it, muttering a command, and Daisy flew backward and hit the wall with a dull thud. She slipped to the ground and started giggling.

"Wheeee! That was awesome, professor!"

"Then I'm sure you're eager to try it. I want everyone paired off and we'll rotate turns and pairs, so you have a variety of tries. Each person has a different balance and a different resistance. You'll find some are harder to throw than others."

Everyone scrambled to find a partner. "Hey, Zixy!" Daisy dashed forward to grab Danny's arm. "Can I try it on you?"

Danny shrugged. "Sure."

Daisy screwed her eyes shut. Then her hand shot out and Danny felt something whump against his face, like getting hit with a pillow. He blinked and rubbed his eyes.

"Oh, nuts! Why didn't it work?" moaned Daisy.

"Wait," Danny said, holding up his hand. He saw out of the corner of his eye that Shai had knocked Aun to the floor with her attempt and was now helping him up. "I felt it. It just wasn't strong enough."

Daisy brightened a little. "Okay, can I try it again?"

Danny nodded. This time the air was stronger and, although he expected it and braced for it, he wavered for a moment, catching himself from getting knocked over at the last minute.

"Almost!" Daisy said. "But it's only fair you get a turn now."

Danny didn't want to reach for the magic, but he changed places with her. Looking at her eager face though, only brought home the feeling he didn't really want to throw her against the wall. "What if I hurt you?"

Daisy giggled. "Not even Nyshlza hurt me. It was fun. Come on, Zixy, give it your best."

"Yes, Zix, I'd like to see that." Nyshlza's soft voice in his ear made Danny jump.

He licked his lips. "I don't want to hurt her."

"Then you won't," Nyshlza answered.

Danny glanced around the room. No one else seemed to be watching them as they practiced with varied degrees of success. He took a deep breath and closed his eyes, letting the smallest bit of the dark magic come to him. His hands tingled and it bubbled up in him, eager to get out. For a moment he forgot what he was going to do and felt only the peace and excitement of the magic. He opened his eyes and the world shimmered in a swirl of magical energies. Each living form was a dark focus.

Daisy gasped. Danny blinked, his concentration shattered, and realized with a sinking horror that he was going to use the magic on her. He tried to cut it off, but already his hand had been twisting, his intent to throw already there.

Part of the magic escaped him and Daisy flew

backwards, landing just short of the wall and stumbling into it.

"Sorry," Danny said, rushing forward.

Daisy stared at him. "For a moment, your eyes turned white like Nyshlza's! How'd you do that?"

Danny shook his head. "You just imagined it. You're not hurt, are you?"

Daisy snorted. "Of course not. Gosh, I wish I could do dark magic like you can." Her face fell. "It's no fair."

Danny shook his head. "Oh, come on, you can do it as well. You just have to concentrate." Her sorrowful eyes—no longer red, but plain dark brown—looked back at him and he felt bad for her. "Here, I'll show you how." Impulsively, he grabbed both her hands. "Reach, deep inside yourself..." He could feel the magic in her, too, only somehow, not being his, it didn't scare him so much. He touched it with his mind and it rushed forward to meet him.

"Oh!" cried Daisy, and he pulled away from it, terrified all over again that he had hurt her. "My hands feel funny," she whispered.

"Then try it now and you'll be able to do it." He smiled at her.

"Change partners!" Nyshlza's cry interrupted them.

"Drat!" Daisy glowered.

Nyshlza stepped between them, pairing Danny off with Brex and Daisy with Tulk.

"I want to go first," Brex insisted. "Tulk never let me try it." Danny shrugged.

"Give me your best try, flower-girl," Tulk said, sneering at Daisy.

Brex's small attempt bounced off Danny's cheek as he turned to watch. Daisy paused for a moment, her face a picture of concentration. Then her hands shot out. Tulk flew into the air and the class gasped as he shot backwards, thwacking against the wall with a loud thud.

"Wow!" exclaimed Aun.

"Way to go, Daisy!" Brex beamed at her.

Tulk got to his feet, rubbing his head, his face bright red. He glowered at Daisy. Danny felt warm satisfaction fill him as everyone ran to congratulate an ecstatic Daisy, and Tulk looked like he wanted to die. *That'll show him for that stupid laundry trick.*

Only then he felt someone's gaze on him and turned to see Nyshlza considering him; and although her eyes were normal, something in her look made him feel deeply uncomfortable.

CHAPTER 14

Out of the Frying Pan and Into Something Else

S till cheering and raving over Daisy's display, everyone headed down to lunch. Danny was relieved to blend in and escape Nyshlza. The happy mood caught him and he laughed and smiled with the others. He couldn't help but be pleased at successfully getting revenge. Underneath, he had a small nagging worry he might be starting to enjoy himself too much, but it wasn't like he'd done anything actually *evil*. Puke waited for him by the entrance of the cafeteria. In a charitable mood, Danny scooped him up and let him sit on his shoulder.

Carly even smiled at them. "I've got something special to show you tonight," she said, giving him an extra plate for Puke.

"That sounds…" Danny wasn't sure if he should say good or evil, although he guessed it was more evil than good. "Exciting!" He smiled at her, hoping he got his words right this time.

She winked at him, like she knew his dilemma. Puke moaned in his ear and Danny hurried away with his food before Carly could screw up an almost okay moment.

"Hey, Zix!" Aun waved Danny over. "What do you think of this?" He flashed a flier at Danny.

Danny took it. It read: *Demon Horse Racing—first meeting this Saturday! Terrify heroes and minions alike with your speed and evil daring on a Demon Horse. Meet in the Dead Field at 10 AM.*

"We gotta do a sport," Aun pointed out. "And I'm sick of everyone asking me to do some kung fu. Racing, now that sounds good."

"I guess…" While Danny knew the basics of riding and horse care, somehow he doubted that Demon Horses would be easy. They sounded a bit dangerous, but at least it was better than troll wrestling.

"Great," Aun said, his almond-shaped eyes lighting up. "I didn't want to go alone."

"Hmph, I thought you were the Fearsome Fighting Fright who conquers all alone," muttered Danny under his breath. But then, he didn't want to sign up for a sport alone either. It felt kind of nice that Aun had asked him to go along, even if it turned out he was just using him.

"Look, it's a meeting of idiots!"

Danny groaned.

Tulk swaggered over, grinning ear to ear. "You wimps ready to be tromped on Saturday? I can't wait to see you troll-thrashed."

Looks like Demigorth found Tulk. This cemented a quick plan in Danny's mind. He set his lunch tray on the table and turned to face Tulk.

"Actually," Aun said, "we're—"

Danny kicked him. "Going to be the greatest troll wrestlers this school has ever seen. One look at those trolls, Tulkie, and you're going to pee your pants. Aun and I could outwrestle you any day."

"But—" objected Aun. Danny gave him his best shot at an evil "shut up, stupid" glare. It worked—Aun shut his mouth.

"Oh really?" Tulk said. "You're full of hot air. And you know what? You just wait 'til then and I'll show you how troll wrestling's done."

"Yeah, you do that," Danny sneered, trying to get the tone just right.

The comment cost him, because Tulk punched him in the gut. Danny doubled over in pain.

"Yeah, I will, Zitty. Don't you forget who's the biggest, baddest first year, snot face." He had the sneer down to perfection.

He must have practiced it for hours, Danny thought through the pain. To his relief, Tulk sauntered off.

"Zixy? You okay?" Aun grabbed his arm. Danny nodded through gritted teeth. Aun shook his head. "You're either incredibly brave or incredibly stupid! What'd you do that for, provoking him? And telling him all that crap about troll wrestling."

Danny figured he'd put his money on incredibly stupid, but he hoped to reverse the verdict by Saturday. The pain in his stomach eased and he stood up. "I told him that so he'd go to troll wrestling. While he's getting his butt whipped, we'll be galloping around on Demon Horses."

"Oh," Aun's expression brightened. "Zix, you're terrifically evil. That's brilliant."

"Thanks," Danny muttered, not wanting to overdo it,

but inside he felt a rush of pride. Aun thought he was brilliantly evil! He couldn't wait to find another opportunity to show off—until he thought about it for a moment. *You're going to get sucked into this evil thing if you're not careful.* Lunch felt heavy in his stomach, although that could have been Carly's usual cooking.

Thankfully, the sight of a goblin seeking him out through the hall distracted him. "Hah!" He grabbed his letter from the goblin's outstretched hand and ripped it open.

"Did you write him back? What's it say?" Aun lit up with curiosity.

Danny smirked—his plan was working. "Listen to this: Dear Zxygrth, Master of Darkness, I am not afraid of you *or* your evil compatriots. Your foul insults fail and recoil upon your own head. All of you will meet a swift and crushing defeat when you come face-to-face with me and my friends. I will discover their identities as well; none of you can escape! We are hunting you down and will find a way soon enough to break your dastardly enchantments. Your Courageous Opposition, Alec the Brave and the Chivalrous Coalition for the Destruction of Evil."

"You mentioned us?" Aun's face lit with evil delight. "Wickedly cunning."

Danny beamed, soaking up the praise. *No one likes being humiliated all the time. This has nothing to do with good and evil.* It was taking a while to get expelled, that was all. There was no reason he should be miserable all this time. "Maybe I'll let your name slip or something in the next letter? What do you think?"

They brainstormed new insults for Alec all the way to the next class. So long as Danny got out of here eventually, it couldn't really hurt to have a good time now and then... could it?

That Saturday, at 4:30, Aun and Danny found themselves with a small group of students at the Dead Field, a large stretch of dead grass behind the stables. Ominous scorches on the field told Danny this must be where the Dragon Riding Class met. Next to dragons, demon horses should be easy.

"Hey, you first years?" A girl with a zillion long braids turned to squint at them. Danny marveled at how much hair she had. Her braids were looped around and pinned back up on the top of her head. She had gorgeous tan skin and deep black eyes that sparkled with mischief. Her loose black silk tunic and baggy black pants both had silver trim in the pattern of leaves. She looked altogether too gorgeous to be evil, despite the lecture on the seductive beauty look they'd had that morning.

Still, she was an older student and therefore dangerous. Danny glanced at Aun, who was staring at her wide-eyed, obviously suffering from the same trouble—and trying not to gawk. Danny gathered his courage up to speak.

"Erm, yeah, um, er, we thought we'd check out Demon Horse Racing, for our sport, you know..." Danny's face burned. He expected a killer, sarcastically evil remark. This girl certainly looked capable enough.

To his surprise, her face lit up with eagerness, her eyes sparkling even more wickedly. "I love racing, and the horses..." She trailed off with a look of anticipation. "You'll see in a minute. They're most beautiful things I've ever seen!"

"You're the most beautiful thing I've ever seen," Aun said in a low whisper that only Danny could hear.

I wish I'd thought of something that good, Danny thought. But as usual, he couldn't think of anything witty to say. They were distracted from the conversation, however, by the sounds of hoofs. Someone had opened the stable. Out rode a black caped figure on a demon horse. The horse was huge and black, with a long, thin tail with a tuft at the end. Its eyes blazed red and it reared up, neighing and blowing fire out of its nostrils. Danny and Aun edged backwards. *Perhaps this wasn't such a good idea after all. At least trolls don't breathe fire.*

The rider, however, kept his seat and pulled hard on the reins. The horse put its front feet down, but snorted another whoosh of flame before coming to a standstill. The rider dismounted. Thin, pale, bony hands lifted up to pull the hood back. The teacher had a mop of raggedy black hair. He laced his fingers together and smiled, showing off fangs.

"Velcome, Velcome," he said in a thin, wavering voice that sent shivers down Danny's back. "I'm pleased to see how many of you have returned to zis great sport from last year. And a special velcome to ze new students." The way he said that sounded more like "fresh meat" than anything else. The horse stamped its hoofs and blew some fire.

The pretty girl started clapping enthusiastically. There were a few half-hearted claps from everyone else.

"Professor Charcula is a world-renowned racer," the girl gushed to Aun and Danny. Her hand brushed against Danny's shoulder.

Danny's tongue stuck to the roof of his mouth and he couldn't find any words.

Aun smiled and nodded. "Impressive, isn't he?"

"Vell, let's get to business. Muahahahahahaha!" Charcula's maniacal laughter was absolutely perfect, making Danny feel small and insignificant in comparison. "Who'd fancy a try at Hell's Wind here?"

"Oooh, ooh, ooh!" The pretty girl waved her hand back and forth.

Charcula gave her a fanged smile. "Queileria! How

wonderful to see you again—you were magnificent at the junior regionals last summer."

Queileria blushed. "Not half so good as you at the professional games, Professor. That first place ribbon in the Flamed Sheol Circuit was astounding!"

"Vell, so it was, if I must say so myself." Charcula bowed.

Queileria rushed forward to take the reins of Hell's Wind. To Danny's astonishment, she held the horse's head to her chest and whispered in its ear. The horse nickered, but didn't blow flames. Then again, if it'd been him held to that chest, he wouldn't have flamed either. The thought made Danny turn scarlet.

"Lucky horse," muttered Aun, and Danny felt his blush creep all the way up to his hair.

The other students rushed to pick horses from the stable. Queileria swung up into Hell's Wind's saddle. The horse fidgeted. Queileria gave it a kick and they were off in a cloud of flames. Danny and Aun didn't have much time to watch, though, because at that moment, Professor Charcula pounced on them.

"Vell, vell, new students. It's good to see a continuing interest in zis sport of all sports. I'm pleased to have you here. How much experience do ze two of you have?"

"Um," Danny said.

"Er…" Aun replied.

"We've ridden regular horses," Danny said, not wanting them to come off as completely inept. He suspected he wasn't succeeding.

Professor Charcula shook his head. "Vell, vell, we all have to begin somewhere, I suppose. But regular horses, tsk, tsk, zey aren't much of a challenge, are zey? Vell, boys, I think I've got a nice pair of beginner horses for you." He smiled at them and it was an evil enough smile to make Danny wish they'd picked troll wrestling after all.

Professor Charcula led the way to the stables. He surveyed the horses left. "Hmm, looks like all ze quieter ones have been taken. No matter, I'm sure I can set you up." He gave them another look over. "Now, what did you say your name was, young man?"

"Zxygrth." Danny refrained from pointing out that Charcula hadn't asked earlier.

"Zaxygrass, eh? Vell now, I zink zis one will suit you just fine—Wrass of Dess."

"Umm…" For some reason, Danny wasn't too keen on riding a horse named Wrath of Death. And from the way Wrath of Death stomped and spit flame out over the top of the stall, he had a suspicion the horse wasn't too pleased at the prospect, either.

"Come here, you rascal," Professor Charcula said. He tried to catch Wrath of Death's bridle, but the horse set his sleeve on fire. "I'll have none of zat!"

There was a cracking noise and a flash of black energy and the horse screamed. Then Professor Charcula came out of the stall, leading the horse. While it walked along with him obediently enough, its eyes blazed bright red like twin suns. Danny gulped.

"Vell, vell, hurry up and mount him, zen." Professor Charcula glared at Danny and gestured to the saddle.

Not wanting to try the professor's wrath, Danny decided he'd take whatever the horse had to offer. He grabbed the pommel and boosted himself up. Wrath of Death tried to rear up, but Charcula held him firmly.

"Now strap yourself in, boy."

Danny noticed the stirrups and sides of the saddle had clamps on them. Not wanting to think what this might mean, he leaned forward, locking them on both legs. Then he grasped the reins and hoped that Charcula was just going to lead the horse around the corral for him. Wrath of Death swished his tufted tail, slapping it across Danny's back, and snorted, but only smoke came out of his nose this time.

"Good, good. Now you check zem." Charcula gestured at Aun.

Aun looked like getting near Wrath of Death was the last thing he wanted, but he obeyed, tugging on each binding. Danny was glad they all held. He had a suspicion he was going to need them.

"Excellent. Now, Zaxygrass, take him around the field, nice and easy." Charcula grinned at him, showing off his fangs. "Good luck." He let go of the bridle and slapped Wrath of Death on the rump.

The horse let out an ear-piercing whinny, rearing upward. Danny clutched the pommel. If he hadn't been strapped in, he would have gone flying. He yelped in terror. Flame poured out of Wrath of Death's mouth and nostrils and then he galloped forward with a vengeance. Danny hung on for dear life, hacking on the smoke.

He couldn't see where they were going. The flames flowing from Wrath of Death's footprints and head obscured the view. Wind blew the smoke into his eyes, almost forcing them shut, but Danny wasn't about to go hurdling towards oblivion with his eyes closed. He squinted against the wind and the smoke cleared. He sniffed back mucus as his nose started to run. They were fast approaching the edge of the Dead Field. Danny yanked on the reins. *Turn, you stupid horse, turn!*

Instead of obeying, Wrath of Death launched into the air. They sailed over the fence and into open land. Grass withered under Wrath of Death's feet and nearby bushes and trees shriveled up, leaving a black scar in their wake. Danny gave up all hope of directing him. Wrath of Death rounded a hill and headed back towards the school. Danny concentrated on holding on. The fence moved up on them again—this time the ground was a bit uneven, sending ripples and jolts through Danny as they moved. Then he felt Wrath of Death's legs bunch in preparation for the jump. As if in slow motion, time slowed down in the air, until the jolt made his teeth snap together when they landed.

Something below him snapped. Danny realized, horrified, that the bindings on his legs had broken. He squeezed his knees tighter to Wrath of Death's side and the horse picked up speed again.

"Heeeeelp!" His cry was torn away by the wind. Wrath of Death nickered and Danny suspected the horse was laughing at him. They approached the barn at a breakneck speed. The fence of the stable yard was coming up on them. Danny clutched the saddle horn with both hands, unsure how he'd stay on if Wrath of Death jumped it again. Instead, the horse came to an abrupt stop, just inches from the fence. Danny's grip was ripped loose from the saddle and he sailed over its head and into a huge pile of manure.

He landed with a terrific splat. It cushioned his fall— somewhat. Every bone in his body ached. Demon Horse racing was definitely not his sport. There had to be something better.

"Wrathie!" chided a voice. "That wasn't very nice."

Danny unstuck himself enough to sit up and see Queileria patting Wrath of Death on the nose. The horse was quiet, but its red eyes gleamed at Danny and he had the feeling he was still the butt of the joke.

"He likes to play evil tricks on new riders," Queileria said.

"I noticed," muttered Danny, feeling his face go bright red again under all the horse poop.

Queileria looped Wrath of Death's reins over the fence and climbed over it. "It's his demon nature. Are you all right?"

Danny nodded. Ignoring the manure, Queileria reached out and caught Danny's hand, hauling him to his feet. She brushed some of the larger clumps off his clothes.

"Um, hey, I can do that," Danny said, feeling tongue-tied. What kind of Dark Lady was she? He started trying to brush off more poop, but only managed to get his hands filthy, as well.

Queileria laughed. "Actually, you did better than my first ride and I was only on Plague of Fire. Those jumps were pretty impressive."

"Ahh, thanks."

Queileria walked back over to the horse. "I think Wrath of Death likes you, don't you, my evil boy?" She kissed him on the nose and he nickered.

"Well, he may be one evil horse, but I smell more foul," Danny said as he climbed over the fence.

Queileria laughed. Unlike the usual dark lord laugh, hers sounded musical. "Say, what's your name, kid?"

Danny felt warm inside. He didn't have anything to lose at this point, so why not try and see what he could get? "Zxygrth. You can call me Zix."

Queileria winked at him. "Well, see you tomorrow for the next practice then, Zix." She handed him Wrath of Death's reigns and sauntered off.

Danny gaped after her, then looked at Wrath of Death. "Looks like I am going to come back and ride you again after all," he said in amazement, hardly believing it.

Wrath of Death winked a fiery red eye at him.

CHAPTER 15

Demigorth, Dungeons, and Detention

The beauty of the moment was short lived. Wrath of Death, evidently pleased enough with his final retribution, allowed Danny to lead him back to his stall, but everyone looked at Danny with wrinkled noses and disgusted expressions.

"Whew! You sure stink," Aun said when Danny rejoined him.

"Yeah, but Queileria asked me my name," Danny bragged. "That's worth several piles of manure."

"Says you." Aun made a gagging motion.

"So what? Did you do any better with your horse?"

Aun fidgeted. "Actually, Charcula got to lecturing me about what you did wrong and he went on so long it took the rest of the practice, so I didn't have to get thrown in the manure pile."

"Well, you can ride him next time because once is enough for me."

Aun didn't reply, but Danny guessed that meant he would be coming again, although a chance at riding Wrath of Death was probably the last thing on his mind. Danny turned around to see him waving at Queileria's back as she walked off, talking to a group of older kids.

"She's too old for us," Danny said, meaning mostly she was too old for Aun.

Aun nodded absent-mindedly.

Danny decided to get cleaned up before Tulk noticed him. He hoped that Tulk had been beaten to a pulp by those trolls. Shaking off as much manure as he could, he hurried across the Dead Field toward the Dark Fortress. Danny ducked through the archway and headed for his room. If he could just get there fast enough, before anyone else noticed his condition…He dashed down the corridor; a few people gagged as he whirled by.

"Hey, Zitty, is that you I smell?" Tulk blocked his way and Danny skidded to a halt.

Tulk looked just fine, no bruises, no scrapes. Danny narrowed his eyes.

Tulk smirked. "What'd the trolls do, poop on you?

"Where were you?" Danny balled his hands into fists. His disappointment at not getting Tulk back burned at him.

"Well, unlike you, the Great Dark Idiot, I managed to stay clean because I am the new up-and-coming champion for minion tossing."

"So you were too chicken to try the trolls, eh?" Danny tried to look tough, but doing that covered in horse manure was a bit difficult.

"Hey, guys!" Daisy chose this moment to show up.

"Why didn't you come to Troll Wrestling? I threw this ugly fellow three times my size...Eww, what's that you got all over you, Zixy?"

Tulk started snickering and Danny, his face red, decided now was the perfect time for a fast retreat. "Gotta run or I'll be late for lunch!" He dodged around them both and sprinted back to his room.

Danny slammed the door and ripped off all his clothes. "Why do I always have to look like a total idiot!" he ranted, glaring at his poop-encrusted hair in his mirror.

"Great Master is not feeling well?"

Danny turned to see Puke staring at him, wide-eyed.

"Gah!" He grabbed a towel and held it in front of himself. "Puke, I'm naked!"

Puke had the decency to look at the floor, tears leaking from his eyes. "Insignificant Puke is very sorry, Great Master. Worthless Puke can wash the Great Master's clothes while he bathes."

Danny sighed. "I wasn't trying to hurt your feelings. Please, stop crying. Yeah, a bath's a good idea. Go ahead and wash my clothes. Then we'll go to detention for Mordryn together, all right?" Perhaps he could avoid more embarrassment if he skipped lunch. The last thing he wanted was to hear everyone laughing at Aun's version of his ride on Wrath of Death.

Puke brightened and bowed low.

The bath refreshed Danny and he felt more cheerful, despite having Mordryn's detention all afternoon and then Carly's final one after dinner—well, final until he managed to cause some trouble to get more. Perhaps he could come up with a good idea during the afternoon one for extending it. Exploding dishes a second time might arouse her suspicions for being repetitive.

Puke riding on his shoulders, he headed to the main hall

to wait for the goblin detention supervisor. The goblin gave Danny a bored glance, then considered his clipboard while chewing on the end of his pencil. "Hmmm, looks like you've been put on cleaning out the secret dungeon passageway. It's certainly been long enough—never know what you might find down there." He flashed fangs at Danny.

Puke whimpered. *Can't be worse than any of what I've had already*, Danny thought. *Not to mention I've heard that line before.* He squared his shoulders and figured that at least being underground was better than clambering over the rooftops again, especially now that he had Puke.

The goblin led them through the twisting halls in the front maze-like area of the school. Despite his resolve, Danny couldn't help but remember his first day at Dark Lord Academy. Igor had mentioned the dungeons in passing, along with executions and plagues. Danny hadn't seen him since and wasn't sure if he was a student, a SICM, or something else entirely.

They stopped somewhere in the middle of the maze. The goblin tapped on a stone wall covered in green slime and it slid to one side with an ominous rumble, revealing a black opening. Puke grabbed onto his hair so tightly it brought tears to Danny's eyes. He reached up to pry him loose.

Reaching into the dark, the goblin pulled out a broom, scrub brush, and bucket. He tapped his claws on the rim, muttering something, and the bucket filled with soapy water. "There you go." The goblin smirked.

"How can I see to clean anything?" Danny hadn't ever thought of himself as a person who was afraid of the dark, but the idea of venturing down to the dungeons in pitch-blackness was not high on his list of things he'd prefer to try.

"Oh, fine, have a lantern if you insist." The goblin reached into the darkness and pulled out a battered one and lit the candle. Its wan light looked hopelessly small, even in the dim corridor. He shoved it at Danny. "Be sure to get all the cobwebs on the ceiling and any bones should be stacked up here by the door. Have an evil time." With a final smirk, he was gone.

"Stop moaning in my ear, you're going to give me a headache," Danny muttered at Puke. He pried the monkey off his shoulders.

Puke sniffed woefully. "Poor, pitiful Puke will perish in dark places."

"You and me both, yeah? I'll sweep, you scrub the stones behind me." *Better get it over with.* With the broom in one hand and the lantern in the other, he stepped into the dark. While barely visible in the corridor, in the pitch-black, the lantern did light the passageway around him with a dull glow, revealing a few inches of dusty stone. Cobwebs brushed against his face, making Danny shudder.

Danny swiped at them with the broom. The lantern in his left hand jiggled, throwing eerie shadows first one way and then another. Grime and dust layered the edges of the corridor and something gleamed white farther down the passage, possibly bones. Puke moaned behind him. Danny tried to sweep the floor, but it proved much too clumsy and ineffective only holding the broom with one hand. When he tried to hold onto both the broom and the lantern at the same time, the flame flickered so badly with the movement that he feared it would go out. Danny sighed and set it on the ground, but that not only put it in danger of getting knocked over or blown out, it didn't let it shed nearly enough light to be so low.

"New plan, Puke." Danny turned to the minion. "You'll hold the lantern up while I sweep, but bring the bucket along and we'll scrub the floor on our way back up." Danny had his reservations giving their only light source to Puke, but obviously something had to be done and it just felt too despicable for him to make Puke clean while he watched.

Danny took better aim at the shadowy cobwebs, although a good part of it was guesswork since Puke was too short for the lantern to illuminate the ceiling. Then he started in on the floor with reckless abandon. Now and then strange items clinked and clattered, but Danny didn't try to see what they were. He'd worry about bones or chains or whatever when they got to the end.

As they moved away from the entrance, the blackness closed in on them like a heavy curtain. It had a suffocating feeling to it, as if the whole weight of the school squatted just above his head. Dust and grime blew up in a dark cloud that looked eerier in the flickering light. Instead of looking round around the edges like a usual cloud of dust, it seemed sharp, jagged, and moved almost like it was alive, unnerving Danny. Dust tickled his nose and he sneezed. Danny rested the ragged end of the broom a moment to wipe it on his sleeve. *Now wait just a minute!* Danny flipped the broom over to examine the end. No longer smooth, it was now jagged and shorter...much shorter.

"What the heck—Puke, give me the lantern a second." Danny grabbed it and bent to examine the dust as it settled. It looked strangely reminiscent of claws and snapping jaws around the edges. Trying to stay close, Danny poked it with the broom. The pile was swept forward a bit, but the broom came away with another chunk of straw missing from the end. *Broom-eating dust?* Danny stared a moment, unsure what to do... he'd run out of broom far before he finished the passageway! Maybe, like the moss, he just needed to be more aggressive.

Trying a war whoop for good measure, Danny slapped

the vicious pile with the broom. Dust flew everywhere, making both Danny and Puke cough and nearly putting out the light. Puke yelped. Ignoring his watering eyes, Danny swept hard, fast strokes across the floor, one, two, three, then pulled up the broom. *Drat!* The dust had eaten yet another hands-width off the end. Now half the bristles were gone.

Danny kicked at it and his boot came away with teeth marks. Danny's stomach tightened. *Watch out or you'll be losing some toes.* He tried gently easing the broom along the floor, just nudging the dust...which only let him see finally in slow motion the dust chomping down on it. Frustrated, Danny smacked broom against the wall.

"Arg! This isn't working. What are we going to do?"

"Humble Puke does not know," the monkey said, his eyes filling with tears. He shivered.

"Wait, wait, it's okay. I'll think of something," Danny said hastily. "Let's...just keep going. We've got half a broom still." Not the brightest of plans, but what else could he do?

Danny attacked the dust again, only his pile was growing and, with its collective size, it turned more aggressive. It rose, snapping at the broom greedily. Danny tried to beat it back and, to his dismay, it ate the rest of the bristles in one sickening *chomp*. Puke gasped and stumbled backwards. Encouraged, the dust pile leaped forward at them, eating down the broom handle in three swift bites. Desperate, Danny tossed the end at it and wrenched the bucket of soapy water from Puke, splashing its contents onto the hungry dust.

The dust cloud let out a high-pitched whine and started shrinking. Puke gripped Danny's leg, almost setting his robes on fire with the lantern, before correcting himself and holding it steady. The dust let out a final sizzle and collapsed down to a sticky puddle of goop. Although it made him nervous, Danny grabbed the scrub brush and gingerly poked it. The dust had solidified into a thick black goo that stuck to the bristles, but apparently was no longer "alive." Danny scrubbed at the edges, but it stuck to the floor like tar.

"Don't suppose you know that soapy water-making trick the goblin did?" he asked Puke.

Puke whimpered, his eyes wide. "P-puke hears something!"

Something clattered in the distance and a draft blew through the corridor, prickling the back of Danny's neck. Turning away from him, Danny stared into the unyielding blackness, listening with all his might. Distant footsteps echoed up the passageway, then went silent. Long seconds passed—still nothing.

"Not the time to be imagining things," Danny muttered. If he gave into that, he'd spook himself far too fast. He had to keep his focus. He stood up. While he doubted it would work, he might as well see if he could figure out the spell. "Here, hand me that bucket—"

Something gripped Danny's shoulder—a hand. Puke screamed, dropping the lantern. It shattered, sending them into blackness. A sharp wind swept past Danny's face. There was a thumping noise in Puke's direction and his wailing was sharply cut off. The only noise was the lantern careening down the passage ahead of them, clank, clank, clank, and Danny's sharp intake of breath.

Momentarily terrified, Danny didn't yet dare struggle against his hidden assailant.

"Muahahahahaha!" Silver eyes flashed in the darkness with uncanny familiarity.

"Demigorth the Destroyer!" Danny yanked away from the hand holding him. "What'd you do to my SICM?" He tried to sound confident, but his voice wavered. His feet crunched on glass and he didn't quite dare to feel around in the darkness for Puke and risk cutting his hands. He'd never been to the school nurse and didn't want to start now. Who knew what they might do to him under the guise of "medicine?"

"Got you good, didn't I?" The voice sounded smug. "Heard you coming a mile away and couldn't resist. You first years are easy bait, just begging for a scare."

White light blinded Danny for a moment. He covered his eyes, squinting through his fingers at his attacker. It was indeed Demigorth, looking much too pleased with himself. The light came from his cupped hands, although whether it was pure magic or some sort of device, Danny couldn't tell, since it was too bright to look at. Annoyed at being gloated at, Danny turned in a circle, searching for Puke instead. The monkey lay unconscious against the wall behind him. Danny supposed that was Nyshlza's throwing spell, only hard enough to knock him out. It seemed pointlessly cruel to hurt Puke—but, of course, that's what villains were, wasn't it? Danny turned back to glare at Demigorth.

"So, bothering Mordryn, were you? I didn't know anyone else had detention today." Demigorth levitated the light so it rose high about them, letting Danny see the most of their surroundings yet. He gulped in a sharp breath at the light revealing an enormous spider shrouded in webs up on the ceiling just a few yards further down the passage.

"Oh, that? That's not all that big. Seen a few twice that size down here before, only not today." Demigorth looked entirely pleased at Danny's discomfort. "Today I've only run into two ghouls and a zombie. Supposedly there's a soul-sucking demon that escaped from hell hiding out here somewhere, but, despite this being my sixth detention poking around down here, I've yet to find it. I don't suppose Mordryn will be kind enough to give me the dungeons again this year." He sighed dramatically.

"Wait...you've had *six* detentions in this one passageway?"

"One?" Demigorth snorted. "There's a whole maze of them, Zexygreth, mirroring the one right above our heads. Or didn't you notice the passageways coming down?" He smirked at Danny's dismay.

Danny's heart pounded at the thought he might get lost down here with giant spiders, ghouls, and zombies. It made him twice as claustrophobic. *That stupid lantern hardly let me see anything.* Danny clenched his hands. *That goblin did this on purpose, hoping I'd get lost down here.*

"Quite something that you've worked your way to the dungeon maze this early in the year. Of course *I* was ahead of you by at least a month last year, but still, nice run on detentions."

"W-what?" Danny grimaced in disbelief at Demigorth, distracted from debating the wisdom of poking Puke awake with his foot.

Demigorth grinned. "I broke the school record for detentions in a single year last year at two hundred sixty-seven. Going at my current rate, I should break the record for a whole Dark Lord Academy career by the end of next year. But I admire a good, hard try—it shows spirit." He thwacked Danny on the shoulder, much too hard for it to be properly friendly. "Looks like Virly has a taste for us snide ones, huh? She's my advisor, too, although I'm her evilest student and don't you forget it."

"Yeah..." Danny rubbed his shoulder.

Demigorth winked. "Well, carry on, I'm off to search out that soul-sucker, may get lucky yet. Have fun finding the way out—they don't start looking for you until you've been gone for a few days." He headed down the passageway, the light following him. The spider scurried away down the passage to avoid it.

"Hey, wait!" Danny called, but the older boy didn't even turn, and within seconds he was left in the pitch black with nothing but some broken glass and the unconscious Puke.

Panic shook Danny as the blackness closed in. Deciding he didn't care about finishing the detention or not, he groped around in the dark for Puke. He was getting out of here now. Rather than listen to his screams, Danny didn't bother with waking him, but just lugged him up the passageway in the opposite direction, hoping against hope Demigorth had been lying about all those turns.

CHAPTER 16

Carly Bakes Some Evil Goods

Danny surfaced hours later in a completely different part of the castle in a corridor full of classrooms. Exhausted, filthy, and exceedingly depressed, he collapsed in relief on the floor. The worst of it wasn't even the dark, the getting lost, or the constant terror, but the horrible news that he could have hundreds of detentions and still not get expelled. Demigorth's gloating over it only made too clear the reality that his plan would not work. *All these detentions for nothing!* Danny ran his grimy hands through his hair.

"Great Master has saved us from the dark and danger," Puke said, throwing himself down by Danny's feet.

Other than the nasty bump on his head, Puke seemed fine. That was something, anyway. While Puke wasn't a very good SICM, he was better than none at all and someone to keep him company when no one else would. Danny grimaced at the realization he was getting to like his SICM's company. *Must be desperation—that and feeling sorry for him.* Puke still irritated him; he didn't need to *care* about him on top of it. At least it proved he wasn't transforming into a real villain. No self-respecting villain would actually feel sorry for his minions.

Danny focused on the problem at hand instead. Missing assignments and mouthing off to the teachers wasn't going to get him out of school. While he could still try to goad Alec into attacking, it seemed far too chancy a plan to put all his hope in it. It appeared he'd have to do something out of the realm of "acceptable evil" to get expelled. He'd have to discard his original plan of causing trouble in the kitchen tonight, as well; he'd need the time to plot something new. Danny considered another bath, but it seemed likely that Carly's detention would get him just as dirty, so there wasn't much of a point.

Somewhere distant in the castle, the bell rang for dinner. Danny decided to skip it instead of put up with questions from the others. He nudged Puke with his foot. "Come on, we better get going. We got our next detention to get to." The last one for a while, too, until he could come up with a fail-proof idea for getting expelled.

When they arrived in the kitchen, they found Carly sitting by the counter eating away at a big plate of food that made Danny's stomach rumble. It made him realize that maybe cutting both lunch and dinner to avoid being social wasn't the brightest of strategies. By this point he was quite hungry.

Carly looked up at him, surprised. "Zixy! What're you doing here early?"

"Er..." Danny didn't want to explain about the horse manure mess, nor the dungeon passageway fiasco.

Carly, however, didn't press him. "Pull up some stools, boy! I've been experimenting. Try some of this stuff out."

Danny supposed it could be no worse than her usual cooking and let her serve him up a heaping plate. He was careful to scoot Puke's stool down a bit, so if the monkey threw up, it would miss him. He'd had enough dirty clothes already.

"Mmm, this is good," he said through a mouthful.

"Lizard Pie." Carly winked at him.

Danny decided he didn't mind.

"Just wait until you try the Cockroach Custard...I did desserts, just like you suggested," Carly continued. "Brilliantly evil, Zixy-boy, that's what you are! I even made up some recipes of my own! Look!" She waved a box of what looked like perfectly normal chocolates. "Poisoned Chocolates, only I didn't quite have the right ingredients so I don't think they're deadly...gotta try them out. I suspect they're too weak and will only give you major indigestion. Here's a genuine Frogspawn Cake, decked with eyeballs. And these!" She grabbed another tray with lumpy objects. "Toffee-covered Scorpions! I bet they'll be a raging success next Halloween! Want to try one?"

"Erm, don't want to ruin my dinner," Danny said quickly, taking another bite of lizard pie. "Maybe I'll grab something later."

"Anything you like," Carly said, pinching his cheek between bites. "You know, I'm gonna miss you, you little brat. Be sure to come and visit often."

"Uh, yeah." Danny couldn't tell if she was inviting him to get the detention extended or not. Either way, he wasn't interested. He pushed back his plate and rolled up his sleeve. "What're we scrubbing for you this time?"

"I thought you could clean out the icebox and the pantry."

"Sounds…" Danny pictured himself sorting through rotting vegetables. "Delightful."

Carly frowned. "What?"

Danny grinned at her. "Don't worry, that was sarcasm. Come on, Puke! Let's get at it."

As Danny sorted through rotting tomatoes and maggoty rice, he tried to think of something evil he could do with all this bad food. *I could use rotten eggs on Vrlyxfrka's office.* But he suspected that all she'd do was make him clean it up, maybe give him another detention. Not worth it. *I need to do something truly terrible and different. Something that stands out— like goading a bunch of heroes to attack the school, only faster.*

The evening wore on and Carly being nice earlier didn't help all the rotten food he had to sort through now. By the time he was finished, he was covered in slime and smelled like the village dump back home. He sighed at his messy robes.

"Sorry, Puke, looks like you're getting more laundry duty."

He glanced over and noted Puke was also slime-covered.

"Insignificant Puke will slave away all night to have Great Master's clothes clean."

Danny shook his head. "Don't worry about it tonight. You can do it tomorrow."

Puke looked nervously back at Danny, his lip quivering.

Danny sighed. "Bathe and sleep first. That's an order."

"As Great Master wishes."

Danny dragged himself out of the pantry and into the kitchen proper.

"Don't forget to treat yourself!" Carly boomed from

behind a large cookbook she was reading, entitled *Great Gross Gourmet: How to Wow the Evilest of Friends with Your Cooking.*

Danny frowned at the disgusting desserts, wondering if he could get away with asking Puke what he might possibly eat. They all looked terrible except those poisoned chocolates, set to one side and obviously not part of her offer.

Then the idea struck him like a pile of rotten tomatoes stacked on the top shelf. He could poison Tulk! Carly said they'd give him major indigestion and the picture of Tulk barfing all over the place or perhaps stuck in the bathroom for hours had a nice, satisfying feeling of revenge to it.

Danny reached for the box, but then hesitated a moment as he had second thoughts. *But what if they're powerful enough to really make him seriously ill?* Then again, that *was* different and completely against the rules. Poisoning someone had to be bad enough to get him expelled! *They have a school nurse if he gets really ill and Carly said she didn't have enough ingredients. This could be my one big chance.*

Danny snatched up the box of chocolates before he could change his mind again. "Thanks!" he yelled. "See you tomorrow at breakfast." He hurried out before she could notice and guess his plan. A warm glow filled him, covering up his doubts. He finally had his ticket out of Dark Lord Academy. Not only that, it'd give him his final victory over Tulk at the same time.

On Monday morning, letting Puke sleep in, Danny stuffed the box of chocolates in with his books. He had worked out the perfect plan. He'd put them out in full view on his desk during study hall. Tulk wouldn't be able to resist stealing one and would eat it right in front of everyone and throw up. Or run to the bathroom. Or whatever sort of indigestion they were supposed to cause.

Danny couldn't help but feel a small sliver of guilt at poisoning someone else, but pushed it away. *Tulk's been awful to me since before I got here—he deserves it!* Besides, if he got too ill, the school nurse was bound to have an antidote.

Danny peeked over his shoulder to see Tulk headed his direction. He sauntered into the cafeteria, smiling and waving eagerly at Carly, hoping that Tulk would notice.

Carly chuckled evilly at him. "Hey, Zixy-boy! I saved the last piece of Lizard Pie for you." She handed it to him instead of the toasted bat wings that seemed to be today's main course for breakfast.

"Great!" Danny winked at her and caught a glimpse of Tulk's narrowed eyes out of his peripheral vision. He turned and smirked at Tulk. "Carly bakes truly wicked stuff...Too bad you're not friends with her."

"I wouldn't touch this glop if I could avoid it," Tulk sneered. But his eyes, drifting down to stare at the almost normal-looking lizard pie, gave him away. He was jealous!

Satisfied, Danny grinned ear to ear. Tulk would see the chocolate and know where the gift had come from. He could have hugged Carly for setting it up so well. He couldn't wait for Study Hall.

Only his first class was History. Professor Screkvox paced back and forth along the front of the classroom, punctuating his points with lightning. His black boots clicked on the stone floor. Despite that, it was hard to stay awake because he was using slides.

Click. Click. "Historically, the most powerful member of a hero party is the Master Wizard!" Lightning rolled from his hands, making the floor shudder. The projector whirred, displaying a tall figure in gray, with a long, white beard and glowing staff. "The Master Wizard is usually an elderly man with magical powers. He is the most dangerous of a hero party, but, paradoxically, the easiest to kill."

Crash! Lightning crackled, making spots of light dance across Danny's vision. Inured to it, Danny blinked several times and tried to keep his eyes open. He'd come a long way since his night on the roof—unless it was close enough to scorch, it wasn't worth worrying about. The projector showed a new image of the wizard fighting a demon.

"Initially, that is!" Screkvox's voice deepened and he laughed maniacally. "In 99% of cases, the Master Wizard returns from death in some form or other to trouble the hero." The projector showed a translucent wizard figure floating in the air, giving advice to a small group of heroes. "Next...the elf figure..."

Danny suppressed a sigh, not wanting Screkvox's temper to shift onto him. But, so close to getting expelled, History hardly mattered. He wasn't going to be around long enough to face the test.

The projector whirred and displayed a blond-haired, green-eyed elf, looking rather self-satisfied for the camera. Danny frowned, thinking back to the few elves who stopped by his father's forge. They were annoying, stuck-up customers who always complained about the price and that the end result was nowhere near as good as their own forges back home. He used to feel sort of awed by them, but now he'd ask them why they didn't just go back to their home and stay there.

Screkvox paced right up to Danny's desk, making him jerk away from his thoughts and actually listen.

"The only worthwhile elf is a dead elf. It's useless trying to turn the classic elf, who has no emotion other than dedication to his pre-determined side of a conflict and his own self-serving ends which he claims are 'for the good of the world.'"

Class dragged onward. Finally, the bell rang and Danny jumped up, snatching his bag. It snagged on the corner of his desk and ripped, spilling his books out over the floor. Danny cursed.

"So stupid you can't even use a book bag, huh, Zitty?" taunted Tulk.

"Get lost," Danny said, kneeling on the floor, trying to scoop everything back together.

The rest of the class hurried past him and out the door, except Daisy. "I'll help you!" she cried, running over. Her foot hit the edge of the chocolate box, spinning it just out of reach at the moment Danny tried to grab it. He dived after it. His fingers almost clasped it when a dark gloved hand snatched it away.

"Now, what did I say about food in my classroom?"

Danny looked up into Screkvox's amused face. "But class is over!" he objected, and realized how lame it sounded.

"That doesn't concern me." Screkvox smiled and opened the box. "Chocolates, how charming!"

"Wait—"

Before Danny could even scramble to his knees or explain, Screkvox popped one in his mouth.

"Scrumptious!" He popped two more into his mouth.

"Professor, those—"

Mid-chew, Screkvox made a strange sound, half-gurgle, half-choke. His eyes bugged out and then he fell forward. Danny rolled away as he landed with a thump on the floor.

"W-what happened?" stuttered Daisy.

Screkvox didn't move. Gingerly, Danny poked him. "Uh, Professor?"

"If he's dead, you're really gonna get it," Tulk said, but the waver in his voice gave away his false attempt at sounding in control.

"He's just faking!" Danny said. His heart raced. This couldn't be happening. Danny grimaced and rolled

Screkvox over. The professor's still-wide eyes stared blankly at the ceiling.

Daisy put a hand on his neck, feeling for a pulse. "Nope, he's dead!"

Between a Rock and a Hard Place

Tulk backed away from them, his own eyes wide. "I had nothing to do with this!" He bolted from the room.

"What're we going to do?" Daisy whispered. "Zixy, you killed a teacher!"

Danny's heartbeat raced. "Carly said she didn't think those chocolates were strong enough to kill anyone. Just cause major indigestion." His mind whirled. *What am I going to do?* Yes, he'd get expelled, but what else might they do if they found out he'd murdered someone? The Executions Department weighed heavily on his mind.

"Maybe if we just leave him, we could pretend we don't know how it happened..." Daisy bit her lip and glanced around the empty room.

"Wait, no, let's hide him." Danny knew they had to act fast, before older students arrived for the next class. "Then, if they find the body later, they won't know when it happened!" He stood up, pushed the door shut, and glanced around the classroom. "Let's stick him in the closet and maybe they won't find him for several days."

Daisy wrinkled her nose. "I dunno, maybe we should tell someone."

"No!" Danny held up his hands. "Do you know what they could do to me? Do you *want* to see me get executed? Daisy, you gotta help me—it's…it's the evil thing to do!"

She thought for a moment. "Yeah, I guess you're right, it would be a bit goody-two-shoes to tell everyone he's dead."

"Exactly!" Danny searched for convincing excuses. "The most evil thing to do is to let the killer go unknown. Let them wonder and worry about what happened to Screkvox until his body stinks so bad that someone finds it! That's what the teachers would want you to do, Daze, the most evilest thing possible. Help me out, okay?" He held out his hand.

Daisy's frown cleared. She flashed her teeth at him and grabbed his hand, pumping it up and down. "Deal!"

Danny let his breath out in relief. "Great! I'll get his head and you grab his feet and let's get him into the closet."

Daisy grabbed Screkvox's feet. "Oof, he's heavy."

"Don't drop him now! We gotta hurry or we'll be late for Strategy class!"

Screkvox was heavy. It took all of Danny's strength, plus Daisy's help, to drag him over to the closet. For a moment, Danny was afraid it was locked, but the door was only a bit warped and with an extra tug it opened. They stuffed Screkvox inside. Danny turned the lock and slammed the door. Thankfully, no other students had shown up—it seemed Screkvox didn't have a class right after theirs.

"Let's get out of here!"

They pelted down the hall and up the stairs, arriving at Strategy class out of breath, just as the bell chimed. It turned out that today Mordryn had enchanted small figures of wood for them to practice battle strategies with. Danny was relieved to get Aun, not Tulk, as his partner, but he couldn't concentrate. Screkvox's dead face, staring blankly up at the ceiling, kept flashing into his mind.

"I win again. Mauhahahahaha!" Aun laughed as his figures trashed Danny's. "Say, Zix, what's the matter with you? I know you can do better than that."

Yeah, now you give me compliments, Danny thought ruefully. He shrugged. "I think Carly gave me something not so great to eat this morning." *If they find out, will they torture me before killing me?* He wiped his sweaty hands on his robes. He kept jumping every time someone scraped a chair or walked by him, but Strategy class passed without interruption.

Danny stuck close to Aun heading down to lunch and noticed out of the corner of his eye that Daisy seemed to be glued to Shai. Aun was raving about his brilliance as a strategist and Danny just kept mumbling "uh huh" and "yeah" whenever there was a pause. He strained his ears for news, but heard nothing about missing teachers or murders.

"Zixy! Where's your little minion? Hope you didn't feed him any of my chocolates!"

Startled, Danny looked up in horror to see Carly peering at him.

"No, no, of course not!" He had been so preoccupied he hadn't given Puke a thought. "I, erm, was actually going to try them out for you on Tulkyzefril, but I...haven't got around to it yet."

He heard a choked noise and turned to see Tulk was a couple of places behind him in line. Their eyes met and Tulk's narrowed, glowering at him. Guilt clogged Danny's throat. He hadn't actually meant to kill anyone, not even Tulk, but an apology seemed inappropriate. He turned back to Carly and grabbed his plate. "But on second thought, I m-might try them on a minion." He dashed away before he could say anything more stupid, his face burning. Had Carly guessed?

He dropped into a chair and thumped his head into his hands several times whispering, "No, no, no."

"What's up with you today?" Aun asked, giving him a funny look.

Danny took a deep breath, saying the first thing that came to mind. "I think Tulk is working up something big to get back at me."

Aun shrugged, digging into his lunch. "Of course he is, that's what villains do, right? You've done fine getting him back, you shouldn't worry so."

"That's easy for you to say," Danny muttered under his breath. "You haven't killed anyone."

Danny didn't end up eating much; his stomach felt full of lead. Instead, he shuffled off to Study Hall and stared dully at his books as the old witch paced up and down the aisles, snapping at people. The words on the book in front of him wouldn't form into coherent sentences and his nerves were frayed like the ends of his sleeves as he kept picking at them until they unraveled. Besides, Tulk sat just desks away, bent over his books, carefully not looking at him. He didn't think Danny had meant to really kill him, did he?

The door swung open and Danny's head shot up. In the doorway stood both Vrlyxfrka and Headmaster Atriz. The headmaster stepped forward into the room; his black robes swished in the absolute silence that had settled over Study Hall.

"Glezvrkxry, may we have a moment with your class?" His commanding tone sent a shiver down Danny's back. He slumped down in his chair, hoping against hope he could remain inconspicuous.

Glezvrkxry bowed and cackled. "Of course, Headmaster Atriz."

"We seem to have misplaced a teacher." Atriz folded his hands, letting his robes cover them. His voice was quiet, but somehow emanated threat. "He was last seen, it appears, teaching his first year class. Most of you are first years. Care to give us a hint as to his whereabouts?"

Atriz's eyes wandered over each of them in turn. Danny swallowed hard, anticipating the moment the headmaster would look at him. Could he keep from giving anything away? A chair scraped to his left and Tulk jumped to his feet, pointing straight at Danny.

"It was Zixygrith! He *killed* him!"

The class gasped and Glezvrkxry's face took on an expression of evil delight. Vrlyxfrka wore one of polite disbelief. Only Headmaster Atriz seemed unmoved. He turned his expressionless face and piercing eyes on Danny.

"Is this true, young man?"

His gaze bored right through Danny. Cold sweat trickled down the back of his neck, but he sat up and met the gaze. There was no help for it now; he had to say something.

"It was an accident." The words popped out of his mouth and he flushed—feeling stupid and terrified at the same time.

"I see. Well, then, young Zxygrth, come with us for a moment."

Danny's stomach churned and he stood up, glaring at Tulk, who now looked pleased with himself. *That'll teach me to feel sorry for him—jerk!*

"You watch it or I'll have Carly stick one of those chocolates in your breakfast," he hissed in a whisper as he passed him. The smirk on Tulk's face faded.

Danny shuffled to the front of the room and Vrlyxfrka put her hand on his shoulder, steering him out the door. "You've been busy, haven't you?" she muttered in a reproving tone. "I thought I told you to keep your mischief within the bounds of acceptable."

Danny grimaced and wanted to run the other direction, but instead his legs kept moving forward with Vrlyxfrka. They headed up a set of stairs and into a corridor with embroidered tapestries depicting various grotesque battles, where demon-like creatures seemed to be torturing humans. A goblin opened a large studded door on one side —the headmaster's office.

To Danny's surprise, it was light and airy, with a polished wooden floor and a red and gold rug. There were several stiff fabric-covered chairs arranged in a semi-circle around a desk. Three sides of the room were mostly windows, looking out on the school. At the far end, smoke poured out of a half-shut closet door. It rumbled ominously, making Danny want to back away. At least a cracked window kept the office air from smelling too smoky. Vrlyxfrka pushed him into a chair and sat next to him, frowning. Atriz, his expression still stony, shut the closet door and sat behind the desk.

"So, tell us, young Zxygrth, how exactly did this 'accident' happen and who were your accomplices?"

Danny took a deep breath. He wouldn't draw Daisy into it—she hadn't done anything, but what about Carly? Would they do anything to her? While she still frightened him half to death, he didn't wish to see her executed. Atriz's piercing stare made him squirm as he tried to think up a good story.

"And please, don't bother me with anything less than the truth." Atriz leaned forward. "I'll know if you're lying, young man. So don't bother."

If they were going to kill him, there wasn't a way out of it, Danny decided. He might as well go down in style. And there was only one person he was willing to implicate as an accomplice. "I, uh, had detention in the kitchen—it was Tulk's fault."

Vrlyxfrka scowled. "I hardly see what that has to do with anything," she snapped.

Atriz held up a hand. "Let him continue."

The whole story blurted out—how Tulk had tripped him, his desire to get back at him, suggesting desserts to Carly to shut her up about gross dinners, stealing the chocolates, Screkvox stealing them away from him—he left out his desire to get expelled, though. He was afraid if he told them his deepest desire, they'd be sure to kill him. Instead, if he painted a picture of incompetence, maybe they'd just expel him. He did have the detentions to back it up.

Danny fell silent after describing pulling Screkvox into the closet. He'd made it sound like Tulk might have helped him, but left it unclear. He doubted Atriz was fooled, but they'd have to torture him to get Daisy's name out of him.

The headmaster didn't press him for an accomplice. He only nodded his head and then snapped his fingers. Smoke swirled around in front of an open chair and Danny's mouth dropped open when he noticed Nyshlza standing there.

"You called, headmaster?"

The left corner of Atriz's mouth twitched upward. "We have need of your help, to, shall we say, remedy a little problem in the History Department." He snapped his fingers and everything dissolved into smoke. When it cleared, Danny coughing as usual, all four of them were in the History classroom.

Vrlyxfrka let go of Danny, walked over to the closet, and tapped it with her wand. The door opened and Screkvox's dead body fell out. Nyshlza started laughing, her velvety voice cascading in a musical, but sinister way. Neither Atriz or Vrlyxfrka looked amused.

"Well, well," Nyshlza said, getting her laughter under control. "This is certainly a new one. And here I thought it was quite creative last year when Demigorth petrified Mystfolyn in stone. You certainly know how to pick them, Virly, although you've really outdone yourself this time." She put a hand on Danny's shoulder and he shuddered. "Zix, I could be really evil and make you help me, but that might put you off dark magic for another year or two and I don't think you can afford what that will do to your grades."

She stepped forward and toed Screkvox's body over onto its back. Suddenly the room seemed to grow darker and fold in on them. The color drained from Danny's face as he realized what she was about to do. He tried to take a step backwards, wanting to be anywhere else, but Vrlyxfrka held him firmly by his shoulders.

Graceful as always, Nyshlza crouched by Screkvox's head, her eyes just visible under the darkness of her hood, solid white again. She touched her slender hand to his bald forehead and started murmuring. The darkness folded in on Danny, dark magic pressing all around him, pushing the air out of his chest. He felt like throwing up, only his body didn't cooperate. He wanted to shut his eyes, but he couldn't.

The magic swirled into Screkvox's body and his eyes shut. The room expanded again, the darkness receding, and Danny gasped in big breaths.

Screkvox opened his eyes, lifted a gloved hand to rub them, and then leapt to his feet, almost knocking Nyshlza over. His eyes darted around the room, then fixed on Danny, full of unveiled fury.

"You!" He took a step forward and stumbled.

Nyshlza put a hand on his arm, steadying him. "Slowly now, Screkvox, you've been dead for several hours and that takes it out of a person."

Screkvox's glare of hatred hit Danny like a furnace blast. "You'll pay for this, *boy*!"

CHAPTER 18

Evil Consequences

Screkvox's glare could have boiled lead, just as Mystfolyn had said a hateful gaze ought to. Danny cringed. This wasn't going to be good.

"Now, then, Screkvox," chuckled Nyshlza. "You have to admit he was original. And you do so like to steal food from the students."

Screkvox didn't look ready to admit anything. However, Atriz stepped between them, holding up a gloved hand. Then he turned to face Danny.

"I must admit, young Zxygrth, I'm impressed. I've not encountered a style quite like yours—so carefully planned."

Huh? Danny stared at the headmaster, unsure what he meant.

"It seems from day one you've been putting things together—Professor Screkvox's little habit of eating everything he comes across, Carly's love of poisonous food —making it all look like an accident, even down to blaming another student for most of it." Atriz's mouth curled up in an evil smile.

Danny opened his mouth to protest that it all really was an accident, but realized there was nothing he could do to make them believe him.

Atriz's eyes glittered with something like malice. "Brilliantly evil—just don't let it go to your little evil genius head. Understand?"

Danny's mouth stayed open. "You're not going to punish me?"

Atriz chuckled evilly. "I'm sure you'll be punished enough having to complete your history course." He winked. "If you keep on this way, I'm sure you'll win the Evil Student of the Year award." Atriz turned away and spoke to Vrlyxfrka. "You may give him a merit award for now."

Fear coursed through Danny, unsticking his throat. "Wait! I killed a teacher and you're not going to expel me or anything?"

Atriz turned back and raised an eyebrow. "And what would be the point of getting rid of one of our most promising students?"

Danny had no response. Atriz waved his hand and disappeared in a cloud of smoke.

"Come with me, you have some chocolates to return," Vrlyxfrka said, her lips a tight line. Still, Danny could tell she was pleased. She pulled him out the door by the collar. While he was relieved to get away from Screkvox, his head was still spinning with the horror of the realization that not only had killing a teacher *not* gotten him kicked out of villain school, it had earned him an award.

Vrlyxfrka dragged him down to the cafeteria. "Oh, Carly!" she called, looking as pleased as a cat with a mouse. "My student has something for you."

Carly sauntered out of the kitchen, flexing her muscles. "Oh?"

Danny pulled the remaining chocolates out of his bag and offered them to her, rather shamefacedly.

Carly's eyes sparkled with evil delight. "Who'd you use them on, Zixy-boy?"

Danny looked at his feet. "Professor Screkvox."

Carly chortled. "That idiot is always stuffing his face. But I never thought you'd have that much nerve, Zixy-boy. Tell me, did they work?"

"Most definitely," Vrlyxfrka said in dry amusement. "Nyshlza had to go fetch him."

"Oh, ho, ho!" Carly looked thoroughly pleased. "So I was right! I did put enough in." She grinned at Danny as he looked up. "I'll keep the rest of these in a safe place—for future use."

Don't worry, I'm not even going to try to find them.

"Oh, before I forget!" Vrlyxfrka reached into her robes and pulled out a small medal on a black ribbon. "Your merit award. May I suggest, though, Zixygrith, that you concentrate on your studies now and don't let all the excitement go to your head."

"Thanks," muttered Danny, slipping it on.

"Well, well, off you go then!" Vrlyxfrka dismissed him.

Danny slunk off, hoping to find somewhere quiet to mope about the failure of his expulsion plans. No such luck. Aun and Shai spotted him and ran over, Daisy trailing them, looking rather grim.

"Hey, Zixy! Is it true? Did you really kill Professor Screkvox?" Aun practically bounced with excitement, his eyes still glowing red.

"Yeah," Danny muttered.

"What're they gonna do?" Shai looked much too eager to be comforting.

Danny squirmed. "They already did it. Nyshlza used necromancy to raise him from the dead."

Daisy let her breath out in a whoosh of relief. Danny wished they had a moment alone to tell her she wasn't going to get in trouble.

"Hey, Zitty!" Tulk had spotted him. "Why aren't you dead yet?"

Faking an enthusiasm he didn't have, Danny stepped forward, grinning. It had suddenly occurred to him that there was one small benefit of his plan going so wrong. He could show Tulk for tattling on him. He tried sneering, although he suspected from the amused look on his other friends' faces he didn't quite have it down right. "Of course not dead, mush brain." He almost winced at the lame insult, but plowed on. "Unlike your pathetic attempts, I'm the real evil deal." He waved the merit award in Tulk's face. "I'm this year's top student! I'm the top student—period. It's not every year that a teacher gets killed. I'd like to see you do something that evil, wimp!"

Tulk's eyes widened at the award. He set his chin defiantly. "You can't be serious! There's no way they'd reward you for murdering somebody."

"Hey, Zix!" Danny whirled to see Demigorth and his friends coming towards them. Demigorth's weird silver eyes flashed. "What's this I hear about you beating my record as the school's evilest first year?"

"Er." Danny didn't know if admitting it or denying it would be a better course.

Demigorth grinned. "I must admit, poisoned chocolate is pretty fantastic. You're one evil little bugger." Then he leaned in and his smile turned menacing. "Just don't be thinking you can outdo me and win the Villainous Student of the Year award, because that one's mine."

"Um, I'll keep that in mind." Danny winced. That hadn't been quite the best of responses.

"Mehehehehe," chuckled Demigorth. "You think you're hot stuff, Zixy, don't you?" He took another step forward. "Perhaps I'll take you down a notch…"

"Hey, Zix!"

They all turned to see Queileria waving at Danny. His heart fluttered and he waved back, although his mouth went dry and prevented him from saying hi.

She smiled at him. "Good going! I heard all about it and you were brilliant! I never did like Screkvox's attitude about horses." She winked. "Well, see you tomorrow at practice." She started walking away, Danny staring after her open-mouthed. She turned and blew a kiss at him, making him instantly go red in the face. Then she continued on her way. Both Demigorth and Aun looked green with envy, Tulk shocked. Shai scowled.

"Who's your new friend?" Daisy asked, grinning at Danny. "You didn't tell me you have a girlfriend."

"She's not his girlfriend!" Demigorth and Aun said in unison, turning angry red eyes at him.

"Well, I gotta go get my books," Danny said hastily. "I left them in Study Hall."

Danny hurried down the hall, wanting to escape before things turned ugly. The positive attention did make him feel good on one hand, but on the other, it was all because he'd *killed* someone. One look down the classroom hall, crammed with students, and Danny decided his books could wait. He started off toward his room, cries of "Hey, isn't that the kid who killed Screkvox?" or "Look, it's that Zixygrith kid!" ringing in his ears. *This is so mixed up.* Was he starting to like being evil? Danny tried to focus on his guilty feelings over Screkvox and Tulk, but the fact that neither of them were particularly pleasant people didn't help much.

"Great Master!" Puke's squeaky voice called out the second he walked into his room. "Look at what Puke has got for Great Master!" Puke held up his books.

"Oh, thanks!" Danny sighed in relief and sunk onto his bed. "That's terrific, Puke."

The creature beamed at him, looking happier than Danny had seen him yet. "What should Puke do now for Great Master?"

Danny glanced around, seeing his laundry was done and folded, even the socks. He'd never had anyone fold his socks before. His mind, however, was blank. "I dunno. I don't think there's anything you can do, unless you can think of a good plan to help me get expelled."

"Great Master wishes to be expelled?" Puke's eyes almost popped out of his head.

Danny shrugged. With his latest plan ruined, he might as well enlist Puke's help—not that he expected much. "I don't want to be evil. I mean, do you?"

Puke's eyes looked like saucers. "Puke must become evil. He has no choice."

"Yes, you do! Everyone has a choice." Danny sighed. If he didn't do something soon, though, it might be too late and he'd end up evil despite himself. "If I can just get kicked out of here...don't you want to get out of here, Puke?"

Puke's eyes started to fill with tears. "Puke does," he whispered. "But please, Great Master, don't tell anyone or they will beat Puke."

"Yeah, well, don't tell them about me either or they won't expel me, they'll do something horrid to me instead. If you think of a way to get out of here, let me know, but otherwise, we didn't have this conversation." Danny grimaced. He was sounding more ridiculous by the minute. He had to get out of here before it made him bonkers. No, he couldn't count on Puke; he had to find a way out of here on his own.

Danny rummaged through his papers for a blank sheet. When in doubt, he at least had Alec. "Here, wait a sec and I'll have a letter for you to mail for me." Danny channeled all his frustrations into inciting Alec.

Dear Alec the Not-so-brave,

Your threats are empty words. The truth of the matter is you are too much a coward to return to face me again. I laugh maniacally at your pathetic skills and my classmates make fun of you and your friends at lunch.

Evilly yours,

Zxygrth, Master of Darkness

Danny stared at the words as they dried. Was it too much? Would the teachers guess what he was doing? *No, they just rewarded me for* killing *someone. They'd give me another stupid badge if they could read this.* Danny folded up the letter, crammed it in an envelope, and handed it to Puke. He'd done what he could, now all he had left was to wrack his brains for a good deed that might be good enough to get him expelled in case Alec was actually a coward after all.

CHAPTER 19

The Trouble With Goodness

A knock on his door interrupted Danny while he dressed. "Who's there?" he yelled. If it was Demigorth, there was no way he was opening the door.

"Me!" shouted Daisy.

Danny sighed, buttoned on his cape, and opened the door.

Daisy grinned at him. "Come to breakfast, Zixy, please. We gotta talk."

"I'm not hungry."

Daisy ignored the comment and grabbed him by the arm. "You haven't heard yet, Zix, but it's going to be awesome. This visiting villain is holding a special Evil

Make-up Presentation! It's going to be so exciting. You're not busy right after lunch, are you?"

"Um…"

"Great. You're coming with me then!"

Danny opened his mouth to say he wasn't doing anything of the kind when it struck him that it would be the nice thing to do. If he crushed her hopes, he'd be acting like a villain, thus tying himself more to the school. If he started being nice to everyone, perhaps it would be hero-like enough to get him kicked out. While not much on its own, it could at least be his first act towards switching his behavior and might help him think of something even more good to do later.

"Okay," he said, smiling at her. "I'll go."

To Danny's disappointment, his celebrity status hadn't abated. Older students continued to come up to him at breakfast, congratulating him on letting old Screk-bag get it. Aun gave him jealous, dark looks and Tulk scowled, although Danny managed to stay out of his way. He tried to remind himself each time he was complimented that being a murderer wasn't a good thing to be known for.

Mystfolyn, in Style class, went on a tirade about how evil deeds were only half-evil if not done with appropriate flair. He scowled at Danny the entire time, making veiled references to Danny's recent deeds. Tulk's expression morphed into a smirk.

"Flair. That is what a Dark Lord or Lady needs, the proper ambiance of atmosphere, an environment of evil, a vivacious villainy!" Mystfolyn tweaked the ends of his mustache. "Not necessary, you say, inconsequential? It is the fine art of style that separates the sophisticated villain from the ordinary thug."

The look he gave Danny made it clear who the

"ordinary thug" was in his opinion. *Are all my classes going to be like this?* The guilt was bad enough without the rest of this.

Fortunately, Mystfolyn then launched into a lecture on using animal characteristics, like horns and tails, to add to one's personal uncharm. He even displayed his own cloven hoof to much oohing and awing from the class. Danny breathed a quiet sigh of relief.

After class in the hall, Aun did a rather irreverent Mystfolyn impression and, although Danny was distracted, he made sure to laugh, hoping this might be construed as a nice action, until he realized he was merely helping insult someone, which was downright villainous. It brought home the fact that he still wasn't sure what was properly good and what was properly evil. If he couldn't figure out something that basic, how was he going to get expelled?

Depressed, Danny wondered if he dared skip Dark Magic, but before he could think of a good excuse to ditch the others, he found they had arrived. Besides, ditching class wasn't a good deed and much more likely to result in a detention with Nyshlza, which was the last thing he needed.

He managed to make it through another session of throwing people without dipping into the dark magic. He also avoided Nyshlza's eyes. With a deep sigh of relief, he let Daisy pull him out of the room the moment class was over to head to lunch.

"I can't wait for painting this afternoon," she said, linking her arm with his. "We're doing monsters from the far reaches of Elyott, *photographs from life*, you know. They're quite gruesome."

"That sounds like fun." Danny tried to look as friendly and kind as possible.

Daisy, skipping along, didn't seem to notice the extra

niceness in his voice. Perhaps he just needed some practice. They had reached the cafeteria line and Danny was careful not to push or shove anyone. When he reached the front, he beamed at Carly.

"Thank you for cooking up such a delicious looking meal," he said, grinning ear to ear.

Carly chuckled as she plopped her latest creation onto his tray. "Now, none of your sarcasm, Zixy-boy. Just because you're a school-wide success, doesn't mean I'll put up with any of your sass."

"But—"

Daisy pulled him away before he got the chance to explain he was serious. "Hey, Shai!" she squealed. "Zixy is going with us!"

Danny could have groaned out loud and it took all his self-control not to roll his eyes. Aun did it for him. "I wouldn't be caught dead learning about make-up," he sneered, doing it passably well.

"Nice sneer," Danny said.

Aun glared at him. "Whatever. Don't keep showing off."

"What'd you mean?" Danny felt a bit hurt by his reaction.

"Don't pretend you don't notice them all," Aun said, glaring, and gesturing to a table of second year girls.

Danny glanced over and saw them all blushing and waving at him.

"Ahh…" He waved back, his face heating up.

"Disgusting," Aun said. "It's just disgusting! Why didn't you tell me you were going to knock Sreckvox off? I would have helped…" He stirred his meal around with his fork. "But, no, you gotta show off all by yourself."

"It was an accident."

"Sure." Aun turned away with a shrug.

Danny winced. If the teachers didn't believe the truth, then why would Aun? "Hey, I promise if I come up with something else really evil, I'll include you next time."

Aun looked up again. "You serious? You're not lying to me?"

"No, I swear. Next evil deed, you're in on it." *But I'm done with villainy, so that's never going to happen. Still, it'll make him feel better and that's good, right?*

Aun brightened and held out a hand. "Shake on it."

Danny grinned. "Not on your life! Who knows what you've got up your sleeves?"

Aun grinned sheepishly. "How'd you guess?"

"You're a Dark Lord, aren't you?"

"Hey, Zixy! Hurry up. It starts in ten minutes." Daisy stood next to him, shifting from one foot to the other.

"See you around," Danny said to Aun and let Daisy drag him off to the Evil Make-up Presentation, hoping he wasn't making a huge mistake.

Daisy and Shai hurried him into a classroom filled with girls. They giggled and twittered like a flock of birds around a bird feeder. Danny flushed, realizing he was the only boy present. Daisy and Shai dragged him over to some empty chairs and Danny felt the weight of the gaze of the girls on him. The girl next to him had red streaks in her black hair and big silver chains hanging from her black dress. She grinned, baring a pair of bright white fangs.

"Say, you're that Zixy kid who killed Screkvox, aren't you?"

The whole room dissolved into giggles.

"He certainly is," Daisy said proudly. "I helped him hide the body."

Fang-girl leered at him, batting her eyelashes. "Need some help killing more teachers?"

"Um." Danny felt his face heat up hotter than Carly's Chili Cockroach Surprise. He was spared finding an answer when a woman with a small suitcase walked into the room. Her face was pasty white and her eyes rimmed in blue and black make-up so heavy Danny thought she looked like she had a couple of black eyes. Her lips were shiny magenta, as were her long fingernails. Danny grimaced, unsure why anyone would think caking themselves in make-up was attractive.

"Welcome, welcome," she gushed. Her eyes strayed over the eager girls and lingered on Danny. "I'm Mesmorelda from Deadly Death Products, Inc. and I'm excited to teach you about all our wonderful products."

She set her little case on the desk at the front of the room. "Deadly Death Products are only available through small home business networks and our products are truly unique and of high quality. Make-up can make any villainess —" she glanced at Danny again, "—or villain stand out. It can increase your confidence and say, 'I'm someone to be reckoned with.' Our unique products also have many practical applications."

Danny suppressed a sigh. He wished he had thought of a good excuse to slip out before she had started the lecture. Wasn't simply walking with Daisy and Shai somewhat of a good deed? Yet his two classmates were glued to every word Mesmorelda was saying and hadn't seemed to notice how good and patient Danny was today. Danny forced himself to attend to Mesmorelda. Maybe the mere fact of a boy sitting there listening to this girl stuff would alert her to his goodness and she would bring it to the attention of the regular teachers.

"One of our favorite lines is the 'Hag by Day, Enchantress by Night.' These villainous aids will make you look ugly and menacing by sunlight and deadly gorgeous by moonlight. They're perfect for preying on unwary travelers. If I could just have a volunteer who'd like to demonstrate for us…"

Most of the girls raised their hands, waving them wildly.

"You there." Mesmorelda picked the fanged girl next to Danny. "Just come up front, honey."

The girl, practically bouncing, dashed to the front of the room. Mesmorelda slathered make-up on half of the girl's face out of view of the group. When the girl turned around, everyone gasped. Half her face looked like it had aged about sixty years.

"Now watch!" Mesmorelda cried, flicking a wand. The room plunged into darkness. Then moonlight streamed from the end of it, lighting up the girl. Her made-up face looked young again, although Danny couldn't tell much different between it and her plain face half. However, all the girls started clapping and talking. It took several minutes for Mesmorelda to calm them down.

"Now I will show you one of our brand new products, our Enchantment Lipstick Line. These not only make your lips stand out, but can enchant those you kiss." Mesmorelda lined several tubes of lipsticks on the desk. "One will turn your average prince into a frog, rat, horse, or dog, and the other—" She held up another set of tubes. "—will restore him to his human form. Perhaps a demonstration?"

She handed the fanged girl a lipstick. "Here's Frog Red. I'm wearing the Restoring Magenta and then, you, young man, come forward." She gestured to Danny. "I assure you, I'll kiss you back to yourself in just a moment." She winked at Danny.

Danny felt his stomach flop. *There're limits to how good I'm willing to be and letting them kiss me into a frog and back is definitely over the line.* "No thanks, I'll, uh, just be going now."

He dashed out the door as all the girls started laughing. His face burned as Mesmorelda called, "But dearie, a little kiss never hurt anyone!"

Danny slipped off to his room and vented his feelings in another tirade to Alec. He hadn't realized being good could be so difficult. The trouble was, any good thing he managed to think of either was behaving and helping him learn villainy or opened him up to being victimized by the villains around him. Danny wasn't inclined to support either. He needed an action that would stand out.

He was still trying to think of ways to get expelled as he walked to Magical Weapons with Aun and Shai that afternoon. Osweggi paced excitedly across the courtyard when the bell rang. She cackled happily when they were all assembled.

"Today, we are going to view the school's magical weapon collection next to the headmaster's office. No touching anything, though, or I'll lock you down in the dungeons as punishment." She cackled, looking suspiciously hopeful, like she wanted someone to try it. "Follow me."

"Awesome," Aun said, grinning at Danny. "I can't wait to see this."

Although Danny hadn't been expecting to be interested in any of his classes at this point, he found he was almost as eager as Aun to see the magic weapon collection. Osweggi led the class into the main hall and up the staircase to a hallway. Danny swallowed nervously as they passed the headmaster's closed door, but no sounds came from within and he was relieved they didn't run into him. If he managed a successful good deed, another confrontation was unavoidable, but that didn't mean he had to look forward to it. To the left an open archway leading to the weapons gallery—the air within the arch buzzed with pale purple magical energy, preventing anyone from walking through it.

Osweggi pulled herself up to her full (but still short) height. She waved her hand and mumbled some words. Purple smoke filled the hallway, making Danny sneeze. When it cleared, he saw the class following Osweggi into the gallery and hurried after them.

"Come along, come along, and stick together," she cackled.

Huge windows on one wall made this easily one of the brightest rooms in the castle. Danny blinked to adjust his eyes. Rows of weapons hung on the walls or were displayed in glass cases or on tables fenced off with wooden railings.

"Remember, no touching!" Osweggi snapped. "Form a line—yes, you, move there. You, come here. Good, now, I'll give you the tour."

They were looking at a row of swords lying on a long marble table.

"These first five are ice swords. See how they are in colors of blue, silver, and white. They are of varying strengths and powers. This one here—" she tapped a big sword with an icy blue stone in the pommel, "—can draw up a blizzard with the right wielder. Most just shoot snow or ice out, or can freeze your opponent. Can anyone guess the powers of this next set?"

Danny looked down at a sword with an orange stone set on the pommel, next to another one with a gold colored crosspiece set with yellow stones. Aun waved his hand back and forth excitedly and Osweggi pointed at him.

"Are they fire swords?"

Osweggi chuckled. "Very good. This is the fire and lightning collection. You must be careful though, because if used wrong, they can fry the wielder."

Danny examined the swords carefully, trying to see if the

one that had singed off half his hair was somewhere among them, but it wasn't. Osweggi continued on the tour, showing them a display of hero swords next.

"This first group are beginning hero swords that help control the actions of the wielder." She frowned at them all. "While at times a person needs a sword that knows what it's doing, some of the these swords had so much magic forged into them, they've developed personalities of their own—sometimes dangerous personalities. Take Stradux here." She gestured at a sword encased in glass. The blade was one of the longest (except for the sword Osweggi carried) that Danny had ever seen. The crosspiece was black and smooth, curving into elegant curls on either side. The handle was wrapped in black leather and a red stone shone dully on the pommel. The blade glinted at them seductively in the torchlight and Danny felt an instant urge to free it from its glass prison.

"Why do we have hero swords here?" a girl asked, breaking Danny's attention from Stradux.

"Well, Dark Lord Academy has the largest known collection of magic swords. Whether for heroes or villains, we find them fascinating." Osweggi grinned. "Besides, it's good to know and study what technology might be used against you."

Danny turned to glance at Aun and Shai and saw they were both still mesmerized by Stradux.

"Even if it was once intended for heroes, magic affects weapons in strange ways. Stradux is an extremely dangerous sword," Osweggi warned. "It can take such control of its wielders that it can send them into uncontrollable battle rages." She shook her finger at all of them. "Stradux doesn't care if he controls a hero or a villain, which has made him too dangerous to use. Next to him you can see several other dangerous swords. Now, to the left are the axes. On the right are magical restraints."

Danny gazed first one way, then the other in fascination. Somewhere in the midst of it all, something stopped him cold.

"What's that?" he asked Osweggi, pointing to a familiar twisted iron collar sitting between several similar objects.

"Faerie collars," Osweggi said. "They stop faerie creatures from changing shape. Unlike humans, faeries are either all good or all evil, depending on their mood and form. They don't have room for both emotions. The collar keeps them frozen in their evil form."

I didn't know Pa knew anything about magical weapons, Danny thought. *Why didn't he tell me?* He found that bothered him as much as the initial shock that Pa might sell or give things to villains.

Trying to ignore his doubts about what else Pa might have kept from him, Danny focused on the rest of the tour and the many amazing weapons—thunder hammers, staffs with magic crystals on their ends, giant maces, crystal daggers, enchanted slingshots with enough power to kill a dragon, pulse rods (wand-shaped weapons that shot lightning out their ends), evaporator rings (the kind that could be twisted to make a beam shoot out and disintegrate enemies)—that he couldn't keep track of them all. His head was spinning as they walked back down the stairs.

"That double-headed ice axe was the coolest thing ever," Aun said, a look of longing on his face.

"I liked that Chinese-style death blade myself," Shai said.

Danny found himself daydreaming of using the various swords, imagining how they would feel in his hand, and eagerly looking forward to the time when Osweggi would let the students try them out. It wasn't until he got to his room that he remembered he wouldn't be here for that if he managed to do something good enough to get expelled.

I wonder if Dicky will get a magic sword when he becomes a hero. I wish I'd been the third son. The thought surprised him because he had thought the hero thing wasn't his type. But it would be nice to be something. Somehow, a blacksmith just didn't feel like enough anymore.

CHAPTER 20

An Agitated Screkvox

The dull light of a gray morning shone through Danny's window, bringing with it no brainstorms in goodness. Danny debated finding flowers to give Vrlyxfrka and Carly, but they'd probably take it sarcastically. Not to mention it was so small as to not make a dent on all his previous evil infractions. *I didn't used to think good and evil were so complicated —maybe I'm just out of practice.* Danny had a horrible moment of wondering if this meant he never had any goodness at all, considering how easily he had gotten mixed up here. It didn't bear much reflection.

"Puke, have you thought of anything yet?" he asked as he straightened his black robes.

"No, Great Master, no good thoughts."

Danny sighed. "Then let's eat breakfast."

Danny was hardly ecstatic about going to Screkvox's class, but he couldn't think of a good plan to get out of it either. Cutting class would only get him more detentions and deeper in evil. He picked at his breakfast.

"I'm sooooo excited," Daisy said across the table from him. "I've been worried about Professor Screkvox ever since you killed him and now I'll see if he's okay."

"He's just fine," mumbled Danny.

Screkvox was more than just fine; he was in rare form. From the second Danny walked into his classroom, he felt the heat of Screkvox's stare. The teacher's bald head shone in the torchlight and he walked back and forth across the front of the classroom, cracking his knuckles.

"What is the number one nemesis of Dark Lords and Ladies?" he snapped out, his gaze settling on Danny.

Danny stopped breathing until he passed on and Screkvox pointed to a girl with her hand up.

"Heroes?"

Screkvox chuckled. "Close. There is a particular sort of hero, the worst sort of hero, one who has no shame or sense of decency, who causes us the most grief. A person who should be our close friend and confidant, a person who, by rights, should not be our enemy and yet is. The child of the Dark Lord!"

He punctuated the remark with a bolt of lightning, making the floor at the front of the classroom sizzle.

"Traditionally, the son of the Dark Lord is his downfall. It is his destiny to become a hero and destroy the father he should cherish. What happened to the heroish idea of 'Honor your mother and father,' you ask? It doesn't apply to villains. If your parent is a villain, it is not only acceptable, but imperative in the hero mindset that you strike him down."

Screkvox paced down the center of the desks to the back of the room, then turned to walk back up to the front, his gaze still lingering on Danny.

"Never have children. Those whiny, annoying little brats have only one thing in common: the desire to destroy you. Even if you think there's no chance of ever having one, you may find out that you do when the brat shows up to kill you. History has proved this, which is why—" Screkvox whirled around, his cape swirling like a black windmill. "Dark Lord Academy accepts no direct relatives of previous villains in this school."

His beady eyes locked on Danny as he said this. Danny didn't know what revenge Screkvox was planning, but he was mighty uncomfortable.

"Now and then, a hero tries to sneak in here, lying about his background." Screvox narrowed his eyes at Danny. "He thinks he might learn some evil tricks to take his poor father down. But we always can ferret him out and take care of him swiftly."

Danny stifled a sigh and started planning his escape from the room as fast as possible. Screkvox waxed on in his tirade, still directing every word of his lecture at Danny until the bell cut him short. The students all jumped up and Danny tried to scurry from the room.

"Zaxigreth!" Screkvox's voice snapped the word out like an epithet.

Danny turned, his mouth dry.

"In my brief sojourn in the afterlife, I learned my *son* is attending this school under false pretenses." His eyes flashed red. "The brat won't stand a chance when he tries to take me down."

Danny wrinkled his brow, unsure what Screkvox was on about. "Well, if I see your kid anywhere, I'll let him know." He started to back away.

He stood up, looming over Danny. "So what's this I hear from Professor Osweggi about you ending up with my magic sword?"

Danny gulped. "An accident." He ducked out of the room and pelted down the hall after his friends. *It would have to be Screkvox's sword. Why, oh, why?* There was no doubt in his mind the teacher planned some sort of revenge. His hands were still shaking when he reached Strategy class. Feuding with Tulk was one thing—Screkvox was more than he could handle.

"Something had old Screk-face in a right tizzy," Aun said, grinning wickedly as Danny slid into his seat next to him. "You think it might have been you killing him?"

"Shut up," Danny muttered, before he remembered about trying to be nice. Too bad it had done nothing except nearly get him turned into a frog.

Aun's grin widened, but he said no more.

"Well now, ready for some action?" Mordryn beamed at them. His red and purple suit was trimmed with gold this time and he rubbed his hands together in eagerness. "Today, we will be trying out our strategies on each other." His eyes glinted in anticipation. "With your SICM, you will direct a group of my insubstantial minions." He gestured at a short, cloaked figure that stood at the front of the classroom. It held a spear and was dressed in a black cape, but had no face, only a foggy darkness where the head should be. "The insubstantial minions will attack each other at your orders and the orders of your SICM and the one with the most IMs left when I call 'time' is the winner." His gaze swept over them. "Play well, because this is your practice for mid-terms."

"Mid-terms," whispered Shai. "And I've hardly studied!"

Danny wondered if letting his opponent win would be

good enough of a deed to get him any closer to expulsion. The idea of running a battle made him queasy enough to wish he could go back to his original plan of flunking out of school. It would be easy to fail History; Screkvox was sure to give him a failing grade just out of spite. It shouldn't be too hard to fail Strategy and he was already failing Dark Magic. Mystfolyn didn't like him in Style. That just left Weapons and Study hall. Surely there was an easy way to fail those too.

The only downside was it would take all year and even then there were no guarantees. It sounded too much like his previous failures. He was going to have to stick this out and be some kind of hero instead. Exactly what he didn't need. Dicky with his slick comments and charm or Alec with his propensity to attack anything slightly villainous-looking were the hero types, not him.

"Down we go to the Dead Field." Mordryn waved his hand over them and everything dissolved into the usual nasty black smoke. By the time Danny stopped coughing, they were indeed in the practice field. Thankfully, there was no sign of the demon horses. He had enough to worry about without Wrath of Death playing jokes on him as well.

"Great Master!" Danny glanced over to see all the SICMs were waiting for them. Puke waved at him, then scurried over. He looked smaller and more pitiful than ever in the company of his fellow SICMs. Puke tripped over Tulk's SICM in his hurry, sprawled on the ground, and started bawling. Danny sighed and went over to pick him up. Tulk's gargoyle creature looked up at him with mournful red eyes as Danny tried to soothe the hysterical Puke.

"Get over here, Ugly," Tulk yelled. "You stupid lump of gray flesh!"

Danny turned to see that Tulk looked pasty and sick. His face was whitish-green and his eyes had a rather dull look, despite his attempt at nasty words. Ugly shuffled over and bent its head before him. Tulk kicked it, but the attempt seemed half-hearted.

"What're you staring at?" he snapped at Danny.

"What's wrong with you today?"

Tulk balled his fists and narrowed his eyes. "I'll show you who has something wrong with him."

That sounded more normal, so Danny shrugged and sidled away from him to go stand next to Aun and Brex.

"Everyone draw the name of your opponent," Mordryn said, sending his goblin around with a small basket full of slips of paper.

Danny snatched one out, ignoring his sense of impending dread. "Hey, I got you, Brex."

"Great," Brex tried to leer at him and lowered his voice. "Soon, you will be begging me for mercy..."

"Yeah, I suppose I will." It took all his composure not to roll his eyes.

Brex punched him in the arm. "You're supposed to have a cutting comeback, Zix, what's up?"

Danny shrugged. "You'll be cake compared to Screkvox."

Aun snorted. "That's not bad. Oh drat, I've got good old Tulky. Wish me luck."

"Break a leg," Brex said with a sneer. "Let's duke it out, Zix."

Danny found it was easier to fail at strategy than he had anticipated. Puke was afraid of his IMs and couldn't be prodded to go and give them orders. Brex's goblin had no such fear and his forces were slicing through Danny's IMs, despite him running back and forth across the field trying to give them orders himself. Loud shouting interrupted his imminent slaughter. Both he and Brex turned to see what the commotion was about.

Aun's minions had Tulk surrounded and were pushing him back towards the black waters of the lake. Ugly directed what was left of Tulk's IMs to try and rescue him, but they weren't cutting through Aun's forces fast enough. Tulk was out of retreating space. He looked both furious and terrified. Then, to Danny's surprise, Tulk started levitating and retreated in the air over the lake. Everyone gasped.

"Swim in after him!" shouted Aun, punching his fists in the air. "Get him!"

Tulk's concentration slipped and he fell into the black water with a splash.

"Help!" he shrieked as he flailed. "I can't swim."

"Now's as good a time as any to learn," Mordryn said coldly. Danny glanced at him. He seemed completely unconcerned.

Tulk shrieked again and Danny saw black tentacles rise out of the water and grab him.

Mordryn yawned.

He's just going to let him die, Danny realized with horror. *I ought to do something! If I save him, that would be a good deed and maybe…wait a minute, this is Tulk! I don't owe him anything. It serves him right.*

But it might get you expelled. Do it! As Danny struggled with indecision, Ugly launched into the air, spreading its little bat-like wings. Ugly's hideous features twisted in worry and it flew out over the lake. It latched its beak-like mouth onto the back of Tulk's shirt and started pulling him upward. The tentacles had a hold on Tulk's legs and the two were locked in a deadly tug of war. Mordryn started to laugh.

Danny snapped into action. It was now or never. He pushed through the IMs and skidded to a halt at the waterline. The darkness within surged into Danny as soon as he reached for it. He hurdled it across the lake into all three creatures.

Tulk and Ugly landed on the far shore. The kraken-like creature got pulled half out of the water. Its tentacles writhed and it slid back into the lake as Ugly dragged a stunned Tulk up the bank.

Everyone rushed over except Mordryn, who gave Danny an evil smile. "You did that just to spoil my fun, didn't you?" He narrowed his eyes at Danny. "I'm on to your little game, Zuxygruth, usurping my role like that. If I see you trying to steal my position of teacher again, I won't be kind about it." Then he stalked away after the rest of the class, leaving Danny speechless.

I was saving Tulk, not "usurping your role." But somehow the words stuck in his throat and he couldn't get them out. Suppressing a sigh, he walked around the lake to join the others.

"You tore my robes!" shrieked Tulk when Danny was close enough to hear what he was shouting. "You dumb idiotic creature!" He was kicking Ugly, which was hunched over and hiding its nose from his feet.

"Dunno what's up with him," Shai said as Danny came up next to her. "All it did was save him."

Aun shook his head. "Don't you remember from our homework? Frthkrixda's first principle of SICMs: No matter what goes wrong, it's your minion's fault."

Shai's cheeks reddened. "It just seems…"

"Like kicking himself in the head, because it just saved his butt," put in Brex. "Hey, what'd you throw them out of the lake for, Zix? It was just getting entertaining."

"What'd it look like I did it for?" Danny snapped, still annoyed with how Mordryn perverted his good deed.

Brex shrugged. "I suppose you were depriving the kraken of its snack, but still, it would have been kind of fun to let it at least drag him under first."

Danny sighed. *Goodness is just lost on some people.* How was he going to get expelled when everyone seemed to interpret his good acts as bad ones?

Tulk missed with his next kick and hit a rock with his foot. He yelped in pain and hopped a step. Everyone broke out laughing. Tulk's face turned bright red and tears danced in his eyes. "I hate you! I hate *all* of you!" Then he turned and dashed away into the woods.

Mordryn chuckled, then turned back to the class. "Enough wasting time—back to practice, everyone."

Danny stared after Tulk. He should be happy that the bully had finally gotten his just desserts, but instead he felt hollow. *A really good deed would be to go comfort him,* he thought.

Danny almost gasped in horror at his own thought. This was Tulk. If he tried talking to him, all the bully would do is hurt or humiliate him in some way. On the other hand, this would be the ultimate good deed and perhaps one that no one could explain away.

"Maybe someone should see if he's okay..." Daisy took a step towards the woods.

Danny knew her well enough to know that whatever she said to Tulk would make him feel worse, not better. Somehow, that's how all of Daisy's "kind" actions seemed to end up. It was her way of being evil. Sparing Tulk her hassling him might make it an even more noble deed.

"Hey, I'll do it," he said, jumping in front of her. "You wouldn't want to miss the other half of your battle."

Daisy laughed. "Why? I'm losing."

"I'm losing worse." He took off running after Tulk before he could change his mind.

CHAPTER 21

A Good Deed or Two

Tulk sat on a log, his head in his hands, crying. As Danny approached, he paused mid-sob and looked up, his sickly face twisting into an expression of hate. "Here to try and make me feel worse? Well, go ahead and try, because things can't get any worse!"

Danny sighed. "I'm not here to make you feel worse," he said in what he hoped was a calm voice. "I'm trying to make you feel better."

Tulk narrowed his eyes. "What're you playing at, Zix?" His fingers twisted into fists. "Go on, gloat, then leave me alone."

"But I really want to help you feel better."

"Why?" Tulk glared at him.

"Because I want to get expelled." Danny blurted out the truth before he could stop himself. He seemed to be doing a lot of that lately.

Tulk's eyes widened. "I don't understand."

Danny grimaced and sat down next to him on the log. "I hate it here—I want to go home. That's why I got so many detentions, only I found out you can't get expelled here for bad behavior. So, I have to do something good to get expelled. Only when I saved you, Mordryn twisted it around. Then, I thought if I helped the person I dislike the most feel better, that might be good enough to get me in trouble."

Tulk's astonishment didn't fade. "You want to get expelled? But you're so popular and successful!"

"I'm what?" Danny couldn't believe his ears.

"Everyone loves you." Tulk sounded bitter. "That Zixy, he's so evil. Did you hear what Zix just did? Even the teachers...why can't you be more like that Zixygrith boy? You've got it made and you want to get expelled?"

Danny shrugged. "I'm just not the evil type. I didn't want to come here in the first place, but my father bullied me into it. I'm always getting embarrassed, harassed—this place is a disaster. All I want is to go home."

Tulk flushed and looked down. "You're probably just lying to me as part of some elaborate prank," he said bitterly.

"That's what everyone keeps saying." Danny glowered. "Why do you think I'm still stuck here? I just saved your life and no one—including you—will believe me that I was honestly trying to do something good."

Tulk shifted a bit awkwardly, but didn't look up. They fell silent for a long moment. Danny picked a bit at the bark on the log and supposed that if someone had saved his life, he might be a bit embarrassed. Tulk still looked miserable—why was helping so hard? He had no idea how to go about it.

"So, what's your deal?" Danny finally asked. "You've looked terrible all day."

"Nothing. Just tired."

"Oh, come on. I told you I've been trying to get expelled. You could make my life loads more miserable than you have been. Least you can do is let me help."

Tulk gave him a suspicious look. "You expect me to trust you?"

Danny sighed. "Isn't trying to stop you drowning good enough proof? What more can I do to show I'm serious here?"

"Fine." Tulk jabbed at the bark with his fingernails. "I—I'm the son of a dark lord."

"You're *what?*" Danny couldn't believe his ears.

"My mother told me just a few months ago." Tulk tossed bits of bark away. "She said I was destined to be a hero and kill my father." He finally met Danny's gaze, his face desperate. "He's my father, no matter how evil he is, and I don't want to murder him. I wouldn't be here if it wasn't for him and—and—I just don't want to do it. So, I got this wizard mentor dude to fix me up an application that would get me in here, so I wouldn't have to. Only now..." Tulk glowered at his feet.

Danny couldn't imagine having to kill Pa, but then Pa was hardly Screkvox. "Let me get this straight, you're Screkvox's son?"

"Looks like it." Tulk scuffed his shoes in the dirt. "Now I know why the old wizard geezer was so eager to 'help' me. He musta known my father was a teacher here. And when they find out, they'll expel me and I'll be forced to wander around until I become a hero and have to come back and kill him."

"Wait a minute!" Danny jumped to his feet in excitement. "I've got the perfect plan."

Tulk gave him a dull look.

"I'll pretend to be you."

"I don't get it."

Danny sat down again, feeling real hope of expulsion for the first time. This had to be a foolproof plan. "Screkvox suspects *I'm* his son because I killed him once already. He said something to that effect after class, but I didn't understand him because I didn't get what he meant until you explained about you. So, if I go on making it look like I'm his son, he'll accuse me of it and then I'll get expelled, just like I want. Then I can go home and you can stay on here and be a Dark Lord."

A speck of life crept back into Tulk's face. "Do you really think that will work?"

"Of course." Danny held out his hand. "Let's shake on it—to our one and only evil partnership."

An evil grin crossed Tulk's face and he grabbed Danny's hand and pumped it up and down. "Done."

"Well, we should pretend we're mortal enemies, just like before," Danny said, standing up again. He dusted off his robes. "That way no one will suspect."

Tulk nodded.

"I will see you later, Tulky-freckle face."

"That's a really lame insult, you know." Tulk rolled his eyes.

Danny grinned. "So's Zitty. Stop being so nice, someone will guess."

Tulk shrugged, his friendly expression disappearing. "Oh, go on and leave me alone, Zitty, or I'll smash you to a pulp next match in Strategy." He raised a fist and Danny headed back to the rest of the class.

Daisy waited for him, hopping from one foot to the

other. When she caught sight of him, she beamed. "Did it work? What'd he say? Did you make him feel better?"

"Um—he called me Zitty again." Danny's mind raced for good cover story. "He was annoyed I messed up his hair by tossing him."

Daisy laughed and Danny found he didn't mind. He felt elated just having a firm plan.

"Great Master!"

Danny turned to see Puke dashing towards him, followed by a group of intent insubstantial minions. Puke climbed up Danny's body in a flash, latching onto his neck and burying his face in his hair.

"Save me, Great Master."

The IMs were still headed towards them at full tilt, armed with spears.

"I better go, see you, Zixy," called Daisy, dashing off.

"Stop!" Danny yelled at the minions. "Halt! Retreat! STOP!"

They didn't.

Danny decided the only good option left was to run. He turned and took off across the field. He dashed past Mordryn, who ignored him; past Aun who shouted an apology and something about having lost control of his IMs; past Shai and Brex who were still finishing up a practice match, knocking their IMs everywhere.

The IMs were gaining on him. Ahead loomed the demon horse stable. Danny put on an extra burst of speed and dashed through the barn door. He whirled around and slammed it shut just seconds before the minions drove their spears into it with a series of dull thuds. Danny slid the bar across the door, locked it, and leaned against a stable door with a sigh of relief.

There was a snort behind him and a burst of light. Puke whimpered. Slowly, Danny turned to meet the curious red eyes of Wrath of Death. He swallowed and took a step back. The horse snorted another glow of red flames and shook his head. Wrath of Death nickered and stuck his head out of the stall toward Danny.

"Who's there, Wrathie?" Queileria came into view and Danny jumped.

"Oh, Zix! You here to visit Wrathie?" She smiled at him.

"Um." Danny didn't really want to say he was here hiding from a bunch of insubstantial minions. It didn't sound very impressive.

"That's so sweet." Queileria winked at him. "Here, why don't you feed him some coal?"

"What?" Danny squinted at her hands and saw they were, indeed, full of coal.

"The demon horses have a real sweet tooth for coal. Here." She put three into his hand. "Now hold it out there to Wrathie and he'll eat them out of your hand."

Wrath of Death nickered again and pulled back his lips, exposing white, flat teeth that looked like they could snap an iron beam. *Maybe he'll eat them out of her hand, but he's more likely to eat my hand off.* Danny took a step forward and Wrath of Death shook his head impatiently, a beady red eye fixed on Danny's hand. Danny gingerly reached out, put a piece of coal on the top of the stall door, and let Wrath of Death eat it off. Then he put the other two there as well. He valued his hands too much to risk them.

"Isn't he sweet?" Queileria held out her hand, flat-palmed, to Wrath of Death and he lipped the coal off of it gently.

"Great Masters tame wild horses," Puke said in a hushed, but still squeaky voice, startling Danny, who had forgotten he was with him. Wrath of Death snorted and tossed his head.

Queileria turned to squint down at Puke. "What's that?"

"My SICM, uh…" Suddenly he wished he'd given Puke a better name.

"This is humble Puke, Great Lady," Puke said, bowing.

"Ooooh, he's so cute." Queileria swooped an astonished Puke up into her arms and kissed him. Danny blushed as badly if it'd been *his* cheek that had gotten kissed. "Well, we'd best get to lunch before Carly runs out of food."

She headed down the stables, still carrying Puke and alternately talking to him and to the horses as she passed them. Danny noticed the bag of coal leaning against a barn post a few yards away. He walked over and grabbed another couple pieces of coal. Taking a deep breath, he walked over to where Wrath of Death stood watching him. He held out his hand, fingers bent back, palm upwards, towards the horse.

Wrath of Death sniffed his hand once, then took the coals from his hand, his teeth gently sliding against his palm, his lips leaving a trail of warm slime across Danny's hand. He slowly withdrew his hand, let out his breath in a whoosh of relief and hurried after Queileria. He glanced once over his shoulder and saw Wrath of Death was still staring after him, watching. Then he raced to catch up, ignoring the many curious horses poking their heads out to get a better look at him.

"Hey! Wait up." Danny hurried after them. "Can I ask you something?"

"You just did." Queleria flashed her perfect teeth at him.

Danny blushed, almost forgetting what he was going to say. "No, I mean…the demon horses, you…really seem to love them."

Queleria chuckled. She leaned forward, her eyes sparkling. "Of course. They're so beautiful, aren't they? And clever, and fun, and intelligent."

Danny squirmed, wishing she was talking about him, not Wrath of Death. "But, caring for them, loving them, isn't that being good, not evil?"

"Oh, that!" Querleria rolled her eyes. "They serve us, right? They're a valuable tool for world domination or striking terror into people's hearts. We're just using our resources to the best of our evil abilities when we take good care of them. Like you do for Puke here, yeah?" She rubbed her hand over Puke's fuzzy head and he sighed in contentment, leaning his cheek against her shoulder.

That did make sense, only it seemed at the same time to be too simple of an answer. Despite the excuses, she didn't seem evil at all. "But, what about love? That's always something good."

"Not always. There's self-serving love, love with unfair conditions. It can be used to manipulate people, get them to do what you want, even if they really don't like it or it's bad for them. They'll do it because they love you and want to please you."

Like Pa sending me here. Scenes from home flashed through Danny's head, now with a new perspective. Did Pa just want to manipulate him? Get him out of the way? Have him show up someday with a cart full of ill-gotten gains to pad his wallet? *No, he also really loved me.* He concentrated on other memories: Pa taking him fishing; Pa showing him how to temper the metal, his hand over Danny's; Pa clapping and cheering for him and Dicky when they once put on a play for him. "But—"

"Don't worry so much about the whole good and evil thing." Queleria gently tapped him on the nose, making Danny's face hot all over again. "The teachers like to harp on it, but the truth is actually really simple."

"It is?" Confusion filled Danny. He couldn't take his

eyes from her lips as she spoke. His mushy brain tried to focus on the subject, but it felt like a sieve.

Queleria nodded and leaned closer, her many long braids falling over her shoulders, dropping her voice to a whisper. "There is no such thing as good and evil."

Danny opened his mouth to protest, but didn't get any words out in time.

"No, I mean it," Querliera said. "Good and evil is just perspective, how we rationalize things. You can make anything sound either way, if you just put it right. That's the secret to it, the motives we claim to our actions. Just think about it for a moment and you can make it sound good or evil, which ever you feel like. Got it?"

Queileria gave Puke a kiss on his fuzzy head before handing him back to Danny. He felt his face getting hot and wished for the first time that he was Puke. She turned without further comment and headed off toward the school.

The monkey, beaming like an idiot, wrapped himself around Danny's neck and they both gave a wistful sigh as they watched Queileria walk off. Yet, something about the whole thing didn't feel quite right to him. Good and evil didn't exist at all? Despite not being able to come up with a way to refute her arguments, some actions just felt inherently good or evil to Danny. Didn't saving Tulk have more weight than Mordryn's evil explanation of it? And what could possibly be a good motive for going to villain school? Wasn't being here inherently bad? Only it didn't quite feel bad anymore—not all the time, anyway.

Danny shook his head, trying to clear the confusion. He needed to focus, get a plan for pretending to be Screkvox's son and get expelled while also appearing to deny it at the same time. He couldn't get sidetracked now, sucked into being a villain, not when he'd worked so hard to get out of it.

During lunch, Danny struggled to think of a brilliant way of doing this, but his mind wasn't cooperating. *When in doubt, just go with something lame and see if you can fake your way through.* He did have a head start—Screkvox already suspected him. Danny waited until almost everyone had headed to class to track down Carly.

"Hey!" he called, poking his head in the kitchen.

"Zixy-boy! It's a delight to see you."

Danny grinned at her and gave her what he hoped was a beseeching look. "I was wondering if you had an extra apple."

Carly chuckled. "Not planning to try and poison any more teachers, are you?"

Danny struggled to hide his surprise. It was like she could read his mind. "Erm, I was going to give it to one of the horses."

"Catch then, Zixy-boy. Anything for my evil lad." She tossed a toxically red apple in the air and Danny jumped forward and caught it.

"Thanks a bunch."

The next morning, he polished it on his shirt on the way to History, taking his time to assure he had a dramatic entrance. While he had no confidence this would work, it was worth a try. Food had started the whole thing, stood to reason it'd further his suspicions again.

"Hey, Professor." He held up the apple. "I've got a little something for you."

The class, already assembled, went deathly still.

Screkvox's eyebrows creased as he gave Danny a stare that made him want to shrivel up and shrink into the floor.

"Since, well, you know, you like food and all…I thought

I'd bring you something," Danny said rather lamely. He extended the apple towards Screkvox and tried to look as if he wished him dead.

After a moment of hesitation, the teacher extended a gloved hand and accepted the apple. He stepped in close to Danny and whispered, "Meddle not in the affairs of Dark Lords, for they are subtle and quick to anger. I've got my eye on you, Zixygruth, don't think you can get away with your little scheme."

Then he turned and put the apple on the corner of his desk. Danny slithered off to his seat, a pit in his stomach, as he wondered for the first time if his plan might end up getting him killed rather than expelled. He slouched down low and tried to stay inconspicuous, but he felt Screkvox's eyes boring into him all lecture long.

CHAPTER 22

Desperate Measures for Desperate Times

Danny waited with bated breath, but no denouncements came. Screkvox still gave him the evil eye every time they crossed paths, but said nothing. *What's he waiting for?* Danny grimaced at his homework while sitting in Study Hall. *At this rate, it would have been faster to fail everything.* He might end up doing that anyway. Tomorrow was the beginning of mid-terms and his brain felt like it was going to explode with all the cramming they'd been doing.

Shai and Aun had taken to reviewing information during meals and they expected Danny to join in. It made Carly's dinners twice as difficult to consume, especially when they were reviewing gutting techniques for slaying styles or the sordid history of Tektorik the Torturous and his fifteen methods for executing would-be heroes.

Daisy, on the other hand, was gearing up for the year's first troll wresting competition after being selected as the school's representative in the junior division. She and Brex, also on the troll wresting team, talked tactics constantly. They kept pestering Danny to help them practice their Dark Magic so that they could move up and face more dangerous trolls. Danny, having no intention of reaching for that center of Dark Magic again, spewed excuses.

Alec took so long to reply to his last letter that Danny despaired of that plan as well. When it at last arrived, he was disappointed to discover it was only a tirade on honor and how, as a Dark Lord, Danny had no concept of it. Not even a hint of a desire to attack again. In frustration, Danny described all fifteen of Tektorik's methods in his reply, promising one for Alec and each of his friends, but didn't have much hope of success there, either. What he really needed was a quiet moment to plan on how to push Screkvox into reporting him as his son.

One afternoon he managed to slip away to his room, but was dismayed to discover Puke bawling in his bedroom. After he managed to calm the monkey into a comprehensible state, he gathered that Puke was failing much more successfully than he was.

"Well, I don't care if the other SICMs don't think you're evil enough," Danny said. "We're trying to get expelled, anyway, so it's fine if you fail."

Puke's tear-filled eyes beseeched Danny. "But, Great Master, I afraid of the minions. They not listen to humble Puke. Humble Puke cannot command them. They do not obey."

Danny sighed. "We don't have a choice, unless you can

find us a way to get expelled before Thursday. Otherwise we have to fight our Strategy midterm."

Puke started wailing again.

"Don't worry, I won't let the IMs hurt you." Danny gritted his teeth. "Stop screeching, okay? It's not like they're trolls or something."

Puke continued to howl like he was about to be thrown to the trolls for breakfast. Danny put fingers in his ears and left the room, disgusted. He leaned against the cold stone wall and shut his eyes. *Why is getting expelled so much work?* He could still hear Puke dully through the thick wall. *Maybe I should throw him to the trolls—I'd get more done.*

That was it! Trolls. If he let a troll loose where it might attack Screkvox, it would look like he was trying to kill him again. Screkvox was surely skilled enough to take care of the troll, but it ought to annoy him into denouncing Danny. Grinning, Danny sprang forward with new determination. This had to work.

While Danny had never been to the troll cages, he knew roughly where they were. He hurried along the corridors, hoping Daisy would be there practicing her moves with Brex. If she helped, it shouldn't be too hard to direct the troll into the History Department. The only downside was he'd have to give her what she wanted in return. Danny's stomach clenched at the thought of bringing up the magic, but if it got him expelled, it would be worth it.

Daisy, fortunately, was indeed at the troll pit. An older girl was facing off with an enormous and very stinky troll while Daisy, Brex, and a group of other students watched and commented on her technique. As Danny paused to watch, the troll jerked its arm out of her grip and lashed out, hitting the girl in the head and sending her tumbling across the arena. He winced as the crowd booed.

"Psst, Daisy." She was too absorbed in the match to hear him. He wiggled through the crowd and tugged on her sleeve.

"Oh, Zix!" Daisy turned to look at him. The students started yelling and screaming at that moment. The girl had gotten another grip on the troll and struggled to trip it. The rest of Daisy's words were lost in the noise. Danny made a motion towards the doorway. Daisy wrinkled her nose at him, gave the match another long look, then nodded and came with him.

"What's up, Zixy?"

Danny's ears still rang with all the noise. "I thought about it and I guess I'll help you with the magic…"

"Oooooh, you will!" she squealed and jumped up and down.

"Wait!" Danny interjected. "But I need you to help me with something in exchange."

Daisy grinned. "Yeah, of course. You don't want to be too kind, huh? Not very villainous."

Danny flushed as her words made him think of his talk with Queleria. He wasn't actually being nice, but using her. Or was he, if he wanted to put it that way? It was too confusing to work out. "Yeah…something like that. Anyway, I wanna put a troll in Screkvox's office, or uh, classroom."

Daisy giggled. "Don't you think he's annoyed at you enough after killing him?"

Danny shrugged, trying to look casual. "Um, well, he can't like me any less than he already does, can he?"

"But you might fail History."

Danny's mind raced for a good explanation. "Er, well, I thought if I did something he could, you know, defeat by himself, he might decide that I'm not all that clever after all and not, um, well, not be so angry at me."

Daisy looked appropriately confused, considering Danny hadn't made any sense. "You think if you set a troll on him, he'll stop being angry at you for killing him?"

"Yeah," Danny said with confidence he didn't feel. "He will, because he can, um, stop me this time."

Daisy rolled her eyes. "If you say so. Zixy, you got the weirdest ideas, but I'll help you out if you help me. Deal's a deal." She held out her hand.

Thank goodness! Danny beamed as he shook her hand. "Deal."

They decided to release the troll at dinnertime, when the students were all in the dining hall and thus out of the way. Danny noticed that Screkvox usually didn't stay to eat in the hall, but took his lunch off by himself, probably to his office, so he figured there was a good chance the troll would find him in there.

Daisy led him to the cages where the trolls were kept. The huge creatures lunged at the bars as they passed, flicking drool over Danny. Somehow Daisy seemed to know instinctively when to step out of the way.

"You get used to them, really," she said. "I think they're kinda cute. Okay, I think this one would be good. I've not tried him, because he's really huge and ornery, but I'm sure with dark magic we'll have no trouble."

This troll was not up against the bars, but leaned on the back wall, his eyes shut. He opened one of them a slit and regarded Danny for a second before shutting it again. Danny swallowed hard, looking at the big fangs poking out of his mouth just below the ring in his enormous bulldog nose.

"You hold them down by the ring, after you ground them," Daisy explained. "That's how you win a match. Okay, so, help me find the center of magic, then open the door, and I'll use it to herd him into the school."

"Okay." Danny took a deep breath. He centered himself, letting go of his present worries and anxieties, and found the dark magic—like a reservoir—deep inside, waiting. It surged into him, making his hands tingle. It scared him how much more pleasant and inviting it seemed than the last time, begging him to be used.

Instead, he reached for Daisy's hands. The magic hummed through his fingers, touching hers and making it rise to the surface. It sang between them, begging so fearfully to be used that it frightened Danny into letting go and dropping it. *Maybe I'll wait until I flunk out of school or just hope Alec attacks after all!*

"Ooooooh," Daisy cried, beaming. "I can feel it! It's so much easier when you do that."

"You've gotta quiet your mind," Danny said. "That's what lets you find it. You have to stop thinking about everything else."

Her eyes widened. "But don't you have to think about what you're wanting to do with it?"

"No, only after you find it." Danny was unnerved by the confidence in his voice, but plunged on anyway. "Now try it on your own."

Daisy shut her eyes and screwed up her face. Even not touching his own magic, Danny was close enough to feel it when she found hers. Her hold on it wasn't strong, but was definitely there. Danny threw open the door to the cage.

"Now," he whispered.

Daisy opened her eyes and grinned. She moved forward, but the troll, who looked as asleep as ever a second ago, charged. Danny threw himself out of the way. He expected Daisy to do so as well, but instead she released the magic at the last moment and it slammed into the troll's face. The troll roared and turned away from her, charging down the row of cages towards the school entrance instead.

"Quick," yelled Daisy, "get the door open!"

She dashed between the cages and around the other side, parallel to the troll. Danny pelted after her. They flung the door open and stood on either side, leaving the only open way for the troll into the school. Danny's heart thumped against his chest. He didn't want to use the magic, but if the troll turned and headed for him, he didn't want to end up troll dinner either. To his great relief, the troll went straight into the school.

"I'll circle around to force it to turn into the History Department—you stay behind it," he told Daisy and took off running again. He sped around the school, through the door by the cafeteria, getting a glimpse of the line, but he didn't have time to check it for Screkvox. He pelted down the hall, relieved not to run into anyone who'd tell him to slow down, and arrived at the correct intersection just in time to see the troll heading toward him.

Danny took a deep breath and accessed the magic, letting it rise between him and the troll. The creature roared and turned down the hall toward the History classroom at the end. Daisy joined Danny. The troll reached the dead end and howled again.

"Make it bust down the door," Danny suggested. "With the magic."

"Sure!" Daisy grinned excitedly and let out another burst of magic.

The troll attacked the door and it shattered. They listened, but no yell of surprise came from the room—only the sound of the troll demolishing the desks. Torn books and chair parts flew out into the hall.

"Maybe he decided to eat in the lunchroom today, after all," Daisy said.

"Drat!" Danny kicked the wall. "We gotta do something to let him know about it."

"Not to mention, I don't know how to get it out of there and back to its cage when it's this angry," Daisy said, frowning.

"Great," muttered Danny. "Just great."

"Hey, I know! Come on!" Daisy turned and ran back towards the lunchroom. Danny followed, unsure if he wanted to know what she was up to. They arrived at the doorway and Daisy stopped so quickly, Danny ran into her.

Daisy cupped her hands around her mouth and bellowed at the teacher's table, "Troll in the History Department!" She then promptly keeled over in a pretend faint.

Danny now had a view of everyone in the cafeteria staring at him, including Screkvox sitting next to Mystfolyn at the teacher table. Danny stooped to pretend to look after Daisy, feeling the burn of Screkvox's glare on him. Silence reigned for a brief moment, then everyone turned back to their lunch and continued eating as if nothing had happened. Danny peeked up to see Screkvox get to his feet and slip out of the room through the door on the far side.

Danny helped Daisy sit up. "Did it work?" she whispered.

Danny glanced at the unconcerned crowd, chatting away like normal. "I guess...no one else seems concerned about it, but Screkvox did look pretty pissed, so maybe."

"Great." Daisy jumped to her feet and brushed off her dress. "Let's go eat then!"

An Attack of Heroes

To Danny's dismay, no reprisals came his direction. The only results of his troll attack were brand new desks in the History Classroom. Danny overheard Mystfolyn complaining to Vrlyxfrka that Screkvox had set the whole thing up as an excuse to get his room outfitted with new furniture and supplies. Had he been wrong about Screkvox noticing him and blaming him for it? He didn't seem any nastier in class, although that would have been nigh impossible, considering how unpleasant he was before the troll.

The upshot of the matter was that Danny was left to struggle on his own through midterms. Although, even those weren't a complete disaster. Spleg's tentacled something-or-other of a SICM got tangled up in its own legs and Danny's IMs obeyed Puke for once and decimated Spleg's, winning Danny's first round. Daisy and Orro slaughtered him the second round, but Danny still passed. While he got a near fail in Style, he made the mistake of filling out his multiple choice test randomly and got enough correct to only earn him a lecture from Mystfolyn on the need to study and practice. Osweggi gave him some nasty bruises, but actually claimed he was improving, despite Danny feeling he hadn't changed one bit. Nyshlza only looked at him with her unnerving white gaze when he claimed he had tried his hardest to levitate an object, but couldn't, and moved onto the next student. History was the only thing he failed entirely.

Vrlyxfrka called him in to review his grades and merely told him the best way to villainy was to try harder and warned him that he didn't want to repeat his first year, a thought that made him nauseous. Worse, Alec still hadn't written him back, making that a dead end as well. By the end of it all, Danny was desperate enough to corner Tulk in the library between classes.

"I thought we were pretending to be enemies still," Tulk muttered, glancing up and down the rows of books. "What d'ya think you're doing?"

"It's not working!" hissed Danny. "He's not denouncing me. The apple and the troll both failed."

Tulk shrugged. "What'd you expect me to do about it?"

"Help me make him think I'm trying to kill him. I need some ideas here."

Tulk's forehead wrinkled in concentration. "You're the smart one. I dunno what to do."

Danny rolled his eyes. Tulk was useless. "How're you gonna stay a villain if you can't even come up with…" He glanced around the room for inspiration and noticed the heavy chandelier above them. "Hey, I got it!" He grabbed Tulk by the shoulder, making the boy flinch. "We'll drop a chandelier on him."

"What? But, but, that might actually kill him…" Tulk paled.

Danny sighed. "We wouldn't actually hit him."

"But you said—"

"What I meant is that we pretend to drop it on him, but miss him." A plan gelled in Danny's mind. "Look, you wait in the main hall and when Screkvox comes by, call to him to ask him a question right when he's about to go under it. So, when he turns away from it, I'll cut the chandelier free and it'll just miss him."

Tulk's eyes went wide. "But what if he thinks I did it?"

Danny groaned at Tulk's stupid timidity. No wonder he stuck to kicking minions and calling people names. "Look, you'll have just saved him by changing his course. Plus, he'll look around for why it fell and see me by the chain holder on the wall. He won't have a clue you had anything to do with it since he'll think I meant to actually hit him."

Tulk looked on the verge of making further excuses. Danny glared at him, desperate to make this work. "You gotta help me. If you don't, I'll rat on you, tell them you're supposed to be a hero."

Tulk trembled. "Fine," he whispered. "I'll do it."

Danny smiled in relief. "First thing after breakfast. Be there."

Tulk nodded miserably.

Danny half-feared Tulk would chicken out on him, but Tulk was there at breakfast looking sulky. Danny poked him in the ribs with his food tray as he walked by.

"You just watch it, Zitty," Tulk said. "Your evil plans will fail with me around."

"Uh, yeah, I'll keep that in mind," Danny muttered.

Aun rolled his eyes at him. "You really gotta work on your comebacks, Zixy."

Danny pushed his blue mushy breakfast *something* around with his spoon. "Like what?"

Aun grinned evilly, doing it pretty well. "That's why my first evil plan is to get rid of you."

"Right." Danny gulped down his food. He needed to get in position. "I forgot my books today. I'll meet you at class."

He slipped out of the cafeteria and across to the main hall, the high-ceilinged meeting place of several corridors. An enormous chandelier hung, glowing with magical light. Danny walked across the hall to the steps going up towards the headmaster's office, where the chandelier's chain was attached to a wall bracket. He stepped back into the shadows.

The minutes dragged out as Danny's heart pounded against his ribs. Teachers and students scurried across the hall in oblivious contentment. Tulk wasn't visible. Danny hoped he was holding his part of the bargain up and waiting out of sight in one of the corridors. Finally, Screkvox emerged from a far corner and strode across the middle of the room, directly under the chandelier. Danny held his breath, waiting.

"Professor!" Tulk came into view off to one side. "Do you have a moment?"

Screckvox turned, taking a couple of steps away from the center of the room. Danny dashed to the wall. His fingers shook as he struggled with the heavy chain. It remained firmly wrapped around the holder. Danny yanked on it, but it didn't budge. Screkvox was now out from under the chandelier, talking to Tulk. In a moment it would be too late. Danny struggled furiously with the chain. His whole plan would be ruined. Screkvox turned away from Tulk and started walking away.

With a cry of frustration, Danny reached for the magic —despite his vow not to use it again. It swelled up, shooting from his hands into the chain, which broke free with a rumble. Still holding it, Danny was pulled into the air. The chandelier plummeted downwards with a rending crack.

"Look out!" screamed Tulk.

Danny looked down to see a paralyzed Shai standing under the oncoming chandelier. Tulk threw himself into her, sending them both rolling out as it smashed into the ground. Danny dangled near the ceiling. Students all around the edges of the room stared at him. Screkvox, who'd turned around, gave him an icy glance, before walking onward.

"I'll help you down!" called Aun.

"No need!" Danny roared, but it was too late. Aun's magic slammed into him and the chain, cutting it free and sending Danny falling. He landed on top of Shai and Tulk.

"Sorry," Danny mumbled as they yelled out in pain.

The bell rang, warning there were only minutes before class began. Some of the other students laughed, but most of them turned away to hurry on to class.

"Let's get out of here, quick," Shai suggested as Danny helped her to her feet.

"Sounds good to me," Tulk said and they scattered off to History.

Screkvox didn't even look at Danny when he entered, but instead launched into his lecture without a hint of anything being different. Danny stared out the window at the drizzling gray courtyard of the school. *I'm never going to get expelled. It's hopeless.*

The warning screech of a strange buzzer interrupted his dour thoughts. "Attention," came a voice from somewhere in the ceiling. "This is the headmaster. There has been breach of security and a group of heroes are in Dark Lord Academy territory. All fifth and sixth year students, please report to the front of the castle for battle instructions. Fourth year and under, please report to the cafeteria. Any student found not obeying these instructions precisely and immediately will be locked in the dungeon until further notice. Thank you."

Danny gasped. Alec had come for him. This was his chance! Hope filled him. The class erupted in a burst of speculation. Danny's heart raced. All he had to do was slip away while everyone went to the cafeteria and find a way out of the castle with the fifth and sixth year students.

Screkvox held up a gloved hand. "Silence. You will proceed to the cafeteria in an orderly fashion. On your way out, I will hand back your last exam and I suggest you spend the time studying those questions you have missed."

"It's so exciting," Daisy whispered. "I wish we could fight."

"Me too," Aun said, his eyes gleaming. "I'd love to see Professor Osweggi in battle action."

"Or Mystfolyn," said Tulk. Danny glanced at him, surprised he was talking to them. None of the others seemed to hold any extended animosity towards him and Shai smiled at him. Danny felt a twinge in his stomach and tried to squash it. Why should he be jealous of Tulk?

"Come on, we can talk about it more in the cafeteria," said Brex, walking up to the front of the classroom after the other students already filing out.

Screkvox stood right next to the door, handing out papers. Danny swallowed hard. He would have to walk right up to him to leave the class. He hadn't been so physically close to Screkvox since he killed him. He tried to squash his nerves—he needed to get out of here quick, before anyone realized his plan.

"Yeah, maybe the heroes will make it up the castle and we'll get a chance to fight them," Daisy said. She skipped towards the front of the room. "Oh, goody, I got a 89%. Thanks, professor."

Screkvox gave her a thin smile.

Danny realized he was at the end of the line—and didn't relish a private moment with Screkvox. He shuffled behind Shai, slipping between her and Tulk. He wished Screkvox would let him slip by without a word, perhaps leaving his test behind, but no such luck. As Shai stepped out, Screkvox took a step forward and switched hands, giving Tulk his paper instead, while blocking Danny's path.

Danny shot Tulk a desperate look, but the idiot had his back to him and didn't notice, leaving Danny alone with Screkvox.

"A moment of your time, Zxygrth?" Screkvox's cold gaze met Danny's and Danny reached up, his fingers closing on the test. Everything around him dissolved in smoke, thicker and blacker than the usual transportation, making Danny cough and hack twice as hard. It cleared to reveal a graveyard.

Dark Lord Academy loomed off to Danny's right, the Dead Field between them and the castle. All around him stood tall gray stones bearing the names of long dead villains. Misty rain blew against his face. Heart pounding, Danny looked across his test to Screkvox. The dark lord's eyes glittered with a hint of fire.

"I told you you wouldn't have a chance trying to take me down." Screkvox's lips curved in a thin smile. "I've been planning long and hard for this moment, *son*." He flicked back his cape, revealing his sword—the one Danny had used accidentally a few months ago in Magic Weapons.

Danny suddenly realized that must have been why the sword had backfired. It recognized Tulk and refused to kill him. Danny, however, had no such immunity. He took a few steps backwards and bumped into the formidable headstone of Headmaster Zoraster, stopping his retreat.

"But professor, I don't have a sword," he protested.

Screkvox flashed perfect white teeth at Danny. "Too bad you didn't prepare as well as I. I've been waiting a long time for this. No one will interrupt us here. I'll take care of business and no one will have any idea what happened to you."

Understanding thunked Danny like Osweggi's sword in weapon's practice. It hadn't been Alec at all; this was too large and organized an attack for a mere student to pull off by himself. "You organized the hero attack!"

"Muahahahaha!" Screkvox threw back his head and laughed. Danny recognized that this was the beginning of the traditional Dark Lord monologue. He glanced to the left and right, looking for an escape route.

"But of course I did," Screkvox began. "I have a few contacts. The disguised message from you, *dear son*, informing the league of heroes of a weakness in the Academy's defenses and a small bribe with the date and time for a convenient attack was the simplest part. They, of course, think they are helping you kill me." Screkvox smirked. "All of it was arranged on my rotation for student duty, should an emergency arise. No one will miss me and most definitely—" Screkvox leaned forward, "—no one will miss you. I shall squash you like the pesky bug you are."

Screkvox drew his sword.

"It's hardly fair to attack me unarmed," Danny protested. He bent his knees, ready to dodge.

"Nice one," sneered Screkvox. "Dark Lords don't have to play fair. Thought you could be a villain, Zixy? You're nothing but a pathetic hero. Soon to be a dead pathetic hero."

Danny opened his mouth ready to protest, but realized before denouncing Tulk as the true son there was no way in heaven or hell that Screkvox would believe him. He'd played his role too well and now might very well die for it.

Screkvox lifted his sword high in a dramatic pose, exactly the sort Osweggi said left a person stupidly open, not that Danny had anything to attack back with. It glittered a moment, then came down in a deadly arch. Danny ducked behind the gravestone. With a clap of thunder, the sword hit Zoraster's headstone, splitting it right down the middle.

Danny fell backward and rolled through the dry grass. "Don't think the Headmaster will be too pleased about that," he muttered.

"Die, hero!" roared Screkvox, jumping after him. The sword whistled much too close to Danny's ear as he dodged again. He wasn't going to last long at this rate.

A whinny rang through the air. Danny glanced to the side and saw Wrath of Death blazing in a trail of flames across the Dead Field as he galloped towards them. Screkvox's sword faltered with the distraction. Danny used the opportunity to dodge backward. Wrath of Death swooped between them and Danny dug deep into the magic, using it to propel himself into the air and onto Wrath of Death's back.

CHAPTER 24

Difficulties in the Headmasters Office

"Wrathie," Danny breathed as he clutched at Wrath of Death's bridle. "I'm so glad to see you, even if I have no idea how you knew I needed your help."

"You can't escape me!" ranted Screkvox. "I'll destroy you if I have to destroy every last villain, minion, and animal in this school. If I have to send it all toppling, I will." He shook his fists at Danny. "You shall not survive!"

Wrath of Death circled around the graveyard, leaving crackling flames behind him, then picked up speed and galloped straight at Screkvox, letting out a stream of fire from his nostrils. Danny yelled, terrified the horse was headed toward his enemy. The dead grass around them blazed up into flames.

Screkvox stumbled to the side, throwing up a barrier of dark magic to protect himself. Wrath of Death cantered past him. Danny felt a surge of magic behind him, a dark pressure growing that would be hurdled at them any moment. Desperate, he reached for his own magic again and it eagerly surged up in response. He turned in the saddle, throwing a hand out at Screkvox and willing it out toward him with all his might. The two magics clashed together with a sound like thunder and made the ground shake.

Danny and Wrath of Death sped out of range toward the back door of the castle. When the horse pulled up at the main gate, Danny was shocked to see Queileria, Daisy, and Puke waiting for him.

"Hey!" Daisy yelled. "What happened to you?"

"Great Master!" Puke exclaimed at the same time from Queileria's arms. "Puke send horse to Great Master."

"Thanks, Puke," Danny said. He slid off Wrath of Death and patted his neck. Queileria passed him Puke and took the horse's reins.

"Screkvox tried to kill me," Danny told Daisy. "And he's headed this way right now. He doesn't care who he kills or how much of the school he destroys in order to get me."

"Wow!" Daisy's eyes got round. "You gonna hide?"

"And let all of you get killed while he looks for me?" Danny pondered it. It certainly had its appeal. Once Atriz got back and saw what Screkvox had done, surely he'd expel Danny for being the son of a Dark Lord and causing all this trouble. "It would certainly be evil of me." *But it wouldn't make me look like a hero, would it?*

"We can't just let him destroy everything!" Queileria said.

"Yeah, it's our school, too," Daisy said. She shook her

head. "I'm not about to let some crazy teacher ruin everything. This is the first place I've ever fit in, you know, had real friends. He's not gonna take that away."

"Yeah!" called Aun from the doorway, showing up with Shai, Tulk, Brex, and Spleg. "Let's fight!"

"What's going on here? You're not supposed to be out here!" Demigorth shoved through the crowd. "It's against Headmaster Atriz's orders. Do you want to end up in the dungeons?"

Danny whipped around to face him. The dungeons didn't seem much a threat compared to Screkvox, but on the other hand, he had a sneaking suspicion that if he explained, Demigorth would advocate just handing him over to Screkvox as a solution.

Demigorth flashed his eyes red. "All of you first years are breaking code. If you don't all get right back into the school, I'm gonna—"

Orro galloped across the dead field towards them, cutting off Demigorth's words. "Mistress!" he called. "Professor Screkvox and an army of Lightning Minions are headed this way."

Daisy's eyes got round. "Ooooooh, I'm gonna fix him good if he burns down my school."

Demigorth looked astounded. "Why would he attack us?"

"He's the one who called the hero attack," Danny said, glancing at all the eager faces of the others, longing for a good fight. Now seemed like the perfect time to lie—he'd worry about good and evil later. "He's betrayed us and changed sides and joined the heroes. Demigorth, if we don't do something, he's gonna destroy the school! You'd better warn everyone."

"But—"

Danny didn't intend to give Demigorth time to think it through and turn the crowd against him. "Everyone who wants to fight, follow me!" He pushed past Demigorth and dashed down the hall. To his relief, the other first years raced after him. Aun caught up next to Danny.

"Where we going?"

"To get weapons."

Aun's face lit up with delight. "Brilliant!"

Danny skidded to a stop in the entryway, noting that the downed chandelier was repaired and hanging as normal. He grinned at Aun. "I told you I'd let you help me next time I did something truly evil. What's worse than disobeying all orders and fighting a teacher? And maybe killing him again." He winked.

"You're the evilest, Zix," Aun said.

Danny felt warm all through. He looked around to see not only his friends, but the rest of his class had joined him, looking eager. Demigorth yelled at them from the hallway.

"Let's go!" Danny pelted up the stairs. The archway to the weapon room was blocked with magic, but this time Danny didn't hesitate. He reached for the dark magic and blasted it into the wall. The air in the arch sparkled and rippled with the energy. "Come on," Danny muttered.

Aun and Shai joined him. "Let's try it all together," Aun suggested. Danny got distracted watching them as their expressions hardened in concentration, then they twisted their palms at the arch. The energy in it twisted and buckled, then the spell broke, sending a shockwave back that tumbled the three of them to the stone floor.

"That was awesome," Aun said, jumping to his feet. The first years hurried into the weapons room, then paused, staring in awe.

"Be careful what you pick," Shai whispered. "Remember

what Osweggi said. Some of these weapons are hard to handle."

"This one looks good," Daisy said, reaching across the ropes to grab one of the fire swords. She winked at Danny. "My mama says I'm a little firecracker when I get a temper."

Danny snickered.

Tulk tugged Danny's sleeve. "What should I use?"

Danny shrugged. "You don't gotta fight."

Tulk shook his head. "You're taking on all my danger for me! I can't let you do that by yourself. It's not..."

Danny laughed. "Honorable? Hey, Tulky-freckle-face, maybe you're a hero after all."

Tulk blushed and turned away to claim an ice sword. Danny selected one of the hero helper swords, hoping it would both improve his fighting skills and make him look more like a hero. The others rushed out of the room. Danny turned to go when he noticed Aun standing still, staring at the wall of swords rather blankly.

"Aren't you gonna pick something?"

"Yeah," Aun said in a spacey voice. "I think I will."

Danny frowned at him. "What's wrong with you?"

Aun picked up the battle ice axe next to him on the floor, but instead of turning to go, he hefted it high, ready to swing. Danny followed his gaze and almost choked. Dark magic swirled around one of the swords in a glass case on the wall—Stradux. Danny's stomach twisted and his breath caught, like the air was getting squeezed out of him.

Aun stepped forward and drew back the axe farther.

"No!" Danny caught his arm. "That one's evil—it'll rule your soul, remember?" *And it will put him in a rage that might make him slaughter all of us.*

Aun's eyes were empty, his expression set, and he didn't

say anything. He shook Danny off, tumbling him to the floor and smashed the axe into the glass case. It had some sort of special spell because it didn't shatter. Aun kept hacking at it, yelling in rage. Dark magic swirled between him and Stradux. Was it too late?

Danny reached for the magic, but, overwhelmed by panic, felt nothing. *What's happened to it?* He took in a sharp breath. What was it Nyshlza was always saying... concentrate? He shut his eyes and tried to block out the feeling like Stradux's magic was a wall of bricks about to land on top of their heads. *Emotion...fear. Will fear work?* He certainly had enough of it and didn't people do terrible and evil things when afraid? *So long as I keep my resolve to fight anyway, not just turn and run.* Terror bubbled inside of him and Danny tried to turn it into desperate resolve.

Determination flooded him and with it came up the magic. Danny seized it and it poured out of him like a geyser and, with the force of his will and a slash of his hand, he directed it at both Stradux and Aun. The room shook and Aun collapsed and the sword's dark magic dissipated.

"Wha—" Aun murmured.

"Sorry, just an accident," Danny said, helping Aun to his feet. He handed him the axe. "Come on, Screkvox is probably in the castle by now."

They rushed out of the room. As they raced down the stairs, Danny heard screams and blasts.

"They've started fighting! We're gonna miss it," Aun said. He picked up his speed, taking the stairs two at a time and leaving Danny in the dust. Danny ran as fast as he could manage towards the cafeteria, but stopped in shock when he reached it.

Screkvox stood in the middle of the cafeteria, throwing magic in all directions. Some of the students fought back, but compared to him, their attacks looked puny and insubstantial. The room also swarmed with hooded figures that periodically zapped out lightning while fighting with students. Danny assumed those were lightning minions. Several of the banners were on fire and the walls and tables were singed. Demigorth and some older students were surrounded by the banners and someone screamed when they went up in flames. The stinging smell of smoke filled the air.

Shai—who had apparently found an evil violin in the weapon's gallery and knew how to play it—lulled several minions into inaction while Queileria took them out with a double-bladed staff. They moved forward to help Demigorth's group, but weren't cutting through the minions fast enough.

Danny was distracted by another cry. Screkvox sent a blast that toppled Daisy and Brex to the ground. Daisy groaned and tried to get up. Brex lay still. Tulk jumped in front of them, hefting his sword, his face pale. Aun dashed up next to him, looking determined to fight despite the terrible odds.

Screkvox threw back his head and laughed. Danny's hands shook. People were getting hurt, and maybe would get killed, all because of him! He had never truly meant to be evil, not once, only to take care of himself. But now he needed to be evil, evil for someone else, for his life, for Tulk's life, for the school itself. He'd worry about the ramifications of it later. He reached for the dark magic with new determination, the magic he had continually denied, sinking deeper into it than ever before. He felt it swirl under his hands, growing thicker and darker, swirling like black smoke.

"I'm over here, Screkvox!" he yelled.

Screkvox leaped into the air using magic to propel

himself across the room, twirling around until he landed next to Danny. His eyes were two bright red gleaming points. *Looks just as stupid on him as on everyone else,* Danny reminded himself. Magic swelled inside of him, powerful and insulating. He wasn't going to be intimidated this time.

Screkvox raised a gloved hand and Danny raised his as well. The air brightened, then rippled as the energy built. It pushed and shoved between them, growing darker and thicker, like a black writhing cloud between their hands. Danny felt his hand shaking, the pressure pushed him backward. He was weakening.

I need more magic. Danny reached farther into himself, let his eyes roll backwards, concentrating on the inside so hard that the outside disappeared, just like Nyshlza had said so many times in class. The world changed—a sea of dark and light energy. Screkvox was the center of a dark knot of magic. It twisted and swirled around him like a cyclone, only now Danny could follow its patterns, understand the twists and turns. With a shiver, he realized he had finally found the center she had so often described to him.

Screkvox cracked lightning at Danny, jagged purple flashes splitting the air between them. But in Danny's new sense of awareness, snapping out lightning back was like child's play—he could feel the magic connected to the lightning rods on the roof, the energy stored and waiting for use. He drew on it and lighting flashed from his hands. The bolts tangled, searing the air with smoke. Screkvox's face twisted in rage, but his hands also wobbled a bit. Danny guessed he must look pretty scary with his eyes turned white like Nyshlza—and it felt *good.* No time to ponder if that was making him evil or not though because Screkvox still was managing to drive him backwards toward the wall. He'd debate it after he survived.

They battled back and forth, first one gaining the upper

hand with the magic, then the other. Screkvox pushed Danny back into the main entrance hall. With his new awareness, Danny noticed something up the staircase—some other form of magic—pulsed, red and violent. It beckoned to Danny, promising help.

Danny zapped another bolt of lightning out, forcing Screkvox to jump to the side. Danny circled so that his back faced the staircase and let Screkvox's next attack push him backward toward the source of the strange magical energy. It wasn't the same form as his or Screkvox's. Danny didn't entirely trust it, but he also sensed it wanted Screkvox more than him.

Using the height of the stairs to his advantage, Danny willed the magic downward, trying to pin Screkvox, keeping his attacks back with the superior position. Screkvox changed tactics and charged with his sword, driving Danny up the stairs with a series of blows so fast that only the magic of the sword moving his arm to block managed to save him. He stumbled at the top of the stairs.

Now Screkvox used magic, a powerful bolt that slammed Danny backwards into a door so hard it splintered it apart. Danny slid on his back across the smooth floor. He yanked himself up into a sitting position and shook his head. The bright light from the windows illuminated a tidy desk and bookshelf; he was in the headmaster's office. To one side, red angry energy boiled out from under a closet door—the source of the strange magic. Only Danny didn't have time to consider it. Screkvox thrust a sword blow at him and, still sitting on the floor, Danny had a difficult time blocking. Screkvox caught the crosspiece of his sword and ripped it from Danny's hands. His magic view of the world faded as his concentration was destroyed.

Battle cries rent the air. Aun dashed around Screkvox

and jumped in front of Danny. "The traitor is mine! You promised it was my turn!"

"You can have him," Danny muttered.

Daisy, Shai, and Tulk burst in after him, holding up their weapons.

"No! It's my turn to take him on," Shai insisted.

"Why don't we take 'em together?" Daisy said, flashing a grin.

Screkvox just stared at the moment as if he couldn't believe they'd just come to Danny's rescue. Danny had to admit that, for a pack of villains, they were pretty loyal. But now was not the time to ruminate on the difference between good and evil. He used the distraction to glance around for where his sword had been knocked to.

"I got to him first!" Aun insisted, swinging his ax. A blast of ice and snow showered Screkvox. The teacher sent a blast of fire from his sword to melt it before it overcame him. Shai played lightning bolts of magic out of the violin so violently that it set the headmaster's desk on fire on the other side of Screkvox. Danny yelped and rolled to one side to avoid getting singed. Screkvox threw up a magical barrier. The energy fizzed and crackled across it a moment, then was hurdled back at Shai, who screamed and twisted sideways. The violin made a sick cracking sound of death.

Tulk raised his sword above his head and a blizzard burst from it, filling the entire room with swirling snow. Danny scrambled to his feet shivering, but still couldn't see where his sword had ended up. Screkvox counteracted it with another blast of heat, but in the distraction, Tulk jumped forward and his blade sliced along Screkvox's arm. Blood gushed from his arm and he howled in rage.

"I'll get him!" yelled Daisy, dashing forward. But she slipped and knocked into Tulk, shoving him accidentally right into the path of Screkvox's sword coming down.

There was a loud bang as the sword recoiled rather than cut into Tulk. The force of it ripped the sword out of Screkvox's hand and sent it flying across the room to slam point first into one of the windows, shattering it. Everyone froze.

Screkvox, wide-eyed, stared into Tulk's pale face. Danny saw realization cross his face as he glanced away to Danny, then back to Tulk, who undeniably looked quite a bit like his father.

"Why you little—" Screkvox lunged forward and grasped Tulk's sword, ripping it from his hand. He raised it to slay the stunned Tulk, who only looked up in horrified disbelief.

"No!" screamed Danny, seeing all his dreams of expulsion crushed once and for all. He plunged into his magic deeper and more aggressively than ever before. Black and hot in the back of his mind, it surged back up into him with a vengeance. Danny put all his will into it and flung out his hands, flicking them towards the boiling red magic in the corner of the room. Screkvox flew backward and sideways, slamming into the closet door. The door shattered.

Screkvox clutched at the broken shards of door, but failed to catch himself. His hate-filled eyes met Danny's a second before he tumbled into an open pit where the closet floor ought to have been. Danny gulped, jerked back to reality despite despising Screkvox. What had he just done? Everyone rushed forward. Flames shot up from the pit and roars and screams wafted up from it. Open-mouthed, Danny turned to meet the astonished expressions of his friends.

"It's a demon pit," whispered Shai. "A connection from our world to theirs."

"Do you suppose that makes him permanently dead?" Tulk asked in a stunned voice.

Daisy snorted. "No big loss if it does."

"I can't believe I just did that," muttered Danny. He was both appalled and invigorated by the victory.

"And I can't believe what you've just done to my office." Everyone jumped at the strange voice and the hint of threat in it. Danny took in the smoking desk, the tumbled and ice-covered bookshelves, bits of paper everywhere like confetti, swirling around in the wind coming in from the broken window. Headmaster Atriz stood in the remains of the doorway to the main hall, arms crossed, mouth pressed tight in a cold look of intense displeasure.

CHAPTER 25

Expulsion At Last

"What has been going on here?" Headmaster Atriz's voice was calm, but his expression stony, his gaze penetrating. Behind him, Mordryn and Vlyxfrka peered into the room.

Everyone stared for a long moment of panicked silence. Now that the moment had come, Danny found his tongue glued to the roof his mouth and his hands shook. *Say it. Say you're Screkvox's son and this will all be over.*

Daisy stepped forward, drawing Atriz's eye. Danny admired her bravery in facing the unnerving dark elf. Whatever else Daisy lacked, it wasn't courage.

"Well, Professor, Screkvox attacked the school. He was

254

trying to kill Zixygrith." She grinned up at him, ignoring his deepening scowl. "So, when he attacked the school with his lightning minions, we all grabbed some weapons and tried to stop him. Then his sword backfired on Tulkyzefril and so he was going to kill him instead and Zixy pushed him down the demon pit in your closet."

Daisy pointed at the demon pit. It burped, sending a little spiral of flame out.

"I see." Atriz's gaze swept over Danny again, then Tulk, who cringed. "Mordryn, please escort Dazidethia, Shaidazgx, and Aundrwtl down to the cafeteria and help Nyshlza get things back to order as quickly as possible. Vrlyxfrka, please go and get Mystfolyn and meet me in my dungeon office since this one—" Atriz scoffed in disgust, "—is unusable. Zxygrth, Tlkyzefril, follow me."

Danny and Tulk exchanged worried glances as they followed the dark elf out of the ruined office, down to the main floor, and then across the school to the staircase to the dungeons. *Is he going to lock us up just like he promised? And does he know Tulk is Screkvox's son, not me?* Danny's emotions swirled. He wasn't sure what to hope for, other than not getting locked up for years on end in the bowels of Dark Lord Academy.

The dungeons smelled heavily of mildew and forbidding steel-banded doors lined the walls. Atriz continued past them to the very end and produced a large skeleton key to unlock the door.

To Danny's surprise, a large white long-haired cat sat right inside the room. It stared up at them with beady red eyes. "Mrrow?"

Headmaster Atriz ignored it and walked in to sit in a black swivel chair behind a desk. It wasn't a dungeon at all, but an office. Danny let out his breath in relief.

Atriz gestured to two stiff metal chairs on the other side of his desk. Danny took the one on the right. The cat followed him and promptly jumped on his lap. It started kneading his leg and purring up a storm. White hairs splattered across Danny's disheveled robes and he sunk his fingers into the cat's fur, stroking it. The vibrating warmth of the cat was soothing.

Atriz raised his eyebrows at the cat, but didn't comment. Tulk slid into the other chair, his face a pasty white.

Atriz drummed his fingers on the desk. "You two boys have caused me a lot of trouble. I just had that demon pit repaired a few months ago and I'm not pleased to have to remodel my office all over again. Not to mention the trouble of finding a new History teacher."

Danny opened his mouth to protest that it wasn't their fault, but then shut it again, unsure what to say.

"And, of course, there's the more serious issue, Tlkyzefrl, of your parentage. Despite your excellent grades so far this term, it is a matter of fate that the sons of dark lords are destined to be heroes, not villains."

"Wait a minute," Danny said. "I'm the one who killed Screkvox, twice even. How do you know that I'm not Screkvox's son?"

Atriz smiled. "Since the beginning of the year I've known one of our final students on the list didn't belong and I've been observing everyone carefully. Screkvox's sword could not properly attack Tlkyzefrl. I've been watching both of you since I heard about the sword incident in Professor Osweggi's class. When you, Zxygrth, killed Screkvox in class, my fears were confirmed by Screkvox's admission both that the sword was his and that his son was attending school." He chuckled. "Besides, Fluff is a villain's cat. You don't see her on Tlkyzefrl's lap, now do you?"

"But," stammered Tulk. "If you knew all this time it was me, why didn't you expel me?"

Atriz's eyes sparkled with mischievous evil. "There are rules to be followed and those that govern the interaction of a Dark Lord and his son are some of the strictest. Once they are engaged in their struggle, it is unwise to interfere. Besides, you must have used some pretty strong magic to foil our entrance tests and have shown great care in keeping up your cover as a Dark Lord in training. By the time I was sure, it was too late to interfere." He shook his head. "But now that the matter is concluded, you will have an expulsion hearing, as well as Zxygrth."

Danny's heart pounded in his chest and his mouth went dry again. This was what he wanted, wasn't it? Then why did he feel so hollow inside? "Why me?"

"Aiding and abetting a hero is a very serious breach of school rules. You have saved his life twice, I hear, as well as aided him in his aim to destroy his father. We take such things very seriously. Your expulsion hearing will be presently, as soon as we have finished setting the school to rights. You will wait here." With that, he stood and swept out of the room.

Danny's mind raced. He realized with a sinking horror that the idea of returning home didn't appeal to him at all. Memories of slaving away in the forge with Amos, Pa's heavy hand of discipline, and, most of all, Dicky's tiresome comments swirled through his mind. Even Tulk, also a hero, had turned out better than Dicky. Here he had friends, as crazy as that might seem. People thought he was cool, someone special, while back home he was nothing but the useless middle child.

But villains are evil! I shouldn't like them and want to stay with them. Only they'd shown him, well, not kindness, but acceptance and companionship. They didn't seem evil, not the way Screkvox had been, even if they didn't seem particularly good, just kids like him. *Don't be fooled, they're going to turn you all into villains.*

Only that made him think of Queleria. She'd said it was just a matter of motives and how you put things. And Danny *had* saved Tulk's life twice, but it was all for the wrong reasons, selfish reasons, "helped" him only to further his own agenda. And yet here was Atriz set on expelling him for it, no matter what his reasoning, for it being an inherently good thing to do. Danny felt more confused than ever about what the difference between good and evil, hero and villain, really was, and no one seemed to have the same answer or approach to it.

He knew he didn't want to be a villain, that much was clear, but did going to school here mean he *had* to? Before he came here, he'd just taken what others said about good and evil for granted, never really explored past the surface of what people assumed about it. It'd turned out a lot more complicated than he'd ever imagined. But was that really a bad thing? What if he could stay here, with his new friends, and puzzle out the real meaning of good and evil, learn more about himself and the way things worked? No one seemed intent on truly forcing him to be anything or anyone he didn't want to be. When it came down to it, that was a choice he had to make on his own. And wouldn't the possible gain in knowledge by staying be worth the risk of possibly giving in to villainy?

A thrill went through him at the realization that he might be able to be here, enjoy all the things that he loved about this place and his new friends, but still have the power to choose his own path in the end. One thing was for sure, he didn't want to be expelled—he wanted to *stay*.

Danny almost smacked himself in the head for realizing all this too late. *I'm doomed to be miserable forever.*

"Mrrow!" Fluff dug her claws into Danny's leg, making him jump. The cat fell to the floor, where she primly stalked away to jump up into the headmaster's swivel chair. She rolled over and started licking her butt.

Danny brushed cat hair off his robes. He glanced at Tulk who looked almost as bad as Danny felt. *So, are we just going to sit here in misery until they kick us out? That's hardly villainous.*

"Tulk, we can't give up. We've still got the hearing." Hope filled him. He grabbed Tulk by the shoulder. "We can argue against their accusations."

"But..." Tulk looked confused. "But we did everything they accused us of!"

"So what? Are we villains or are we heroes? Just because we're guilty doesn't mean we have to get convicted." Danny's excitement grew. "I've talked myself out of plenty of stuff this year. Besides, what do we have to lose?"

"Didn't you want to get expelled?"

"I've changed my mind." Danny swirled his cloak. "Mwehehehehe."

Tulk rolled his eyes and cracked a grin. "You still need to work on that."

"Well? Are you with me? Or do you want to be a hero?"

Tulk shrugged. "Not really. I don't care that much for either, but I'd rather be a villain than a hero. At least I'm not bad at it."

"You're pretty awesome in Style."

Tulk's whole face lit up. "Thanks!" He offered his hand to Danny. "Another evil partnership?"

"Done!" Danny pumped his hand.

Someone knocked on the door and a goblin entered. He snickered at them. "Time for your trial, little trouble makers."

Danny took a deep breath. *This is it.*

Out in the hall, Puke sat on Ugly's shoulders, waiting for them. Danny winced—he'd forgotten their SICMs would get trouble as well. The goblin led them down the hall into another basement room, an enormous amphitheater, lit with skeletons holding torches. Behind a judge's bench at the far end sat Headmaster Atriz. On either side, upon raised platforms, sat twelve of the thirteen teachers of Dark Lord Academy, Screkvox unsurprisingly being absent.

The SICMs waited by the door while Danny and Tulk entered the room. Two small chairs sat in the middle of the semi-circle, waiting for them. Tulk clutched Danny's arm.

Danny stood in front of his chair, too nervous to sit. Tulk sagged into his.

Headmaster Atriz pounded a gavel. "We are assembled for the expulsion hearing of Tlkyzefrl and Zxygrth. Tlkyzefrl is accused of being the son of a dark lord and thus is at the school illegally for the purpose of murdering his father—Zxygrth of aiding and abetting him in his goal of the destruction of his father. Students, how do you plead?"

"Not guilty," Danny said, looking straight at Atriz. The other teachers muttered to each other, but he didn't let that distract him. "I wish to present our defense."

Atriz didn't change his grim expression, but his eyes sparkled with amusement.

Danny cleared his throat. "To begin with, Tulk did not know his father was teaching at Dark Lord Academy—he only wanted to follow his dearest dream of becoming a villain. From an early age, he didn't know the real identity of his father and only at the very last minute did his mother shatter his dreams, revealing his father was a Dark Lord."

Danny had no idea if any of this was true or not, but figured it didn't hurt to make it up as he went along. "What could be more evil, more villainous, than forging one's papers into villain school? Is it any surprise that Tulkyzefril is one of the best students in our year? He's been completely villainous since the moment I met him." *At least that's true.*

"Never once did Tulk move to attack his father, nor did he have any desire to. Tulk only wanted to be a model of villainy to his fellow classmates." The logic felt a bit shaky to Danny, but he plunged ahead anyway. "Tulk only became involved in the duel between myself and Screkvox by accident."

Now came the tricky part, his own role in everything. Danny shoved his sweaty hands into his pockets to prevent himself from playing with them. "Screkvox, impressed by my first evil act of killing him, took me on as a special student." *A special student to kill that is.* "He was my dark mentor and I turned on him and attempted to kill him when I felt I had learned as much from him as was useful, as all respectable villains do."

There were several surprised gasps at that and Danny felt a rush of warm pride over having come up with the argument. Paying attention in History class apparently *had* done him a favor or two. "As far as the evil partnership between Tulk and myself, there was no goodness involved. Once I learned his secret, I needed it to remain so, because if it were found out, Tulk could possibly ruin my chances for slaughtering my dark mentor. What sort of villain would I be if I let him do it for me? I used Tulk to learn more about Screkvox to ensure I could kill him."

Danny felt his arguments were so transparent they were hardly existent, but it was true that he had saved Tulk's life twice completely for his own personal ends. That had to count for something, didn't it? Atriz's stony expression didn't change.

"I swear that both of us have acted with pure villainy and thus with confidence do we swear there is nothing heroic in either of our actions this year, despite all looks to the contrary." Out of arguments, Danny sat down, figuring he'd done all he could.

"That was a most…creative defense," Atriz said, drumming his finger again on the judge's bench. "The two of you may wait outside in the hall while we deliberate."

Danny stood and, on shaking legs, led the way out of the room. He leaned against the cool stone wall and shut his eyes, trying to stifle his nerves. Puke came over to clutch his leg with a death grip while Ugly lay down next to Tulk. Danny remembered guiltily that Puke still wanted to get expelled. *Well, too late now. It's out of my hands.*

"You were amazing," Tulk said in a low voice. "All of it was nonsense, but it was still amazingly clever."

"Hey, have a little hope." Danny tried to muster some of his own while he said it. "We might win."

Tulk shook his head. "I'm the son of a Dark Lord and nothing I can do will change it. But I hope they let you stay."

"Me too," muttered Danny. "Me too."

Tulk sagged down. "I just don't know what I'm gonna do if they kick me out. My mother doesn't want me, never did. She got tired of me and told me to go off adventuring to be a hero and kill my father and not to come back until I did."

Danny couldn't stand to see him so miserable. "If we get expelled, you can come home with me. You've got a good build for a blacksmith, so Pa could take you in as an apprentice. I bet you'd be better than me at it." He kicked the wall with his free leg. Pa would be furious if Danny got himself expelled.

"Do you really think I could?" Hope flashed across Tulk's face.

"Of course. You work hard, learn fast—Pa could always use someone like you."

They fell into silence again. The minutes dragged out, feeling like hours. Danny paced back and forth (having transferred Puke to his shoulder), longing for a verdict one way or the other. Yet when the door opened, he jumped in surprise and his heart galloped away faster than a pissed-off Wrath of Death.

The teachers filed out, none of them looking toward Danny or Tulk except Nyshlza, who winked at Danny. He swallowed hard. Then Headmaster Atriz came to stand before them.

"Tlkyzefrl, no matter what your intent, evil or heroic, the school rules are firm. No child of a Dark Lord may attend. You shall leave us today. However, we bear you no ill will, beyond that which we bear to all sentient beings. You are free to go your own way. The dark chariot will carry you to any reasonable destination of your choice."

Tulk nodded and stared at the ground.

Atriz turned to Danny. "Zxygrth, while you have broken a large number of serious rules, you will not be expelled."

Danny let out a gush of air in relief.

Atriz held up a hand. "However, you are on probation. If you study hard, improve your grades, and restrain your evil aptitude for trouble within the reasonable bounds of this school's guidelines, you will be permitted to stay. We shall evaluate your progress at the end of the year and decide if you can be taken off probation."

"Thank you, sir," Danny said. Looking up at Atriz, he felt good (or was that evil?) about being here, being allowed to stay. He looked forward to bragging about his brilliant defense to Aun, Daisy, and Shai. And maybe Carly would have something reasonably edible for him as well. Then, with a sinking feeling, he remembered Puke. The poor monkey-like creature would be forced to stay here.

"Uh, sir, I was wondering…" He flushed, hoping the request wouldn't be presumptuous.

Atriz raised an eyebrow.

"Would it be okay if I traded SICMs with Tulk? I mean, poor Puke is really not cut out to be in command of anything and Tulk's creature seems much more evil. I was thinking perhaps, if Tulk would take him, that Puke could leave with him…He'd really enjoy doing something else, I think."

Atriz was silent a moment. "All right, in this case I don't have any difficulties in letting you switch SICMs. Your Puke is free to leave with Jared here and you keep his SICM." He paused a moment. "Was getting a better SICM all part of your master plan?"

Danny grinned. "Of course."

"Yes, of course. Remember what I said about probation. I want you to go to Vrlyxfrka's office where she shall give you the details. Jared, the Dark Chariot is waiting for you outside the castle drawbridge. Move along now." He turned and headed upstairs.

"You're Jared?" Danny asked. "And you don't mind if I take your SICM? Or if I send Puke home to help you in the forge and learn blacksmithing?"

"You mean I can still go to your Pa's place and be apprenticed?" Tulk's voice trembled.

"Of course. I'll write you a letter of recommendation right now. You really don't mind about the SICMs?"

"No, go ahead and take Ugly." He gestured at the gargoyle. "She's really smart and not even that ugly…I just was trying to name her as evilly as possible." Tulk blushed. "Oh yeah, and my real name *is* Jared."

Danny nodded. "A good name for someone ordinary, like a blacksmith. Maybe you should rename Puke, too, actually…Let's get some paper and a quill and I'll write a letter. After I explain, Pa'll be overjoyed to have you." He peeled Puke off his shoulder. "Listen, Puke, you're gonna get to leave. Jared is going to be your new master."

"Humble Puke understands," the monkey said.

"I think your SICM is kinda cute, actually." Tulk blushed.

Puke burst into tears and threw his arms around Tulk's neck. Tulk grimaced and pried his fingers off, readjusting him so he could breathe. Danny grinned, patting the gargoyle on the head. It butted his leg gently. They headed down the hall and up the stairs. Waiting at the top, Danny could see their friends, wanting to hear the news.

Tulk paused for a moment halfway up and turned, blocking Danny's path. "You're being really nice to me," he said, looking baffled. "Not that I don't appreciate it. This is the best thing that's ever happened to me, but aren't you supposed to be villainous? Why are you being so nice?"

Danny thought of Pa's iron hand, his constant bark of orders, the terrible heat of the forge, how his muscles ached every day after working, and Dicky's constantly snide and irritating comments.

"Sometimes," he said, "a little kindness can be more evil in the long run.

ABOUT THE AUTHOR

Ardyth DeBruyn is a native Oregonian with a restless nature and a degree in Anthropology. After hiking over 1500 miles across Europe and living on the Mexican border for a year, she settled back in the Pacific Northwest (for now) to write fantasy stories. She has decided she can type herself into adventures faster than walk. She has fiction published in a number of webzines and two published novels.

Website: www.ardythdebruyn.com

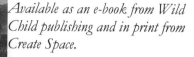

Available as an e-book from Wild Child publishing and in print from Create Space.

Reina's brother Austyn has been declared the Child Warrior, but he's only six. What's a big sister to do?

Allowed to accompany her brother, Reina discovers they're in deeper trouble than she thought-the Gold Wizard isn't shaping up to be the guide he's supposed to be and the Red Wizard's harpies and snakewolves are on their trail. If anyone's going to find a way to track down the elusive Sword of Chivalry for Austyn and get him into the Red Wizard's castle to fulfill whatever it is the obscure prophecy insists must be done, it's got to be Reina.

Made in the USA
San Bernardino, CA
06 December 2012